THE ASH FAMILY

A NOVEL

MOLLY DEKTAR

Simon & Schuster
New York   London   Toronto   Sydney   New Delhi

Simon & Schuster
1230 Avenue of the Americas
New York, NY 10020

First Simon & Schuster hardcover edition April 2019

SIMON & SCHUSTER and colophon are registered trademarks of Simon & Schuster, Inc.

For information about special discounts for bulk purchases, please contact Simon & Schuster Special Sales at 1-866-506-1949 or business@simonandschuster.com.

The Simon & Schuster Speakers Bureau can bring authors to your live event. For more information or to book an event contact the Simon & Schuster Speakers Bureau at 1-866-248-3049 or visit our website at www.simonspeakers.com.

Interior design by Carly Loman

Manufactured in the United States of America

10 9 8 7 6 5 4 3 2 1

Library of Congress Cataloging-in-Publication Data

Names: Dektar, Molly, author.
Title: The Ash family / Molly Dektar.
Description: New York : Simon & Schuster, 2019.
Identifiers: LCCN 2018011339 | ISBN 978150114468 (hc) | ISBN 9781501144875 (tp)
Subjects: LCSH: Communal living—Fiction. | Missing persons—Fiction. | GSAFD: Mystery fiction
Classification: LCC PS3604.E388 A84 2019 | DDC 813/.6—dc23
LC record available at https://lccn.loc.gov/2018011339

ISBN 978-1-5011-4486-8
ISBN 978-1-5011-4488-2 (ebook)

To my mother and my father

fall

CHAPTER I

Bay and I approached the farm at dawn. The first sun churned sideways through the trees, catching in the previous day's rain, which the wind now shook down from the Carolina silverbells, the beeches, and the poplars. I rolled down the window and heard the forest fizzing.

Bay had taught me one of their songs in the car: "Come, my soul, and let us try, for a little season, every burden to lay by, come and let us reason." He sang the harmony and drummed his thumbs on the wheel. I couldn't hold the melody and my voice kept slipping.

Before I met Dice, before I met Queen and Pear, he was the whole Ash Family to me, and I promised him: my soul, with which I would try. We repeated the song till I could maintain my line. When we turned off the paved road, the low sun lit up every strand of his hair, so that, as a result of its extreme disorder, it looked like a giant, bright halo. He had rescued me, I thought.

Bay drove maybe a mile more up a road so bumpy that my

head kept hitting the ceiling. We passed four signs warning hunters not to come near, *BEWARE LARGE DOGS*.

"Here," he said. "We're here." In an instant the gold light broke, and here was my first view of the farm. The house crouched in a whirl of yellow leaves from the biggest hickory I'd ever seen. The wind spun the leaves in the air as thick and self-contained as the liquid in a snow globe. I felt like my eyes were failing. I stumbled out of the car. Bay took my hand. I'd gotten a splinter in it the day before, and I felt like he'd shoved a stake through my palm. A light went on in the house.

On our trip up through the mountains Bay had told me that I could stay at the farm for three days or the rest of my life. His family—intentional family, not born family—sustained itself communally, off the grid, in the old way. This was the real world, he explained, and if I stayed I'd get a real-world name to replace my fake-world one. He said I would come to understand that there was no definite self: in the Ash Family there was no selfishness, so there were no possessions, no children, no couples.

"What if I stay longer than three days but want to leave after?" I said.

"Why would you want to leave, when you'll have more freedom here than anywhere else?" he said. The family's father, Bay said, was Dice, and Dice would understand me the way a lightning bolt would understand a rod.

I was ready to believe it, all of it. Bay could see, as no one else had, the yearning I felt for a more essential life. To me *essential* meant a life more connected to wild nature. I'd always known there was magic on the margins, there was a world beyond my mother's world, where a dinner that "went off without a hitch" meant a dinner where no one talked about anything that mattered. My mother cared about manners and appearances and above all she wanted me to go to college so that I would "have a better future." She wanted a life of safety for me, as though safety were still possible on the choked earth. Safety was a relic from before humans destroyed the world.

Some part of my mother was riven; I kept stumbling along the edges. Once my ex-boyfriend and I had found a broken-down shotgun in her dresser drawer.

My ex-boyfriend, Isaac, told me that my desire for a more essential life was meaningless unless I was fleeing from *and* fleeing toward. I'd had so much trouble discerning the toward. I was looking for the toward. Then I met Bay. Next to him, in the yellow-winged morning, it seemed to me that everyone in Durham had told me just what I'd needed to leave them behind.

The hickory leaves pattered against our backs and adhered to the house's clapboards. "Will I meet Dice now?" I said.

"Not for a little while, I think," said Bay. "Let the fake world fall away."

His arm was around me, and I watched his breath enter the air. The cold had broken records for September. I didn't know where I would sleep, what I would eat. I had no money and no possessions. Three days or the rest of my life, I thought. We stood listening to the leaves, the sheep's plaintive calls, the cows' exasperated moos. A white dog loped toward me—it was huge, almost my height—and butted its head into my chest.

"Let me see your watch," Bay said.

I held out my arm. He unbound the watch from my wrist and slipped it into his pocket. I liked the feathery feeling of his fingers on my arm. Then he pulled away from me. "Stay," he said as he walked into the house. At first I thought he was talking to the dog.

I stood alone in the courtyard, under the shedding yellow tree. I could hear a whip-poor-will and the creaking trunks of trees. Across from the house, the L-shaped barn filled up my vision from end to end, dim against the glare of the sky so its detail only gradually appeared, a dusky bronze color with a tiny tower on one end, topped with a tin wind arrow, slowly turning. Between house and barn, there was a storage house on crooked slate stilts, with a triangle roof like a child's drawing. Mountain slopes rose on two sides, holding the buildings like a folded palm: what I would come to know as the holler. It was all tidier than I'd imagined, and older. I'd expected tarped buses and pelt teepees leaning in the woods, but this was a quiet old-fashioned farm tucked into standard pastures.

The wind streamed down the slopes, eddying and rumpling in the longleaf pines and on the weather vane, so that it turned this way and that, not indicating anything.

Bay stood on the porch. I started when I noticed him there, a tall broad shadow, like a black bear—I'd heard there were many bears in these mountains. I wondered how long he'd been watching me.

"We're ready for you," he said. "Just remember, don't tell anyone your fake-world name." He led me across the threshold. I noticed the dirt on the floor. The walls were milky yellow. I followed him through a meeting room filled with chairs, and then into the dining room.

And here was the family, two dozen young people. They all wore dun sweaters or canvas jackets; they all had the same short sloppy haircut, the same broad hands, the same rawboned faces and vivid eyes. They seemed to be moving slowly, their gestures drifting through the air; they reminded me of astronauts who had to strap themselves down to rest in space.

"A sister!" Bay said. They looked up at him and smiled. Every face was beautiful.

"Who's this?" a black-haired man said.

"Berie," I said. Then I remembered I wasn't supposed to say.

"She's fake world, through and through," Bay said. He laughed. My heart lurched and seemed to budge the splinter in my hand that I'd gotten yesterday, during our trip here. "Sit here," he said to me. He turned to the others. "I found her by the bus stop. I thought she was Cassie for a second, didn't you?"

"Who is that?" I said.

"Very curious," said the black-haired man.

"What's easy for you is hard for us," Bay said to me, in a singsong. "What's hard for you is easy for us." The family members laughed.

I smiled along, though I did not understand.

But I had secret knowledge too. What none of these people knew was that he'd kissed me the night before. Maybe there were no couples here, but he'd kissed me.

Bay took a seat at the far side of the table. I sat, too, and the women on either side smiled. "You must be tired," said one.

"This is the hardest part," said the other, so gently that I felt my face flush. "Have a little bread. We make it ourselves." She said her name was Sara. She was a beautiful woman with a grown-out buzz cut and big eyes with delicately veined eyelids. She buttered a piece of bread for me, but I felt too nervous to eat. I looked around. Laid out on the table were steaming red-clay cups and silver bowls and jam jars, berry branches and fall leaves, basket-embossed loaves of bread.

What would my mother think of me here? I hadn't yet learned to control my thoughts, so she rose up, unbidden. She still thought I was on my way to college in Richmond.

I was fleeing from: my mother, whom I constantly disappointed. She worked at two different gift shops. She bought our groceries at the discount store that carried unpopular products from major brands—Welch's jam with chia seeds, double-protein Philadelphia cream cheese, pumpkin spice Cheerios. She liked to speculate about why these things didn't sell, always trying to reassure me that they were just as good, better, more special than the full-price versions. As a rule, the less confidence she had in what she was saying, the more she repeated herself. She said everything she did was for me, all so I could afford college and a better life. She said that over and over.

My mother owned three precious things, a matching jewelry set from her mother's mother: a necklace of white gold and garlands of pearls and diamonds, and two stud earrings, big fat diamonds clenched in white-gold claws. She kept the set bedded in red silk velvet in a Colonial Girl Sandwich cookie tin in our house in Durham. My mother might have hated the jewelry, which did not keep her fed sufficiently as a child, did not send her to school, did not save her from the desperation that led her to marry my father. But instead she loved it; she pierced my ears when I was ten so I could wear the earrings and necklace together when we went out on glamorous occasions, which meant a stroll through Duke Gardens in the spring, among the college students, dogwoods, and magnolias. She must have asked me if I wanted piercings and I must have said yes, but she never understood that acquiescence is not the same as desire, and by asking for permission she forced my hand.

In January, she had begged me to apply to college. I did, even though I barely had the grades, even though I didn't want to. It was her dream, never mine, kicked off by her own mother, or her mother's mother, the long line of women who never got out, but instead grew old and stiff as boards and knocked over one onto the next, leaning hard all the way to me.

In May, she sold the necklace to pay for what the financial aid wouldn't cover.

In September, she bought me a plane ticket for Richmond. "I always knew you'd manage," she said, driving me to the airport on the gray slopes of I-40. I could have taken the bus to Richmond but she wanted me to arrive like the best students. I thought I was doing the right thing by accepting her offer. It seemed cruel to say no.

Four days before I met Bay, when we parted at the airport, she spent a while searching for something in her handbag, clearing her throat. Because she was a big-boned, broad-shouldered woman, her handbag, like her floral cap-sleeve dress, looked funny on her, though for once I felt sorrier for her than ashamed for myself. She seemed to find what she'd been looking for. "Take this," she said. She handed me a little photograph.

It was a picture of my father, yearbook-style. Cloudy gray background, chin up, face to the side, and eyes front. He had a high fade and the calm looks of a man who knew how to shoot.

"So you can remember him," she said.

I didn't want it. I hadn't seen my father since I was six. I didn't want to remember what he looked like. I tucked his face into my wallet.

I could not forget the sight of my mother standing there on the other side of security, watching me head away. Her arms straight at her sides, purse on the floor. Her neck pulsing. Her reflection in the linoleum.

Oh, my mother. I should have hugged her.

I wanted to make my mother happy but I knew there was something more for me than college.

I was fleeing toward the *something more*. Once, alone by the Eno, I'd found two bucks with their antlers wedged together. I'd approached them as they lay panting and I'd jostled their antlers till they separated. I remember kneeling on the dead mauve leaves, watching the bucks stagger to their feet. I remember feeling all of the forest moving through me. School, college, my mother were a dam on the river of a vivid life; out of doors the dam would break and I would tumble in the current.

The Ash Family rose from the breakfast table to begin their chores. I sat alone at the enormous table, worried I'd been forgotten. But soon the woman I'd met at breakfast—Sara—came to find me.

She hugged me as though we had not seen one another for a very long time. "Little one," she said. She looked ethereal, but she stank like a tramp. She led me across the yard. I kept stumbling on the ridged ground. I felt clumsy, delirious. Four days ago I'd been college-bound and now no one in the world knew where I was.

Sara opened the stable door. "Good morning, horses," she said. The sun came in behind us and the barn was filled with whirling gold chaff. I inhaled the warm sleepy scent of the animals and felt the quickening of an uncommon happiness. It was a moment of apprehension of all the forms life could take—it felt like remembering, but I'd never been so close to horses. Two of the horses were white with black pinpoint spots, and two were red, with white blazes splitting down their long heads. I'd later learn that the red ones were Suffolk mares and they pulled our plow.

"Dice is dynamite," Sara said. A red horse pressed its nose into her temple and she laughed. "Found me when I was seventeen, when he was feeding all the people. I was the first to join him. I knew I'd been saved." I thought about the man outside my high school who once handed me a comic book he said would save me. Then he tried the girl next to me, and she said, *No thank you, I have already been saved.* I wanted to be saved—then and now.

"How did you know?" I said.

Sara rubbed the horse on its blaze, and it sampled her shirt collar with its dark lips. "Dice knew this cold was coming, and we put the blankets down on the fields. He let it come. He can change the weather with his mind."

I wanted to believe her. She was polite and stern, like a nurse; there was something entrancing about her easy kinship with the horses, her strength, her calm. "He actually used to work as an engineer at a power plant," Sara said. "When he realized that all the fish downstream from the plant had died, he quit and went to the Arctic to learn from the glaciers. But he felt he couldn't keep propping up the fake world forever." She laughed and shook her head, like we were both in on a joke. "He wanted a new world, where he could live the right way. So he moved here, and I came along."

We approached the three henhouses, where dozens of hens burbled and squawked. She showed me their water and grain, and moved from task to task without bothering to make conversation. "By the way," Sara said suddenly. "Did you know that glaciers roar and thunder as they melt?" Her lack of etiquette made me trust her. She said the cooks rose at five and everyone else at six, something like that—"Only Dice has a watch." Work started at seven and continued for four hours. Then lunch, and break, and work till dinnertime, then singing or a story.

For the next short while, she said I was going to look after the sheep and the chickens and the pigs, while most of the family prepared for the action on the mountaintop. Dice found out that a coal company had planned to burn thousands of acres of forest nearby, in Tennessee.

"They're burning the cottontails off, the flying squirrels off, the wolves off, the pumas, the bears, the salamanders, the spiders, the deer, all off," Sara said. "In less than a week, now, the coal people are going to blow the top off the mountain with millions of pounds of dynamite, blow off five hundred feet of what they call overburden, right down to the coal." I took pleasure in a moment of imagining how my mother would think Sara was crazy. Here I was, talking with Sara: my mother would think I was crazy too.

"They keep getting closer and closer to us. The old forest is almost all gone," Sara said. "But they can't get a good price for the soft coal. The industry is dying. You know why they're doing it?" She fixed her large eyes on me.

I shook my head.

"They're roaring and thundering," she said. "You have to watch out for the half-dead wolf, you know. We see them around the land sometimes. Dressed like scientists. Looking in our rivers. Digging in the woods. There's no coal here, but the roads have gotten better, and they want to develop. It's already too bright to see the Milky Way." Her tone made my skin prickle. "Once the biodiversity is gone, it's gone. After a catastrophe it takes millions of years to come back."

"Do you really think you'll be able to stop them?"

"Let me tell you something Dice told me," she said. "We animals are more like fungus than like plants. We are descendants of big groupings of cooperating fungus cells. We are not single selves, just tendencies, groups. And so we do think we can stop the catastrophe, because we are not working alone. The fake world is not a match for us." When she turned away from me I saw her buzz cut was grown out in the back like a rat tail. In that moment she was the most beautiful woman I'd ever seen.

I wondered how they would stop the mining, the developing. I imagined a march through the center of town, like my ex-boyfriend and I had done against the bathroom bill and the ag-gag. "I'd like to come to your protest," I said.

"We don't really do protests," she said. "We do direct action." She stooped to stroke a hen's broad red back, and it hunched, stilled by her touch. The hens ate soft mangoes and passion fruits. They jabbed their beaks into grapes. Sara showed me how to collect the eggs, feeling around in nesting boxes, under the warm feathers and sturdy legs. She watched me and said, "Bay was right to bring back someone who loves animals. I bet your family didn't see that, did they?"

"My mother wanted me to focus on school," I said.

Sara touched my face. Her hands smelled like horses. "I am glad you found us," she said.

We tracked through the barn, a maze of low-ceilinged wooden rooms of irregular sizes. One room was stacked floor to ceiling with pieces of PVC pipe. As we walked past, the pipe ends looked like rolling eyes.

We fed the four massive pigs, dropping down crates of lettuce and kale and bagels and strawberry Yoplait. "From the free store," Sara said. "The Dumpster."

"Do you travel to town often?" I was remembering Bay: *three days or the rest of your life.*

"That's a silly question," she said. "We're traveling at six hundred miles a second toward the Great Attractor." She laughed when she saw my face. "Get relativity," she said. "It's one of our lessons."

The pigs raised their fleshy noses and snorted as I emptied yogurts onto their heads. The sheep ate fermented tight-packed hay, silage, in a big round cage. They walked to the front of their stable to look at me as we approached. Dark eyes and white muzzles, side-springing ears. I touched the fine down on their cheeks. I'd never touched such gentleness, this wool, these horns, these gold eyes, built out of grass and water. I was used to carnivores like cats and dogs.

Past the sheep we tossed carrots and cabbages, loaves of bread, straw to the cows. The cows were silver with black noses. We climbed into the wide food trough between their rows, and Sara pulled a ladder down from a ceiling hatch and planted it in the tall hay. I followed her feet upward, feeling a cool breeze coming down the ladder. We emerged into a space that was as vast as a cathedral, windy and dark except for slivers of light coming in the loosely constructed walls. "The largest barn of its era in the Appalachians," said Sara. "A monumental work."

Hay piled up almost to the ceiling. I felt a long, deep thrill that mounted as I shuffled my feet over the uneven plank floor and fell into the bales to smell their sweetness, to feel their prickles in my hair. Isaac used to say that there are times when things are positive or negative, or times of simple intensity, when those distinctions dissolve. That was how I felt when I first fell in love with him. And here was the feeling again, after a long dormancy. I wanted to run out to the hills and press my face into the soil. I felt I would finally be swept away in the river of a vivid life. As we picked our way across the floor, every new view proved to me how perfect the place was and how right my feelings were. "This is where you'll be sleeping," Sara said. "All new arrivals sleep up here, in the hay."

"How many are there?" I said.

"Haylofts?" said Sara, though I felt she knew what I was asking.

"No," I said. "New people."

"Everyone is old at something and new at another," she said.

I could stay here three days and then take a bus to Richmond. The semester had started yesterday, but maybe it wasn't too late to enroll.

"You belong here," Sara said. "I can tell." The future had been a wall, and now the wall collapsed and I could see the huge range of weathered mountains, and the structures of the farm like the eyes in a face.

I could stay three days, or I could stay the rest of my life.

We descended the wobbling ladder. Sara showed me the leader ewe, whose loyalty I would have to capture if I wanted to herd the flock. The ewe was blind in one eye, which was white and brimming over with scar tissue. Her other eye contained a horizontal rectangular pupil in a gold-colored round. Her large compliant head took up so much space. Her horns were warm, as though they were filled with blood. "When the weather's good, you'll herd," Sara said. She looked out the window. "Today, for example."

"By myself?"

We opened the barn doors and the sheep coursed out into the

sloping meadows. "You're going to have to do it when we're away," Sara said. "So you'd better learn."

"I've never even met a sheep before today," I said. The bleating flock slowly headed north, stretching and gathering. It was early afternoon.

"If you lose the sheep, you'll lose the sheep," said Sara. "So just don't lose them." She took off her scarf and wound it around my neck. "If it gets too cold, the sheep will find a warm hillside," she said. "They're good at that."

"Don't leave me," I said. My hurt hand pulsed.

She took off her canvas jacket and draped it over my shoulders. "The more you dawdle, the harder it will be to catch them."

The sheep had already disappeared over the ridge. I'd have to run to catch them.

"Stand in front of the ones that are going the wrong direction," Sara said. "And if they don't heed, shake a stick and shout. If you belong here, you'll love it. Earn our trust."

My wounded palm was hot, and I used it to try to warm my freezing fingers.

"You're still cold?" she said. She took off her sweater and handed it to me. I didn't want to accept it, but it was so warm in my hands. She took off her skirt, pulled it over her boots. She took off her turtleneck, exposing her prickled skin, her pale stained undershirt. She held her clothes out to me. I couldn't look at her face, but then she turned and I wished I had. I no longer had any idea what she thought of me. I no longer knew whether I was safe. I wished Bay had been there to guide me.

Sara walked almost naked back down the long slopes.

CHAPTER 2

I'd met Bay at the bus stop three days before. I'd been taking a Greyhound from Asheville back to Durham. I was going to ask for refuge at Isaac's squat, since I couldn't tell my mother I'd decided not to enroll at the college I'd gotten into, in Virginia.

I stood waiting on Tunnel Road, eyes watering, feeling tight and drawn, as though I'd survived a great ordeal. I didn't even have the money for gas station chocolate.

A man was standing next to me at the bus stop. He didn't have any bags so I guessed he was waiting for someone. I didn't look much at his face to begin with. He had long wide scars running the length of both of his arms, from elbow to wrist, evidence of what could have been mortal wounds.

I remembered Isaac telling me that the right way to cut was "down the lane, not across the street." Isaac's gruesome knowledge gave him power, and I loved to feel like there were alternate uses for arms and knives, like the world was full of objects that, reimagined, could tip us away from safety. I liked glitter in an envelope as a prank and I liked a pinhole in a shoebox as a camera lens. I liked the way a rope tied high above the quarry could become a terrifying swing, or an arm pushed against a door frame could start to feel weightless and rise of its own accord. I liked high-jumping so high that mistakes badly hurt, and taking my mother's food to Isaac's squat, and, at the animal shelter where I volunteered, petting the death-row dogs I was supposed to ignore.

As I looked, the stranger tried to hide the scars, which made him seem good.

"Let me guess, Greyhound girl," he said. I started. He was talking to me. He had some kind of accent. "Heading home, but you don't want to." It was a Southern voice, a mountain voice.

I gazed at him. I was sad to be so easily legible.

"I bet your dad left home when you were younger. No"—he sized me up, and I couldn't help smiling—"your mom."

I shrugged. He had a busted-looking face and gentle canine eyes. "It wasn't really a home," I said. The first words I spoke to him were all he needed to build a connection so strong it seemed magical.

"I like to hear people's stories," he said. We stood smiling at each other. He gave me a piece of chocolate with a pink candy coating. "Want another?" he said. I nodded, but he waited a minute before he handed me the bag.

He told me his name was Bay.

"Nice to meet you," I said.

"Rest assured, dads don't like me." He laughed. I felt like I was in a scene I'd often noticed in parks, a squirrel looking down at a dog, the dumb communion of animals, their mismatched understanding.

"These are good," I said, even though the chocolate tasted like oil. I swept a horsefly from his shoulder. He shook my hand off, and I stepped back.

I was starting to realize that no, he wasn't at the bus stop waiting for someone else—he was waiting for me.

"I bet you think you know all about men," he said.

Isaac had been my first and only boyfriend. He was a photographer; I was his model. In the conversation that had led to our breakup just a few weeks before, he'd accused me of stagnating. He told me I needed to get out more and see the world. He said he thought college would be good for me, but I wanted to find my way back to the forest where I separated the bucks: there was another way to live. He had used to talk about smashing windows and destroying institutions and reinventing the world from the ground up. And now he was a studio art major at the University of North Carolina, part of the system. I said, "Your hypocrisy is unbelievable." He explained that even a hypocrite could be an agent of change, an idea that, for a time, liberated me from understanding that a life without hypocrisy was desirable or possible.

He even got a claw tattoo to match mine—"to honor our relationship," he'd said. Before I knew him I'd gotten two chickenlike claws on my shoulder blades. I'd wanted proper talons, but they'd come out fleshy and small, like something you'd fry. In March, when things were still going well for us, I'd accompanied him to Sirius. They're not supposed to give you a face tattoo till you have one somewhere else. Yet suddenly I was holding his hand while the tattoo man pounded his left temple with the needle.

Even with the claw curling around his left eye as a sign, I'd thought, of loyalty, he told me I was stagnating. He told me when I was posing for a long exposure. I was wearing a nightgown and he wanted me to flit slowly around a candle that he'd placed on the floor. Only my feet would be legible in the photo. Well, of course he thought I was stagnating—I was his model; it was my job to stay still.

If the conversation had gone differently, maybe I would have applied to UNC with Isaac. My favorite part of school was track and field. I high-jumped. High-jumping was scary and I liked scaring myself, losing myself in the effort. Over time, I got good. Good enough that my teammates would gather and watch once I beat all my opponents and kept jumping just to see if I could beat myself. When I stood on my medical-tape marker, everyone liked to touch me to wish me luck. Back then, I could jump five feet six inches, which meant I could jump over my own body if I had to. "You're flying!" my coach would say, and it was true, this was as close as I could get.

I liked biology, too, but only certain things about biology: when we debated the ethics of keeping the brain-dead Nebraska woman alive so that her baby could gestate; or when we dissected a cow eye and found the *tapetum lucidum*, deep in the knot of corded white appeared this mother-of-pearl, this rumpled surface of glittering azure; or when we learned about the horror of climate change, the visions of superstorms punching into the stratosphere, the low-pitched warning of the inundated Outer Banks.

For climate change, I read, we'd have to adapt, and to mitigate, and to suffer. All three. But it was impossible to figure out what I could do that was big enough to help the migratory birds unable to find their resting spots, the bears starving to death, the ancient oaks dying off because of the relentless heat, the exterminated coral reefs, the pelicans caught in the black ooze. Not college, surely.

I wanted to keep talking to Bay. I said, "Tell me about your family." And I leaned against the wall too, a little closer to him. He said he'd tell me everything. The Ash Family, they called themselves, because they got their start in Asheville, and because Dice, the father, said they were the leftovers from the purifying flame. "The heavy bits," Bay said. About thirty people and growing. Sixty sheep, thirty cows, four pigs, twelve geese, sixty chickens, a raw-milk dairy, an orchard, a vegetable patch, an old farmhouse in a holler, a whole mountain to graze, a little utopia.

"We share everything—clothes. Money, our minds, our bodies," he said lazily, appraising me. "It's a real family. No one is ashamed of anything."

"Well, that sounds nice," I said.

"Does it?" he said.

"Sure," I said. Isaac used to favor *sure* because it threw my weight back on me—*Are you less angry now?* I'd say, and he'd respond, with a shrug, *Sure.* This time, though, I meant it. The farm did sound nice.

"Look at you, you're so lost! I like lost souls. I get along great with lost souls." He laughed at me. I liked it. He was right.

*   *   *

Two days before I was supposed to leave home for college, my mother had tried to bake a yellow layer cake. She said it was for me; I said I didn't want it. The cake came out flat, with a chewy rind. While I was trying to thank her for making it, she pushed it with two hooked fingers all the way along the countertop till it fell off the edge and onto the floor, where it landed with a thud.

"It didn't turn out the way I wanted," she said. Her face trembled, her loose eye bags and loose mouth so delicate and fine, the finest material in her vinyl and linoleum house—finer even than the jewelry.

She left the kitchen with the cake on the floor. I scraped it up, and sampled it from the dustpan, and it tasted like nothing. I'd never seen her waste food. I thought I was kind to leave her, so she could take better care of herself. Or I thought I was unkind to leave her, but I needed to stop living in her pain.

My bus arrived, blue and silver with tinted windows, blasting a warm toxic smell from its undercarriage. There were only six passengers. Bay picked up my backpack and my suitcase. "What do you have in here?" he said.

Peter Pan shirts and oxford shoes, a jacket, cold medicine, a Xeroxed copy of *Evasion*. "Nothing," I said. I wanted him to leave my bags on the ground. I wanted him to invite me to meet his family.

"Doesn't feel that way," he said. He hoisted the bags into the hold. "You'll want to keep your wallet," he said, taking it from my backpack.

I looked searchingly at Bay. Behind him, the entrance of the tunnel arched over him, and the two rows of gold lights pointed right at his head. In the hills above him, a hawk fell like a spear.

Bay closed the hold's door. "Why don't you catch your bags in Durham, since there's nothing in them," he said. "There'll be another bus in an hour." The driver climbed into his high seat. He was going to carry away my bags, and I was not going to stop him. I watched the bus fall into the tunnel. Clouds blew over the sun, seeming to stop and start. A cold air was settling from the highest part of the sky. "Can I have my wallet?" I asked Bay.

He withdrew my wallet—an embroidered, Velcro-closed thing—and opened it. There was no money inside. "So I'm paying for dinner," he said.

"I'm leaving in an hour," I reminded him.

He found the photo of my father. "I was wrong, earlier," he said, turning it back and forth in the light like a prism.

"I guess," I said.

"He looks good," Bay said, "like a good man." My father and I didn't have a relationship. He'd vanished, leaving me with a blurry assortment of sensations—it must have been him who gripped me by the arms and whirled me around when I was so small it didn't hurt. He was the one who gave me a pair of glasses that turned all points of light into hearts. Or maybe I was just remembering what my mother told me.

"I'm glad he left," I said. I'd thought this many times, but I had never said it aloud.

Bay shook his head, disapproving. Isaac's disapproval angered me. Bay's disapproval made me feel as though I had something more to learn. Bay slipped the photo into his pocket and said, "How can you be so sure?" And he gave me a long hard look.

I wondered if Bay found me beautiful. I knew from biology that forensics workers appreciate suspects and victims who easily lose skin cells—because they leave their DNA everywhere. If I had beauty, it was this kind. I was always trailing strands of hair, smudging my clothes with my dye-dissolving sweat. I was easy to track.

"Let me tell you about one of our favorite ideas," he said. I wondered about the word *our*. "From a Renaissance tramp doctor named Paracelsus. He said, 'You who know nothing, love nothing. The more knowledge is inherent in a thing, the greater the love. You who imagine that all fruits ripen at the same time as strawberries know nothing about grapes.'"

We sat in the dead-streaked grass next to the cinder-block Greyhound building. The sun tilted over the trees. The leaves were already starting to turn. In Durham, where my bags would arrive without me, I knew my mother and Isaac could sit under green for another month.

I thought about sixty sheep, thirty cows, four pigs, twelve geese, sixty chickens, a raw-milk dairy, an orchard, a vegetable patch. I tried to understand what Bay was saying about strawberries and grapes. It seemed ecological, which I liked; but no, he clarified, it was about love. He led me to his car. "The more knowledge you have, the more you can love," he said. "Love comes from understanding, not from ignorance."

I was in Bay's car now, which smelled like the state fair—

like manure, peanuts, ice cream. Isaac thought I couldn't choose, but in reality I'd always known what I wanted. I wanted to be pushed around, pushed onto the ground to break with a thud. Bay helped me put my own will back into it. I chose to be his passenger.

CHAPTER 3

Bay said a cold snap was coming, and his car had no heat. "Never been this cold in this time of year," he said. He gave me his long-underwear top and I wrapped the arms around me as we drove past shorn fields, trailers, tobacco stands, and subdivisions with enormous cheap houses and spongy sculpted grass.

I'd loved traveling with Isaac. We'd driven to Bynum to see the wooden giraffes with silk-flower eyes and to Lucama to see the fifty-foot whirligigs. Isaac always forgot to toggle the switch from vegetable oil to diesel when he turned off his car, but you couldn't get the car started on vegetable oil, so one of us would have to open the car lid and suck on the fuel line to the engine until the taste of vegetable oil gave way to the taste of diesel fuel—really, more of a feel, a scalding evaporation. The insides of our cheeks bruised black.

I was quiet, next to Bay. I was overflowing with questions about the Ash Family but too nervous to ask the wrong thing. Finally, I introduced myself. "No way are you a Beryl," he said. In his voice it sounded like *Burl*. "I will never call you that."

"What will you call me, then?" I said.

He looked over at me and tilted his head. "Dice will decide," he said. "You'll have to show yourself to us somehow. For me, Dice said I was a bay, like a harbor."

"What's your real name?" I said.

"I forget," he said.

At last, Bay pulled up to a mountain cabin, a rich-family one, with red shingles and white-frosting eaves, a redwood deck and large windows facing into the gloomy Smokies.

"What is this?" I said.

"The free store," he said. "We need coats."

He parked the car, and we walked to the door. I raised my hand to the doorbell, but he shoved me aside.

He took a plastic card to the lock and opened the door into a dark, glossy foyer, exhaling heat.

"Are we stealing?" I was breathless from the shove. *He's a farmer*, I reminded myself, *a shepherd*.

He said, "No one's been here in months."

"I saw lights on."

"That's just automatic."

"To keep people from stealing," I said.

"Listen," he said. "If you want to fall down the hole of believing in property, in a sense, you're stealing from me. Because I'm taking care of you."

"You wanted company, you said."

"Did I?" He smiled. "Do you think society is unequal?" He

peered down the hallway and shifted his head like a snake. "Would you go to a rally?"

"Yeah."

"Would you break a big-box window?"

"Yeah."

"Would you shoot an oilman?"

"No," I said. I wasn't violent. I didn't even eat animals; Isaac had taught me to be a vegetarian. Isaac used to say, *It's easy to be an activist when you're heartbroken.* He was talking about the people who smashed windows, whom he did not respect. It's easy to imagine that rage against one person and rage against society are in sync. I didn't know how to explain this to Bay. "Think about the oilman's family," I said at last.

"You've got to fight violence with violence," Bay said. "Image-fare." I thought then that he was speaking metaphorically. He stepped farther into the hall. He looked bizarre next to the foyer table with its arrangement of dried billy buttons.

"You're going to get caught," I said.

"No one's been here in months," he said. "See that doorknob? No prints, cleared off by the rain. That takes weeks and weeks. And moss won't grow like that on a front walk that's been recently stepped on."

He turned to enter the house, and I stood there for a minute, my tongue pasted in my mouth. Then I went around back. I looked for a stream or a rain barrel. It was almost night. I felt pricks of what I thought was rain, but it was snow, astonishing at this time of year. The flakes landed on my hands and didn't melt. I found a rusty tap and fell onto my knees in front of it. When I spun the knob, which shrieked and emitted no water, a shard of rusted metal entered my palm, burning hot.

I dug my fingers into my thigh, trying to stay quiet. The splinter had sunk deep, and I was afraid to squeeze it out. It was worth entering the house to clean out the wound, but just then Bay came out, carrying a heavy load, and kicked the door shut behind him. "Let's head out," he said, and set off back down the walk.

"I need to get this splinter out," I said. My voice was raspy. "It's metal." My palm already shone with swelling, and I felt faint.

"Another thing wrong with you?" he said. He softened. "I'll teach you how to fix it later." He held out a winter coat, a down-filled performance jacket of some kind, expensive.

I grabbed it.

"Give that back to me," he said, smiling, but I could see he was unhappy with me. My hand burned.

"No," I said.

"Trust me," he said.

I handed him the jacket. He admired it while I shivered. He reached into the pockets.

He reminded me of Isaac, taking away something I wanted. The Christmas I was fifteen, my mother had bought me red rubber boots. She already had a pair, except hers were from Walmart and my new ones were from Belk. "We'll match," she'd said. The rubber was thick and expensive, carmine red like a quince flower.

I showed the boots to Isaac and he laughed. "Hideous," he said. "You don't want those." He hadn't yet met her. But Isaac was good at freeing me to feel new disdain or new love; that was why

I liked him so much. "Let's give them to someone who actually needs them." He drove me to Ninth Street and we deposited the boots next to a sleeping man with a cardboard sign, even though they would not fit him. It hurt me to give them away, to look back and see them standing on the curb, pertly upright.

When my mother asked me why I never wore the boots I said, "I donated them." I hadn't known how important they were to her. But she didn't talk to me for a week after that, and I learned it was better to lie.

I looked out over the Smokies, soft layers of taupe and gray. "Here you go," Bay said. He was just like Isaac, but better. After all that fuss, Bay'd just wanted to dress me himself. Nothing had ever hurt so badly as pushing my swollen, frozen, hot hand through a coat sleeve. I didn't let it show. I thought he might turn the car around. I was all his. He zipped me up, pulled the cords. "It's warmer when someone does it for you," he said gently.

I closed my eyes in the rush of heat.

He caught my throbbing hand and lifted it to his eyes. He looked at it just like he'd looked at my father's photograph, tilting it. My left palm was too swollen for me to make a fist, and in the middle of the red, the splinter was rimmed in rigid lemon-white.

"Hey," he said. "You'll get a scar, and you'll always remember this time. Hey, Beryl," he said, more softly. "I know these things. It'll be okay."

I floated, pinned to the earth only by my hand.

*　　*　　*

That evening, he parked in a Pisgah National Forest lot. He brought a folded tent from his trunk, and I saw that the trunk was full of gleaming empty bags of gas station chocolate, the same kind he'd offered me.

"Over in Asher land, we eat our own animals," he said, "but we're mostly a dairy farm. The worker reaps the best rewards. In the fake world, we only eat vegetables, except roadkill. Bet I can find us a raccoon or opossum for tonight." We started to hike up a narrow pine-needle-floored trail into the plum-colored twilight. He carried the backpack and I carried the tent and water, taking care not to use my left hand.

"Sure," I said, though I was a vegetarian. I just wanted to watch him eat it. I liked how Bay kept transforming things: woods into bedroom, raccoon into nourishment, someone else's jacket into ours. I wanted to live like that, borderless, every object taken on its own terms.

We hiked a mile in and set up a camp. The blue night glittered through the trees like a chandelier. While Bay hunted, I held stream ice in a bandana. My coat and hood wrapped me in happiness—I was happy again—the night with Bay was better, his caretaking, the strangeness of homemaking in the middle of nowhere. I thought about deer beds near the Eno, the tamped-down meadow grass.

Bay didn't bring back a raccoon. He heated water on the camp stove for ramen.

"Does Dice shoot oilmen?" I said.

Bay smiled at me. He put a floppy rectangle of ramen on a paper plate for me and crumbled the seasoning over it. "The short answer is no. He's peaceful at heart. The FBI used to watch him because he gave out too much free food. He fed all kinds of people, thousands, the homeless, protesters, everyone." He paused. "But don't you know sometimes people bring violence on themselves? Or maybe you've never seen police in riot gear."

"I've gone to a lot of marches," I said. "My friend lived in a squat, actually."

"A real good girl," he said.

I lay down before he did, and watched his flashlight play over the tent's vibrating blue walls. When he unzipped the door, my heart jumped. He smelled like diesel fuel. The kind of smell near which you shouldn't strike matches. He took off his shoes and the space filled with the vinegar smell of unsocked feet. I waited for him to undress, but he lay down in his clothes. His pants, formerly chinos, perhaps, were as waterproof and shiny as an oiled canvas. "Washing your clothes takes all the fight out of them," he'd said.

In the morning, I paddled my way out of the sticky Pertex and emerged from the tent caped in steam. My left hand was empty of sensation. On the camping stove's soft blue flame, Bay boiled organic oatmeal with organic dried cranberries. Food from the rich people's house. He said he was going to town.

"Am I coming?"

This made him smile, and only later I knew why: I was so eager to let him set the terms.

"Go for a walk," he said. "You need to get better used to your body. You have the distinct look of a person who doesn't know anything about her body." He shook my shoulders. "That's my personal challenge to you," he said. "You always stop short, don't you?"

I loved his touching my shoulders.

"How's that going for you?" he said, and slung on his backpack.

"Don't leave me here," I said.

He looked at me and smiled. He said, "Dice always talks about breaking down the door. Break down the door. What's behind it?" He set off down the trail. The woods became bleaker and my jacket felt warmer.

The autumn sun was unexpectedly low, and I didn't know how to use it to track my path. The sun was pale gold. The remainders of snow had mottled the ground, destroying my depth perception— the forested hills rose like a wall of gneiss. I felt myself panting loudly; I developed a stitch in my side. My hand was melon-heavy. I tried to remember what I'd heard about splinters finding their way to the heart. The woods were young, the ground a knit of jug plants with heart-shaped leaves. The narrow trees trembled in the wind, without enough substance for the wind to bend them.

In these woods every tree seemed exactly the same, and the wind ensured that I couldn't hear myself or smell myself, and it would have been easy to lose faith in myself entirely, except that every pump of blood jostled the metal wedge in my palm. I kept moving forward.

The sun had gone behind a cloud. I trailed spiderwebs like finish-line ribbons as I walked between saplings. I passed a stream overhung with boulders, and twenty minutes later, I passed it again.

I tried to reacquaint myself with my body. But I didn't feel anything, except for the pounding in my hand. I sat this time, and lifted my hand to my face and examined it, testing the skin, which seemed hot and fragile as the skin of a fermented fruit.

I found a row of trees marked with orange spray paint and followed their jagged path till I came out suddenly on the shoulder of a vast deserted highway. Along the sides, busted tires curled like snakeskins. The woods were so shallow after all. One car drove past but I didn't rise to flag it.

I tried to remember what Bay had said: *You who imagine that all fruits ripen at the same time as strawberries know nothing about grapes.* I knew I would never see Bay again, and I was sorry. He was a dream person.

I grounded myself by breathing into my scarf. Memories darted around the brown trees, thousands of them edging up on me. The past for me was 100 percent sad, the way that sometimes weather sites say it's 100 percent humidity outside, but it's still not raining.

I heard a far-off echoing pop, a truck backfiring or a gun, and tried to find my way back to the road again, and failed. The setting sun revealed itself, ducking under the cloud cover, and I walked straight toward it, over streams and logs. Then far away I saw the low blue dome of our tent. I struggled forward, suddenly exhausted.

Bay sat by the tent, smoking and boiling rice. "There you are," he said, and I wanted to kiss him. "What's up?"

"I got lost. I thought I'd never see you again," I said.

"Oh, I envy you," he said. "That's the best place to be."

"I didn't like it," I said. In my absence, Bay had gathered branches for a fire. He built a high, airy stack that lit immediately. No snow: no tent. We sat wrapped in our sleeping bags. My face and chest burned. My backside felt icy and vulnerable. I let my gaze crawl over his long ugly scars.

"How'd you get those scars?"

"From a fight with my dad."

"Did he fight you with a *knife?*"

"Scissors," he said. "Before the Ash Family, I told people I'd fought with a bear." He'd never looked so large as in that moment. He shifted the fire with a branch, compiling the flames into an upward torrent. "What about your folks?"

I saw my mother lifting gems into my hand. "My mom is fine," I said. It felt childish to tell Bay the details.

He nodded. "Well, little sister, you'll fit right in," he said.

"Little sister?" I said.

"You don't like me calling you that."

"I think you're younger than me," I said, though I was only nineteen and Bay seemed twenty-five, or twenty-eight.

"Get away from the calendar." He breathed with a lot of movement. "None of that matters," he said. "We're going to a place of real love. Dice will show you. The borders between you and me?" he said. "Porous. The definite self? Doesn't exist."

I nodded, unsure.

"Dice will understand you like a lightning bolt understands a rod," Bay said. And again he talked about Dice, whom I pictured as a hippie, professor, or priest. I wondered whether Dice would have anything to teach me, because I was looking for someone who could weave together all that I was with all that I wanted to be—a seeker, maybe, but uncertain about my direction, someone moving peripatetically in the direction of nature, wildness, fear, desire, like the weird crosshatch of scratches on the diffraction glasses my father may have given me—I liked to think he did, I was somewhat certain—glasses that turned all small bright lights into hearts. Isaac had told me that the degree to which you can be moved by aesthetic experience seemed, in studies, to have a genetic component. That was my principal heritage, my main virtue—whatever it was, I had so much of it: I could be moved.

After years of lying low, Bay said, Dice was ready again to take action in the world, to wage war on behalf of nature. Bay stopped talking about Dice and looked at me. The fire had calmed. I felt loose and easy, like I'd just been kissed all over the face and neck.

"It's been a big day," Bay said. "But you know what? You've let your guard down. This getting lost is just what I hoped for you." He smiled. He seemed to be taunting me. "Little sister," he said again.

I pushed back. "I could have fallen and died in the woods. I could have gotten shot by a poacher," I said. Or I could have chosen to hitchhike away. Since he'd bothered to talk to me at the bus stop, didn't he want to preserve me? I needed to know that I was not interchangeable, that there was something to me that he liked, something he liked beyond my willingness.

"Beryl," he said. My name was an insult. "I thought you'd understand the Ash Family needs you to go beyond your comfort. Honestly, I was going to bring you there tomorrow. But, you know." Firelight animated his silhouette, his rough hair, his dark slimy coat. I searched for the gentleness I'd seen at the bus stop. He'd once had calm eyes and a frightening face; now it was the opposite: his eyes were tracers, the lights that smear your vision with afterimage; his eyes were bright with malice. "We can give up."

This wasn't what I wanted. I could already feel the shame of returning to Isaac, to his narrow room in the squat, the train pushing through the woods right past the gardenia bush that suffused all our years of courtship with its heart-wrenching heavy gorgeousness. In the summer, even naked, even with the fan, our bodies got sticky as tape. He didn't like the people who smashed windows, but when we lay together and he let his hand drift over my neck and touch me so lightly I could barely stand it, I'd picture him throwing a rock into a wall of glass, and how the shatter seemed to happen not radially but all at once. He was studying at UNC, he wanted me to study, too; he didn't feel the call to a more essential life. I needed to go home changed or not at all.

"For the time being," Bay said. "Not *give up* give up. It's just good sometimes to let yourself go out with the current. Let the tide recede." He shifted tactics. "How's your hand?"

"I think I should go to a clinic tomorrow. It's just getting worse. Though," I added quickly, "I'd like to believe what you said, that it will be okay, and just scar."

"A clinic, like a hospital?" The mood had darkened again somehow. He straightened. "Well, if you go to the hospital, you're going back."

He was agitated and I didn't know why, so I pushed it. "Are you making me choose between you and my hand?"

"We don't deal with institutions like hospitals. We can't be numbered."

"My hand is rotting!" I said. "Look!" My hand was puffy and seemed about to split open.

He rose, so tall he seemed to be on stilts. He pulled his Ka-Bar knife out of his pocket and unsheathed it. In his shadowy hand the shining blade was a small pointed length of fire. In one quick motion, he turned and jammed the blade deep into a tree. The tree stayed still, impassive, but someone cried out: it was me.

When my emotions were hot like this I couldn't tell good from bad, all I could tell was that I was shivering, and I liked that. All elements melt together at a certain heat.

Bay turned around with a smile. "Here, sister. Let me sanitize that hand."

He put more wood on the fire. He sat beside me, pulled my back against his chest so I was almost in his lap. He held out our hands together in the light. "Christ, that's a deep one," he said. "It's metal?"

"Yeah," I said. "I thought you said it would be okay."

"Do you trust me to help you fix it?" he said.

I told him I did.

"Look at me," he said. "Do you trust me?"

I looked at his fire-blurry face. I had that feeling again that I was communicating with an animal. His eyes were fierce but his brain was blank to me. "Yes," I said.

He squeezed my wrist and held my hand flat, grabbed a long burning branch from the fire, and crushed the flame end into my hand.

It didn't hurt at all, really, certainly no more than it was hurting before. He lifted the branch away and we both looked at my ashy palm. A second later, the pain hit, but I could handle it by then. The splinter hadn't budged, though the skin around it quickly blistered. I wondered if this was how he'd intended to fix it. I could still feel the warmth of his hand compressing my wrist, of all things.

"There," he said. "Sterilized."

If I were him, I'd have been sorry, or at least solicitous. But he stretched out on the ground, calm again, just like after he'd shoved me at the rich people's house, shoved me and then instantly forgotten, perhaps. I ran to get my frozen water bottle from the tent so he wouldn't hear me gasping, because now it did hurt—I'd been skinned.

I approached the fire again, numbing my hand against the bottle. It occurred to me that you could learn tolerance to pain the way that you learn math, and I found the thought comforting. I told this to Bay.

"You're right," he said. "It's a life skill. You can learn to make a fire with sticks, too. I practiced every day for an hour, and in a year I could do it. And in the Ash Family, there's a guy who bootstrapped his tools from scratch. You know how to do that?"

"Using sticks?" I said.

"You make a really crude lathe. Then you make crude tools and make a better lathe. Then you make better tools. Lathe your way to a better lathe. Come down here and sit by me, baby."

He kissed me on the lips. He pulled my hair down till my head rolled back and then he kissed me on the neck. "You're nice," he said. "I want you to come meet my family. You'll fit in well. I can't wait for them to meet you."

I smiled. I thought that this was my victory. I thought I'd gotten something from him.

CHAPTER 4

On my first evening at the farm, the sheep guided me home. It was dusk when they whirled past me. Several men exited the barn, calling and gesturing, and the sheep shambled in. A man laid long handfuls of grain in the feeder trough. He saw me watching and said, "Not enough pasture this time of year." I wished he would congratulate me on bringing home the herd.

No one paid me much mind inside the house, either. Warmth and smoke and a frying-onion smell billowed from the kitchen, but there was no space for me there—an older woman kneaded bread at the table, a man flipped vegetables in an immense black pan, another sliced a licheny cheese.

I was looking for Bay, and looking for a place to wash my injured hand, which was hot and sore. I hung Sara's scarf, sweater, and jacket on knobs in the entryway. There was a tray on which sat an orange-lettered plaque that said *September*, and a little box below with the plaques for the other months. I walked through a dining room, a meeting room, and four bedrooms. Each bedroom contained seven bunk beds heavy with pilled blankets. At the other end was the only room with a door, and the door had a lock. I knew because I tried to open it.

I hated that they were hiding a room from me. I missed Isaac's squat, the cat-torn corduroy couch on the porch, the loft beds with granny-square blankets in garish polyester, the walls adorned with paintings of centaurs and rats, the kitchen ceiling a bramble of Christmas lights and drying herbs and dusty feathers, the roof and porch swing always occupied by smokers, the mosquito coils, the incense, the sage, the *palo santo*, the hornet infestation, the bath with its border of hundreds of melted-down red candles, the freight train's loud breathy whistle, the play parties during which Isaac and I hid out in his narrow white room, just listening. In Isaac's squat, nothing was off-limits. I tried the locked door again.

"My friend!" someone called behind me.

It was the black-haired man who'd stared at me during breakfast. He said his name was Gemini. He was emaciated, crouched, in his thirties maybe. "Welcome," he said, smiling at the window, the ceiling. "Dice wants to show you around the property," he said. "You're lucky. Sometimes people wait days to meet him." We sat on the wide-planked floor.

"So what's your story?" I said. I wanted a name like *Gemini*. I was envious of the confidence it signaled.

"My story?" he said. "There's no such thing as the definite self." He shrugged and smiled at the ceiling. "Dice will teach you how to see things fresh." He stood and repositioned a shank—deer, probably—that hung, drying, from a beam. He sat next to me again. "Are you cold?"

He hadn't looked at me yet. "Yes," I said. "I'm cold."

Gemini sprang up, relieved, it seemed, to have a task. He pulled a wicker bin out from under one of the bunks. He tossed me a high-necked taupe sweater constructed of thick waxy yarn. "Raw wool," he said. "Repels more water than a slicker." He tossed me a pair of black work trousers. I couldn't tell if the knees were moth-eaten or worn down from labor. He found a pair of boots. "Put them on," he said.

"Now?" I said.

"Are you embarrassed?" he said, finally raising his gaze to me. There was something canny in his look. I took off my jeans.

A man came into the room, and I hurriedly buttoned up the pants. I knew it was Dice before I looked up.

He was a small man with a slow smile. He was not a hippie. Not a professor. Not a priest. Not any of the ways I'd pictured him. Instead, he was a boxer. He seemed to have his fists up against the world. I couldn't read his expression, whether he was assessing or prowling or lost in thought. I did not notice when Gemini vanished.

I took off my sweatshirt and pulled the sweater over my old Peter Pan blouse. The raw wool scratched my neck and wrists. The trousers were thick and unyielding, molded to a foreign person's shape. The boots felt huge in the toes. I recognized how flimsy my old clothes were. I let my hair down over my shoulders. I was the only one on the farm with long hair.

"Hello," I said.

"Cassie used to wear that sweater," Dice said. So that was his voice: textured and cottony. "And Queen. Pear. And before that Bip. We don't have possessions."

He looked at me intently. He stood straight as a plumb line, the kind of straightness called exactly true. He was an unadorned man with buzzed silver hair and a concerned, falconlike brow, a look so intense it was almost cross-eyed.

He took out a knife, reached high—I backed away from him again, jumpy—and cut a ribbon of meat from the dangling shank. His hands were bright and raw, each finger the size of two of mine. He handed me the piece, dry and textured like grosgrain. I wondered how to tell him I was a vegetarian. Isaac had persuaded me to give up meat with a conversation about minimizing suffering, incremental change. Surely I could explain myself to Dice.

"Eat," he said, fixing his eyes on mine. I was disarmed by his attention. He and I were alone—Isaac, who was a hypocrite, had nothing to do with it. I ate. The meat tasted like the landscape distilled into salt. Water shot onto my tongue. I felt like a dog. It was my first brush with Dice's power: he aroused in me a violent desire to please.

Dice said, "I think you like it." He ushered me out onto the porch and into the navy-blue night. I could hear the cowbells and sheep bells, now sporadic as the animals lay down to rest. "Who taught you to tie your shoes in runner's knots?" he said.

I looked down at my laces, blushing. I didn't know how to react to this quality of attention and so my body defaulted to shame. "My coach," I said. "I'm a high jumper." It seemed essential that he know this, as though the fact would somehow make me adequate. This walk felt like a test, and I was nervous.

"Was," he said. I looked up at him, puzzled. "I *was* a high jumper," he said softly. "Queen will show you how to move around in the tree canopy with a throw rope." He smiled and whistled, calling something. "After you've been here a little while you'll never want to think about the fake world again. Trust me on that." His tone was complicated. He seemed to be making fun of his own seriousness. Of course this was a test: he was widening and widening his circle till I entered it. But I didn't know it then.

Three dogs cantered through the woods. They were enormous and white, as though all their color had been filtered away.

"They kill hunting dogs," Dice said. "That's why we have all those signs up."

I drew my hand back from the dog's ear. "They're all right with you," said Dice, "just don't approach them while they're eating." The dogs, I would learn, ate deer and wolves, and sheep who sometimes suddenly died. They would leave rib cages, bloody legs, pelvises strewn across the farm. By the forest border, we were tripping on bones and stained fur. Dice said, "Did you know that over the past hundred thousand years, humans have been getting tamer? We're breeding for lighter limbs, smaller teeth. We're taming ourselves. And when we're as old as bacteria—that's about four billion years old—we will be as radically interdependent as they are."

"You think we'll get to four billion?" I said.

Dice nodded. "I've spent a lot of time with fossils. I know how things linger. Did Bay tell you I used to work in a coal plant?" He paused. "Tell me about your family," he said.

I told him it was just my mother and me.

"I bet she puts a lot of pressure on you," he said.

"Yes," I said. I could see her now, her tall stomping walk and the pleasure with which she oriented her solar-powered queen of

England figurine on the kitchen windowsill. The queen wore a blue skirt suit and the sun made her little hand wave daintily. My mother adored that thing, which came from one of the gift shops where she worked. "But I think she tries her best," I said. I almost cried as I told him.

"You have to tell yourself a new story," he said softly. "That's all you're crying over—a story you've made up."

I wondered if this was true. My mother and I had both wanted the same thing for me—a better life than hers—but we disagreed about what *better* meant.

He was silent, maybe waiting for me to speak, and I surprised myself by pouring out all the details of my lies—the planned trip to Richmond, the bus to Asheville instead. He asked why I didn't simply refuse to go to college.

I thought about her waving goodbye at the airport. "I didn't want to hurt her," I said.

"You're good to chart your own way," he said.

"I don't think so," I said. Our disagreement was a formality, a game. I knew Dice would win, since I wanted to be good, to believe, to be saved. But—and the Ash Family was always this way for me, beginning to end—even if it was a game, it was more honest than anything else. I hadn't told Isaac, my mother, or anyone else my true feelings about college. And Dice had gotten it from me immediately, with no effort at all.

I wondered if he understood me like a lightning bolt understands a rod, which is what Bay had said would happen. I wondered what that meant, exactly. If I thought too hard, the sense unraveled: maybe Dice was the energy, and I the metal that pulled him safely to the ground. Or maybe it was my job to wait all day for Dice to gather over me.

"Your life in Durham, your mother's life, was unconsidered," Dice said, a little heat edging into his voice. "She bought into the idea that more is better. More schooling, more exclusivity, more credentials, more more more. But *you* are special if you can see beyond that."

I didn't want to hurt her, I'd told him. I imagined how hurt she'd be if she heard Dice saying this about her. I imagined her in Durham, bending over in pain, as Dice's words struck her like a spell. I shook my head, but I was blushing.

He watched me closely. "Let me show you." He reached toward me—"May I?," and I nodded—and touched the center of my forehead, spreading my brow, smoothing out the furrow. My eyes closed. His hand was warm. Dice withdrew his hand and I opened my eyes. "Have you ever walked through a forest on a summer evening?" he said. "Have you seen the does with their spotty red fawns in the tall grass?"

"I have," I said.

"Good," he said. "Listen closely. Like a guided meditation. You know that awakeness? The lightning bugs in sparkling array. Remember walking on a curving road at the peak of summer." I pictured Hillsborough, its hilly old farms. "The plants are gently respiring, releasing all their dew." He savored the words. I felt caught up in his delight.

It might have been how hungry I was after days of meager food, or how tired I was after herding, how torn up by all the newness, or his soft, urging, repetitive words, or something remaining from his fingertips against my brow, but I began to feel a tingling in my fingers and toes. I was no longer cold or hungry on an unfamiliar mountain farm, I was awestruck under a wild star-smeared sky. Dice's voice was an incantation, guiding me down a gravel path. "You are passing a stream," he whispered, "and now you are on the edge of a quarry." I could see the quarry on the Eno in Durham, green-flooded and eternally deep. "You stumble, and begin to fall down the sheer side, against the rocks." I could feel the immense pain in my ribs. His voice was a hush. "Now you disintegrate. You sublime into particles and loft into the air. You become one with the whole world."

I came to in a gust of cold air, and my eyes seemed to reattach to my brain. My ears rang. We had stopped to sit on rocks by the crushed lanes of a vegetable garden. Half of it was covered in white sheets, insulating against the unseasonable cold. Collards and kale showed faintly like huge black flowers. I felt slightly embarrassed. Dice said, "Sometimes you are so fully seen that you disappear." Later, on the edge of sleep, I thought this through and did not understand it, but at the time it was a revelation, a key: if only we all knew this, there would be no war, no warming crisis, and no extinction.

He stood. "Look at you," he said. "So open." He laughed. I was glad he laughed; I was tired of being so serious. "Let me tell you about the family rules. Not my rules," he said. "I don't have rules. Rules from the people who live here." I could just see the white dogs in the distance, wearing each other out running up and down the slopes, snapping at the spaces between each other's mouths. We began to walk again, but it felt different, as though

I were sailing over the ground, frictionless. He said, "I know Bay has your wallet, and I know there's nothing in it. But utopias often fall apart from lack of funds, so new arrivals sometimes choose to donate to the family." I was trying to keep track of each new piece of information. I tripped—a branch, or a bone—and he pulled me up; it was like being winched up by a crane, irresistible. He cupped my elbow in his hand.

"Second," he said, "utopias fall apart from love problems among members. It is important you don't fall in love." He was teasing me. I thought of Bay by the fire, his mouth on my neck. Dice was so much better at talking than Bay, and all kinds of considerations and judgments seemed to run in him like an underground stream; he was precise, controlled. "No couples," Dice said, "and no children—there's enough people on Earth already."

We were walking now past the low twisted trees of an orchard. The dark, bone-humid night, the orange windows in the long house, the clanging bells, the piney wind: they were all his vision.

"Utopias fall apart because their buildings burn down," he said. "We don't bring fire into the barn." In his voice *fire* sounded like *far*. "We don't promise a perfect age right around the corner, either. Don't expect New Jerusalem to come down."

I watched a crowd of bobwhites hustle past. I hadn't been paying full attention. I wanted practicalities.

"What about leaving?" I said. "If someone wants to go away and come back, maybe?" It sounded more like a challenge than I had intended. I still felt as though I was coming out of a trance, not quite aware of myself in my new clothes, in this new place. He glanced toward me. In this dimness, his face was just an outline.

"Why would you want to leave?" Dice said.

"Maybe to see my mother?" I said.

"Why would you want to see her, when you're here among family that truly loves you?"

I noted distantly that I was no longer in the mood to defend my mother.

He continued on, with rules against reading and writing, phones, mirrors, soap. Rules about volunteering for hard tasks. About sacrificing for the land, facing pain for the land.

"No fake-world medicine," he said. "No hospitals." Especially not antibiotics, which were distorting the evolution of bacteria and creating new strains we could not defend against. He said that old witches often had the right idea: the willow-bark tea that predated aspirin, the foxglove that fixed hearts long before digitalis.

"What if someone breaks their arm?" I said.

"It's important that we not reveal ourselves haphazardly to the fake world," he said. "People would be threatened by our way of life and try to destroy us. We can't be numbered."

"You certainly wouldn't let people"—I couldn't say *die* in front of him—"wouldn't let people stay sick," I finished lamely.

"Beryl," he said, his warm hand against my cheek. I hadn't realized he knew my name. "I do not let people stay sick."

I blushed again. "But can you fix my hand?" I said.

"Didn't Bay?" Dice said. His tone was cross. "There's a healer, Pear. She'll look if it's not better next week. Pear's the one who fixed Bay's arms."

"After his dad stabbed him with scissors?"

Dice let go of my elbow. "Bay," he said, "was trying, incorrectly, to build a bomb for me." This wasn't what Bay had said, but I had the feeling they were colluding; there was some intention behind these conflicting stories. "He got a thousand pieces of glass in his face."

"A bomb?" I said.

"Sometimes you have to fight violence with violence," Dice said. "Do we prefer violence? No. But consider what's at stake." I blundered after him. Would I bomb mining machinery? Would I bomb a house if there was no one in it? I would not bomb a house if there was someone in it.

"I used to work in a power plant," said Dice. "Did you know you pulverize the coal into fairy dust before you burn it, so it's hotter? I used to clean the fly ash out of hoppers. It's as soft as water. It clogs in your mask. It's what's left of the ferns in the wet forests and it's radioactive, no one knows that coal plants are a hundred times worse than nuclear. No one knows it because everything you read about climate change is so boring. Why is it all so boring?"

I shook my head. It didn't bore me; it made me sad.

"It's because climate change is so big—so extra-human in scope, Beryl," he said. "And the solutions are so mundane. Change your lightbulbs. Bike. Recycle."

"I wish nature could beat people up," I said.

He smiled. "Exactly, exactly," he said. "And let me tell you something true. This is the best conversation I've ever had about our rules."

I flushed. My mother told me the right response to a compliment isn't to try to deny it. Just to say thank you. But I couldn't even say that to Dice, I was too excited. "Really, the best?" I managed.

"If you stay on here you will find another solution," he said. He nodded. "A real solution." We passed the hickory and stepped through the yellow leaves. Dice said, "In school they teach you that natural selection is all competition, but cooperation, cooperation is equally strong. Cooperation determines which animals live and which die, and what form they take. This is dangerous knowledge." He paused. I wasn't used to so much thoughtfulness. Emotion was easy and planning was hard, and most people, activists or otherwise, never moved from one to the next. *The more knowledge is inherent in a thing, the greater the love*, Bay had said at the bus stop.

"But don't you think," I said, emboldened by his compliment, "don't you think moving off the grid means you can't have a real effect on the ruling class, on politics, on the workers?" That was something Isaac would have said. That was how he defended his decision to stay in Durham, to stay in the system, change it from within. I followed Dice up onto the porch.

Dice didn't ask me what effect I'd had recently on the ruling class and politics and workers. This was a kindness. He nodded. "Marx said he didn't want to write recipes for the cookshops of the future. The people will find their own best way. We found ours."

We walked through the bedrooms to his door. I remembered how Isaac used to reassure me, when we worried we weren't doing enough good. "My friend used to say that even a hypocrite could be an agent of change," I said. I thought he'd nod again. Instead he rounded on me. His low brow had lowered farther and his eyes were shadowed.

"Who said that?"

"Someone I know in Durham." My heart was pounding.

"A fool," he said.

Dice unlocked his room, which smelled, unlike the rest of the farm, soapy and piney. A loud cat with too many toes sat in the middle of his floor, and he picked it up tenderly. "And after all these years," he said, his tone turned kind and gentle again, "the developer company, Delta, is closing in on us, and we're not going to let them take our land. You'll see."

His room was furnished with a pink velvet love seat, a bookshelf topped with a row of needle-sized bones. He showed me his bathroom. A stove with blue and white tiles occupied much of the space. The tiles showed fish becoming horses, and trading ships with all their sails.

He sloshed a vat of water from the stove into the tub. The steam was so thick it was almost a froth. He poured in a cap of lavender oil, distilled in pits, he said, a light oil sparkling in the water. "Few people know it's a tonic, not a relaxant," he said. He lifted my wrist, his touch shocked me, I laughed. He was looking at my splinter.

"Do you have tweezers?" I said awkwardly, not quite willing to take my hand away from him. That was how my mother took care of splinters.

"Just let your hand infect a little, and the splinter will slide out on the pus. That's what the infection is for," he said.

He paused and looked at me. In the light, he reminded me of a mossed-over weatherworn statue in the cemetery. It was hard to look at him—he was too attentive. "You can take a bath if you want," he said. "Hot baths are a rarity around here."

"Is it just luck, or did I earn it?" I said.

He looked me up and down. I held my breath. "Beryl," he said. "No, if you stay, your name will be Harmony."

He left and closed the door. I turned the lock behind him though I knew he had the key.

The water tugged in circles around my knees and chest. Below its line I was gravityless. I scrubbed myself and the tub filled with grit. The soap was white and loamy and peppermint scented: cow-fat soap. My ribs were bruised—I remembered my fall into the mine, and then remembered it was imaginary, part of the guided meditation. I poked the dark spots in confusion. I realized I hadn't asked him what happens to people who break the rules.

Isaac would laugh at this *Harmony*, a soaring name for a girl who was known to be a problem. Maybe things were different here, I thought. I lay back in the steam and felt my body was pouring upward with it, diffusing into the air.

I must have been seven or eight the last time I'd had a bath. At that age, I remembered, I once collected magnolia seed cones, hairy pods with hot-red seeds spilling out of them. I carried them indoors, dirtying the table, and my mother hurled them out the window, one by one, into the black air of a thunderstorm, as if she could wound it.

CHAPTER 5

When I emerged from Dice's bathroom, wearing my new clothes with the lavender water dripping off the ends of my hair, Sara, not Dice, was waiting for me on the couch. I felt the quick heat of disappointment. She led me across the dark courtyard. I had missed dinner. I was trying hard to accept everything and didn't tell her how hungry I was.

Sara showed me to the barn with a flashlight and we climbed up into the hayloft cathedral. When the flashlight's blue-white beam hit the columns, monstrous dark shapes flowed over the walls. Sara kissed me good night on the corner of my mouth. "If you ever have any problems," she said, "Dice will be there for you, all right?" I lay down on a bare mattress under a blanket that warmed me like fire. My ribs ached. All night I could hear the animals sighing. And screech owls, who sometimes sounded just like human babies.

I must have fallen asleep because I woke with ice on my eyelashes, ice in my nostrils. My injured palm felt slick and oily. The sky began to lighten and I examined my hand—the splinter was gone. The narrow verticals of sky turned cobalt, then mauve, then white.

Sara reappeared and handed me a tin cup of hot milk and honey. She sat with me on the mattress, which, under the stains, was lustrous with blue jacquard roses. The mattress half lay over a shut black trapdoor. "Where does that little door go?" I asked Sara. "To a stable?"

"It's locked," she said, as though that was an answer.

We could hear someone ringing the big bell in front of the long house. "Breakfast," Sara said, and we descended. We lined up in the meeting room. I was last. Someone near me smelled like artificial butter. Someone else like freshly sharpened Ticonderoga pencils. Like new plastic bags. Like molasses. The smells came from clefts, places where the body folded. You could smell people across the room. I wanted a smell, too.

The family members prepared quickly for breakfast, a long centipede row of arms tidying, arranging, setting. I was still trying to guess the right ways to help. The mood in the room was excited—everyone talked quickly. About pipes? About chains? About mountains? Through the window I watched three men haul roadkill deer back to the house, pulling them over the gravel as though they didn't know about wheels and carts.

Two other men with shaved heads unlidded large portions of sheep cheese, quinoa, late pawpaws with chestnuts, salted sheep's ribs, and candy roaster squash pies with deer tallow scraped from hides. I tried to select vegetarian items, though I didn't know if I even was a vegetarian anymore. I would learn that our food was mostly preserved or Dumpstered or foraged.

Bay was there, joking and smiling and expounding on something, but Dice wasn't. I noticed one woman with a frightening tattoo, a straight line that fell from her chin down her neck and past the collar of her shirt. I averted my eyes. I sat between Gemini and Sara. They both called me Harmony and smiled strong happy smiles with their lips, no teeth. I would find out later that teeth-smiling scares sheep.

I listened to Bay. "You wrap a chain around your wrist," he was saying, "and a chain around your neighbor's wrist." He gestured with a bitten-down bone. "You put your arms into a pipe and lock the chains together. So the police are helpless. They can't reach the carabiner and they can't cut through the pipe because then they might slice through your wrists."

I remembered the PVC pipe in the barn—thousands of pieces. I met Bay's eyes and smiled. He seemed not to see me. I sat there, stupidly blushing. Well, couples weren't allowed, but he'd kissed me. If he didn't want to be kind to me in public, then I would pretend it didn't matter.

"What's going on?" I whispered to Gemini.

"Protest," Gemini said. As he talked, he tore a piece of brown bread into many smaller pieces, and rolled the pieces into tiny balls, and then ate them, sparrowlike. He explained that Dice and his contacts were planning a log blockade, a sit-in and a hunger strike, all over the enormous site that the coal people had burned and wanted to rip up, almost two thousand acres. "We're just trying to get in the way," he said.

I'd never seen a protest like that. What had Isaac and I been doing, running around taking photos and stealing food from my mother's kitchen for the squat? I felt ashamed for thinking our work had been so important.

"Is everyone going?" I said.

"A few people need to stay behind."

"Can I go?" I wanted to prove myself to the family. I wanted to put my body on the line for nature—like Dice had said, not just recycling and LED bulbs, something more essential. I imagined telling Isaac about the blockades and the pipe arms.

Gemini wouldn't meet my eyes.

I knew Dice had arrived by the sudden quiet. The family members put down their silverware. I wondered if they just did it naturally—and if one day I'd find it natural. He stood in the doorway, surveying us. Slowly he made his way around the table to me. He placed his hands on my shoulders. My skin was burning from that feeling where all emotions run together and all I feel is heat. His fingers were warm through my shirt. He smelled like ash. "Let's welcome this young woman," he said. Two dozen faces turned toward me, and I felt stupefied by their bright curious gazes. "She's a good one," said Dice.

"We know it!" said Sara.

"Her name will be Harmony, if she wants to stay," Dice said. He squeezed my shoulder and I felt limp. I could feel my heart flickering in his palm. Quietly, so I almost couldn't hear him through the ringing in my ears, he said, "We will never limit you like your mother did."

My eyes filled with tears. I wondered if my mother had limited me or betrayed me or let me down. Not exactly, not specifically, but that didn't make Dice's grip on my shoulder any less true, and I began to forget how much I loved the flecks of rainbow twirling off those diamond earrings, my inheritance from her, her love of small beauties. The family watched me expectantly—and there was Bay, watching too, willing me to nod, to agree, to acquiesce. I felt myself crying. I may as well surrender, I thought. The gale came into me, and blew all my doors and windows open.

After dinner, the family pulled the chairs into a square and paged through long maroon songbooks. Nothing else I'd seen at the farm had words on it, other than the calendar with its wooden plaques for the months. Sara gave the key at the beginning of each song—"Fa, la, so," she sang, and then the sound blossomed as everyone matched their voices to her. The songs were eerie, clamorous, with wide rifts between the chords, and fugues during which the melody circled through the group. There was no tension at all in the harmonies. I couldn't follow the music so I watched the family's faces. Some, like Gemini and Bay, knew every word and barely looked at their texts. Others looked tentative, following along with a finger. My favorite song that first night was "O'Leary." The singing frightened me a little and I loved the feeling, the same feeling as looking at Bay's scarred arms.

How will my heart endure
The terrors of that day,
When earth and heav'n before His face
Astonished shrink away?

Afterward, the women put on nightgowns and the men long johns and they carried candles to the bedrooms. No one seemed to have a claim to any particular bed.

I climbed the hayloft ladder alone and found the way to my mattress. The night wind sobbed in the hay. I thought of my old bedroom in Durham. Together, my mother and I had decorated the walls with nature magazine photos—octopus suckers curling in a gloomy sea, a sand-filled old house in the desert. The pages had stiffened and curled and lost their gloss. My bookshelf was shoved full of castoffs from the gift shop where my mother worked. I had wind-up chattering teeth, magnetic lettuce, a pig-shaped flashlight with two LEDs in its snout, and well-worn cardboard-framed heart-diffraction glasses.

I had taken barely anything with me when I left Durham. That morning, I'd packed winter clothes and over-the-counter cold softgels, little cabochons to set in a brooch, orange for the day and blue for the night. I stuffed plastic jewelry into a Ziploc. I rolled my French Toast schoolgirl blouses and wedged them into my oxfords. I paced my room, cupping old possessions like eggs: my extra track spikes and varsity J, my pearly contact sheets from Isaac, long exposures of me snow-angeling on dark ground.

That afternoon, Isaac had taken me on a farewell trip to the quarry. We'd broken up a few weeks before. Neither of us knew how to interact now, so we behaved the same as ever, except weighed down with a melancholy so intense I felt I was acting in a play. He drove past the park where I'd posed for him over the hurricane-swollen stream.

The Eno had flooded the old quarry with an unknown depth of rich, jelly-green water. We jumped into the water for the express purpose of evaporating on the shore. Plunging through the cold, flimsy water, for a second I forgot how to swim.

"I can't believe you're leaving, Berie!" Isaac said too loudly as we paddled to the edge. The water at my feet was cold, and at my chest it was hot and green. I couldn't tell if he was angry. I had done just want he had wanted—what my mother wanted, what everyone wanted.

I said, "I'm sure it'll be just the same as being here."

Later we lay in the buzzing leaves, watching four small boys swing themselves from a rope into the water. The air smelled like cinnamon from the black and yellow millipedes. I heard Isaac's shutter click. He aimed at me through a gap in the weeds. When I reached for him, he said, "You're going to get to college and you're going to like it."

"Maybe," I said. A drip dangled from his earlobe and I restrained myself from kissing it away. I knew his skin would be sulfurous from the water. I knew his face better than I knew my own, his hammerhead eyes, his peculiar softness.

"Don't let the strawberries die while I'm gone," I said. I'd cultivated them for years in the vacant lot next to his squat.

"Well," he said, "if we ever get married, this is where we'll have the ceremony."

I laughed.

With Isaac I first learned to commit to something. I remembered the first time he'd coaxed me to jump off the quarry's cliff. I remembered holding the coarse rope in my hands, swinging myself over the flooded depths, and dropping down into the deep green water. If you don't drop down at the right spot, you'll smack yourself against the cliff, Isaac said. But the water looks so far below, and the plunge takes all of the air out of your lungs. This was training for my future life. Before Isaac I'd never been such a good high jumper; I'd always been afraid I'd fall wrong. He taught me it only takes one split second to commit to fearlessness. I'd learned that lesson—I'd learned it too well. I could no longer stay with Isaac listening to the trains make their way through the woods, hosting the punks who came off of them but never quite leaving myself.

My third day at the farm came, cold and bright. The family rested. Tomorrow they were going to chain themselves together in Tennessee. I led the sheep out, then worked with three other women to make pemmican for the voyage, grinding salted venison into brick-colored powder, mixing it with warm fat and raisins and honey, and pressing it into little balls. We wrapped each ball in a waxed bedsheet. The men tied together the PVC pipes like bales and stacked them in the back of a pickup.

After lunch, I searched for Bay. He'd been ignoring me at meals, and I was tired of acting like I didn't mind. I was going to say, "Did you miss me?" I wanted to ask if they really meant it, *three days or the rest of your life*, and if he'd noticed I'd been here three days. I searched the cold bedrooms, and around the hickory, down to its last leaves now, and the stables, and the dairy.

I found Bay in the storage house. The walls were stacked with Dumpstered food—cans of corn, condensed soup, oatmeal. *The worker reaps the best rewards*, Bay had said. Bay was sorting through crates of carrots half-buried in sand. I stood on the threshold, suddenly afraid to call him, to seem too eager. Isaac and I had moved through this phase—the phase of unequal affections—so speedily that I couldn't even remember who had been in charge.

I was turning to leave when he noticed me. "Sister," he said. "So what's it going to be? You need me to bring you back to Asheville?"

"I have to decide today?" I said, disingenuously, just to get his response.

"We'd miss you," he said. "I, personally, would miss you."

"I like being missed," I said.

"Stay," he said. He leaned onto me. I could feel the cool intake of his breath as he smelled the part of my hair. "You'll stink like a real Asher in no time," he said.

Isaac said that even a hypocrite could be an agent of change because that was what interested him—the lifestyle, the feeling of being different. But he also wanted all the normal things, buying things and earning things, a house and kids. We'd gone to marches and then what had we done? I'd never been to an action with water cannons and rubber bullets. But Dice had, and Bay had, and the family had. Dice had said they had *another solution, a real solution.* I'd always known there was something more.

And here was Bay, asking me to stay.

"All right," I said. I was hoping for a kiss on the mouth, but he only kissed my forehead.

CHAPTER 6

A girl I'd seen the previous day, the girl with the tattoo, woke me before dawn the next morning, when the black trees were just a slight perturbation on the blue-black sky. She brought me a cup of cream, like sweet white grease. "They're heading off," she said, "so you've got to help me with the milking." She said her name was Queen. I again examined that tattoo down the center of her throat and into her shirt collar, a thick dark line, finger width, so it looked like she was sliced in two. She was young. My age.

A school bus idled in the courtyard, and the family members hustled out to it through the clouds of exhaust, lit orange and red. Before I'd blinked the blear out of my eyes, they were gone: the bus, Dice's truck, and Bay's car. Now I could hear the cowbells and the sheep bells, the rooster.

Queen wouldn't tell me how long they would be away. She had pink cheeks, a round face, lank hair grown-out pageboy length, perfectly round nostrils, and a slow, dazed way of talking. Queen roused the enormous, sleepy cows and showed me how to clean their rears with a stiff brush, how to wash their teats with a sponge and warm water. I asked her what the cows thought of us, and she said they could tell I was nervous. The sun came in, and the hay-clotted air became, abruptly, a gold mine. Queen showed me to a thirteen-year-old heifer, and instructed me to set down my stool and bucket in the straw, and to grip the bucket firmly between my legs so she wouldn't ruin the milk by kicking it over. "Good," Queen said as I pinched and squeezed the cow's warty teats. But within a few minutes, pain wore out my tendons. Meanwhile Queen had milked a whole bucket.

She glanced over at me. "Not everyone can get the milk out," she said. She seemed to be assessing what to say next. "You can just rest. We won't be in any rush till they all get back."

I knew I shouldn't want to rest, remembering Sara saying *earn our trust* when she held out her clothes to me, but with Queen's permission, I stopped. I rubbed my forearms in relief. The patient cow gave me a brown-eyed look. I asked Queen about her tattoo. "I was on drugs," she said. I watched milk issue from her fists. "I came here to be free," she said, "freedom in the mountains." She flushed and patted the cow's flank.

"And you found what you wanted?" I said.

For a long time all I heard was the hiss of milk into her bucket. "I'm more free than I was before," she said, "but wherever I go, I find myself." Unlike Dice, unlike Sara, Queen seemed to be still working things out. She smiled again. "Even though Dice says there's no such thing as the definite self, did he tell you that?"

I nodded.

"You remind me of a girl I used to know," Queen said. "Cassie. She was a watcher too."

I moved my stool closer. She began talking to me about actions that create authenticity. For example, she said, once you get a tattoo, you're the kind of person who would have a tattoo. For example, she'd never been sexy, never felt sexy, and then she had sex for the first time and though she felt just the same, she knew she was now sexy. The action made her so, incontrovertibly. I nodded along, though I didn't completely understand.

"It's just like the Ash Family," Queen said, and she was smiling again, at something that seemed in the past or future: "If you try to be a part of it, you are," she said. "You have to be open."

"Dice said I am open," I said.

"Start by telling me about how your mother let you down."

"What do you mean?" I said, so quickly I didn't have time to consider it.

Queen tilted her head. "Yesterday, at breakfast, Dice said it." Queen's tone was determined. "She left you alone, right? She abandoned you?"

I remembered my mother's reflection in the linoleum at the airport, such a big solid woman made small and uncertain by a trick of the light. It felt like someone was pressing two fingers into the base of my throat. "Yes," I said. "She was horrible." Maybe, in a certain light.

Queen patted my shoulder the way she'd patted the cow.

I said, "Why didn't you want to go on the action?"

She smiled. "I didn't want to fast," she said. "I'm afraid of going hungry, so Dice didn't make me." She squeezed my arm.

Like Dice's, her grip was so strong it felt mechanical. "I know it's a lot to take in at first," she said, "but no one here will ever make you do anything you don't want to do."

I looked at the ground and nodded.

"Believe me," she said. Her eyes were pink.

She let go of me. A cow bellowed, its voice breaking. Queen wiped at her face. I wondered how she got that name but I was afraid to ask. "Do you think they'll manage to stop the mountaintop removal?"

"I'm not sure," she said, tilting the udder. The cow licked its blue nose. "But Dice has performed many miracles." She paused. "He got me off drugs, right when I thought I would die. I was at the end of the line." She was distant, thoughtful. "He heals without fake-world medicine."

This reminded me that I needed to go to a store. "Is there a car around? Can you take me?"

Queen said, "Why would you want to leave, when we have everything we need?"

"I'm going to get my period soon," I said.

"We don't have to leave for that."

"I'd love to pick up a few other things," I said. I craved so many foods, foods I planned to steal or eat right at the cash register: Peach Looza. Coconut water, the sugary, viscous kind filled with white cubes of pulp. Chocolate chip cookies, lined up in a plastic rib cage. I was going to put lotion all over my raw hands. "Come on," I said. "Dice didn't mention any rules about errands."

"Most of the women here can't get their periods anymore," Queen said. I was surprised. Everyone on the farm seemed young.

Instead of a trip to town, she brought me to the storage house and pulled out a cookie tin. She showed me the little rubber cups for the most of it, and special store-bought soap to clean the cups, and then reusable pads with snaps on the wings, hand-sewn out of novelty fabrics, dogs flying airplanes, dancing skeletons, to hide stains. We could dump our blood in the humanure wooden toilet box and cover it with sawdust, like anything else, she told me. "Listen," Queen said. "They're not going to be straightforward with you about whether you can go to town. They'll say, 'Why would you want to leave, when what you're looking for is right here?'"

I thought back—Dice had said that; Queen had, a minute ago.

"I've learned it's better not to ask," Queen said. "Sometimes you might go, accompanied," she said. "They don't like it when we leave. If you try to leave, they follow you. And then if they think you've closed off, they do this thing called a rebirth."

I wondered if she was speaking from experience. "What's a rebirth?" I said.

"It's a ceremony," she said. She shook her head as if to clear it. "Dice wants to keep the family together, that's all. And if we're open enough, we'll be able to fix the world. It sounds crazy," she said, "but we've all seen this light around him, he glows a little bit."

Queen closed the tin, red with silver reindeer, which reminded me of my mother's tin, and that necklace with its silver garlands, and the earrings, and how I was supposed to be in Virginia, learning expository writing and pushing my way into a future more auspicious than a knickknack store. Then she tucked the tin back among the gold bottles of peaches and tomatoes.

Queen looked me over. "Let's cut your hair. Get that padding off the brain. And for the family resemblance, you know."

"Cut it right now?" I said, lifting my hair, which felt like satin in the cold.

She watched me, smiling vaguely. "I promise, you'll really feel like you belong."

She used the sheep shears. The shears were two facing knives connected by a U of bendy metal—no hinge, like scissors, just a hooklike structure she squeezed with her hands. She held my skull with her fingertips, tilted it back and forth as the shears crunched into my long hair. With each clip my head lightened, bobbing up like a spring.

There wasn't a mirror around to check what I looked like. In the compost toilet room there was a burned cookie sheet nailed where the mirror would have been. I kept seeking my face in it.

"I bet I look like a mental patient," I said.

"You are one!" Queen said, and kissed me on the head.

I could feel the cold breeze blowing on my skull.

Only five of us were present at lunch. I didn't recognize the other three. They ate quietly, standing with their plates by the sink, their heads bent.

In the afternoon, I followed the sheep higher up the mountains. I was learning. A few headstrong ewes led the flock, and so it really wasn't sixty sheep I had to control, but four. When a sheep turned the wrong way, I'd run to stand in front of her, and sometimes that was enough. She'd shift direction without even acknowledging me, like a cat. When that didn't work, I'd stand in front and yell a little, "Ay ay ay." When that didn't work I'd stand, yell, and shake a branch, making myself look bigger. If I had to escalate, I'd try jumping, throwing sticks, yelling, running right at the sheep, and pushing on their heads and shoulders. I had an innate advantage, because sheep already fear anything with eyes at the front of the head, instead of at the sides. Front eyes are for predators.

That afternoon, the sheep tromped over a stream, frozen on top, moving underneath. My knees and hands cracked the ice as I splashed into the water. I looked up and I saw a heron, the blue slashes along its narrow head, the long white curved throat, the massive tucked body, dipping its foot in the stream.

I was in the mood to believe. The family had made me receptive to new possibilities—yes, they'd done their work. It was getting lost in Pisgah, it was Dice's spell, it was everyone telling me, over and over, that I had to be open, and that they could tell if I wasn't. I lost track of myself; I felt I was becoming the heron. What a relief it was to move from looking to being. So this is what it's like to be a bird, gravity so light on my hollow bones, my long curled neck readying for a strike.

The heron startled and took off, a rigid white kite. I could hear someone rushing through the woods behind me, a girl's voice cursing, then a shuddering crack, and the heron jerked in the air and followed its own neck to the ground. Queen emerged from the woods, carrying a rifle. She walked through the stream and approached the heron, which beat its wings helplessly against the stream bank. "Hey, Harmony," she said, and laughed at my aghast face. "I've got dinner."

"You can't eat a heron," I said.

"Yeah, you can," she said. "They taste like frogs' legs." Some dark blood trickled into the stream, which pulled it quickly away, toward Tennessee. She slung the immense corpse into her arms. One wing spilled whitely to the ground. "We eat otters, beavers, raccoons." I searched her face for remorse and found none. "You're all right. Go on," she said. "Go on and bring the sheep back."

That night, the compost bucket under the sink was filled with blue feathers. Queen had dredged the bird's long breast in flour and fried it with mushrooms. I ate the heron, dead blue angel, because I was here to understand how it all worked—the processes of stars, trees, and animals, the way to wring out a living from dirt. I'd eaten deer; this was the same. I had this idea that if I found everything agreeable and easy and comprehensible, then my redemption wouldn't be real. It had to be hard, to hurt, like my hand. So I would be okay with not leaving. I would be okay with no modern medicine. I would be okay with no couples. In the fake world, people competed to live with perfect ease and that was why the Earth was dying.

And I could look in any direction and see goodness. The following morning, I woke to find every needle of pine jacketed by a low frozen cloud, sparkling with rime. The extended laugh of the yellow-shafted flickers echoed upward, with their endless tapping. I reached the kitchen before anyone else, and while I made pancakes for the five of us who were left behind, the clouds drew back raggedly from the lavender-blue sky, and all the mountains shone.

It was not restful, but it was ascetic, which could be mistaken for restfulness.

Soon Queen came to work beside me. I admired how quickly she lit the woodstove. She cored apples, filled them with butter, and baked them till they collapsed, red skins turned leathery gold. I liked her again.

"Changing weather," Queen said, nodding at the sun on the sleet. "Sometimes here there's a double rainbow, and there's a third rainbow and a fourth rainbow, always in the same place if you know where to look, around the sun."

"That can't be true," I said.

"I promise. I'll show you," she said. "Did you know Dice can change the weather with his mind?"

"Sure," I said. Queen seemed naïve, but I couldn't make sense of that: she'd tried out more lives than I had. "Later," I said, "will you tell me more about your life before you got here?"

She looked surprised. She smiled at me, stroking her vertical tattoo. I wondered if it felt different from her other skin. "We're not supposed to talk too much about the fake world," she said.

"Does everyone always follow the rules?" I said.

She gave me a long, probing look. "Don't mess with me, Harmony," she said.

"I'm not!" I said. And she surprised me by bestowing upon me a glorious sunbeam of a smile. That moment set the pattern for what would become the center of our friendship: we recognized in each other the person who might lead us astray.

Breakfast was quiet. We knew our brothers and sisters were planning a hunger strike, sitting on the cold ashy mountaintop all chained together, in frost, in sleet. I turned at little sounds, like that wind arrow caught in the holler bluster. No, it was just the dogs on the porch; no, it was just the pine branch scraping at the window; no, it was just the wind.

Queen milked. I collected eggs. We fed the pigs. "Did you know these pigs are guarding something?" Queen said.

I shook my head.

"See that door behind them?" There was a door in the back wall of their stall—I hadn't noticed it.

"There's a room back there. That's where Dice buries departed friends," Queen said. "I mean, his faithful dogs, the good rams."

"Oh," I said. "For a moment, I almost thought you meant people."

She laughed. "You don't think dogs and sheep are as worthwhile as people?"

I shook my head uncertainly. "Have you been in there?"

"No," Queen said. "It's locked." She snaked her arm around me. "Last year, when the room got full, we milled up some old bones and used them in the garden, for phosphorus. He's thoughtful about everything," she said. "I like thinking that nothing gets forgotten."

The family returned that afternoon. The bus arrived, then the truck, then Bay's car, and Queen made me help her fill up the largest cauldron with water to boil. The family came out, dirty, gaunt, and terribly quiet. They removed their clothes, standing on their toes on the dead grass. They wore underwear or undershirts or nothing at all under the subdued half-light of the afternoon. They were like a conquered army. Dice tested the water, then the family washed, with buckets and dippers, in water slippery with cow-fat soap.

Bay walked toward us. I looked at his scars, like countless shining splinters. My heart lurched remembering he'd kissed me.

"What happened?" I said.

"Wait for Dice to say," he said.

We ate salami and bananas and grits for dinner. Dice ate nothing. Afterward we pulled the chairs in a circle in the meeting room. A circle of chairs meant a story; a square of chairs meant singing.

"I want to talk about failure," Dice said. "You might think we failed, but I'm not so sure." He spoke very quietly. "Once I saw a corpse in the desert and it was only dry bones but it lay atop a patch of flowers." In school, we always avoided looking at the teacher. But here, our attention made Dice a radiating star.

"There aren't many wild places left in these mountains," Dice said. "Look for the clean trunks. To the missionaries who first scouted the Blue Ridge," he said, "these trees were a hundred feet tall. Four hundred years ago North Carolina was wild grapes as far as the eye could see, sugaring a horse's legs to the knee, and you could catch a passenger pigeon for dinner just by swinging a heavy pan through the air." The family hummed and sighed together. "Remember what you're struggling for," Dice said. "We'll find the ennobling conflicts that will convey us to a better world."

Out of the thousands expected, Dice said, less than a hundred showed. The first day no media came either. So for the eighty or so present, there was extra pressure to fast and stay, and so many disappeared in hunger and frustration till it was only the twenty of the family left. The next night they unchained their arms because no one cared one way or the other. "But is this failure?" Dice said.

And then when the journalist arrived, Dice said, he didn't have his cameraman. "Is this failure?" Dice said again.

The mountaintop was going to fly off today. He said, "By what standards did we fail? I believe a protest can have five goals. You can have a protest to disrupt a harmful thing." He spoke soberly, as though he was not trying to get anyone excited.

"Yes," we said.

"Or have a protest to get the message to media."

"Yes!" we shouted.

"Or have a protest to show your enemies that you exist."

"Yes!" Almost everyone was crying. Even Bay's face glistened.

"Or have a protest for self-expression, or have a protest to live differently for a little while." When I blinked tears fell onto my cheeks too. My heart pounded as though I was scared, and I felt that hot undifferentiated emotion, and it took some time to untangle what I was feeling: fear, regret, but above all, elation. "Any of these five forms of protest can have real outcomes, and we are three for five, and this is a success if we are willing to call it one. Even one would be enough."

He spoke as though he hadn't noticed he'd brought a roomful of people to tears. "We'll plan another," Dice said. "We'll step up. Cooperation is just as important as competition. This is dangerous knowledge. Cooperation, consistency." He said that the migrating monarch butterflies zigzag over Lake Superior to avoid a mountain that vanished millions of years ago. And this wasn't a failure. The more efficient you are, the more fragile. Dice had told me that all of life is storytelling, and now I saw how the protest hadn't been a failure at all, but a step toward justice.

We sang the song called "China." Sara led it. Her hand wavered as she beat time.

Why do we mourn departing friends?
Or shake at death's alarms?

The floor shook. I remembered seeing the family at the breakfast table my first morning, less than a week ago, their peaceful communion. Now I saw how that communion could be unpeaceful, ungentle. They all felt the same emotion at once; they had that mass brain like the monarchs. Dice said, *Cooperation is just as important as competition.* If Dice had asked me to run back to the mountaintop just then, I would have done it.

While we sang, Sara opened the doors and the windows of the long house, so the songs could go out and the stars could come in. Light snow was falling. The wind came in strong and the snow came in too, as though nature itself were penetrating, invading, shuffling in, leaving its tracks all through the house.

winter

CHAPTER 7

I spent that winter getting to know the sheep, laying down straw
for their beds, mucking out the stalls in the morning, herding
them out in fair weather, distributing silage and dusty hay into
their long troughs, and then, soon enough, helping with the
lambing. I'd find lambs in the ewes' enclosure in the early morning, staggering around and bleating.

I couldn't tell if I was happy or sad. All the clutter in my head
was gone. I felt free and easy and able to focus on new things
besides my mother and Isaac and college and old necklaces and
solar figurines. Dice told stories: about Tennessee miners freeing
convicts and burning company buildings under cover of night,
about women saboteurs dynamiting their textile mills, about bea-
ver lodges you could crawl into, and the sandstorms he'd experienced where there was so much static electricity he had to pull a
metal pipe behind him in the sand, to ground the current.

The weeks passed, then the months. We ate bread with chicken
fat. Once a week, stack cake, layers adhered with applesauce made
from dried apples. Sometimes we had boiled beans studded with

mean razorback. Sometimes shavings of country ham, cured from last winter's hog slaughter in a pillowcase of ashes. Thick sweet butter. Chinquapin meats prised from their spiky hulls. Bannock bread, sorghum-sweet. Fresh cheeses, still jiggling like gelatin. The worker reaped the best rewards.

I became a glutton for experiences. Experiences so real they felt unreal. We heated water for cleaning our dishes and dairy and bodies with two wood furnaces. In the winter, a water pipe below the shower split along the seams, and we couldn't bathe there while one of the men repaired it. So again we boiled water outside in a copper tureen in the fire pit, and now I too got to take the hottest bucket bath as I stood naked in the snow. I could slough off handfuls of dead skin and oil and dirt, smear it onto my hands—the filth had the waxiness of oil pastels—then rub my hands together and it would roll up like dough. I'd never been so dirty or so clean, so protected, so exposed. The flickers tapped in the woods, the cotton snow fell from the boughs and melted on my shoulders.

The days reached the shortest point and we filled the dining table with candles and drank melted chocolate. Gemini made new bullets out of bits of lead. "For hunting?" I said, and he shrugged, which was like him. The bullets popped out of the mold brilliantly shiny and silver, but when I reached for one, he cautioned that they were hot enough to melt my skin.

For toothpaste, we used baking soda mixed with four thieves oil. For medicine, we used Pear's tinctures and poultices and teas—plantain for swelling, witch hazel and mullein for a stuffy head, sassafras, kerosene.

I laughed to remember myself that first night, worried about eating a strip of venison. Now I ate grubs from the woodpile—boiled, with butter on top. I ate crickets, deshelled and delegged, roasted on skewers. I ate ant eggs.

Who lived like this, and who would believe me if I told them? I don't mean believe, exactly, but believe and care. Who would?

In the early months, sometimes I wondered still why hadn't I gotten on that plane to Virginia. I had not been in the habit of surprising myself like that. But as the days passed, I knew it was this. It was this, I thought in the steely forests, my feet ringing on the hard-as-iron ground. It was this, I thought as steam cascaded upward from our dinner table. It was this, I thought, holding Sara's hand as she led me to my hayloft. I felt as though I'd sidled through some force field into the world where I'd always belonged.

One evening I sat in the kitchen, watching Pear knead the bread for the first rise. I admired her ropey forearms. Almost every night, Pear made eight to ten loaves of a kind of spongy, soft-crusted bread. Those ten pounds of flour and water took thirty real minutes of kneading, or else the bread came out crumbling and structureless.

It was after dinnertime, after singing, and the kitchen was quiet. The air smelled like cinnamon, tea, and our sweat. I sat near the green-tiled stove, watching Pear and keeping track of the fire. Wind roared across the top of the chimney.

"My, that fire can draw!" Pear said. She smiled and I saw how her teeth overlapped in the front. I'd felt sorry for Pear because of the name Dice had given her. She was middle-aged and lumpy. But when I admitted this to Queen, she told me about the pears at the tops of the trees, which only farmers know about, pears you never find in stores, as big as footballs, as sweet as bleached sugar, so soft your fingers sink right through the skin when you try to pick them.

I opened up the door of the stove and dropped a heavy log right onto the center, so the embers jumped up. Strangely, the heaviest logs didn't always burn the hottest.

"A lamb only lives two months around here," she said. "Do you think his life is, on the whole, a good thing?" She had flour up to her elbows, and her arms looked both solid and ghostly.

"Are you asking me?" I said, surprised. I hadn't, since that first night, been asked to speak my mind, which was fine with me, since I never had an idea what I was supposed to say.

"Oh, Harmony, yes, I'm asking you," she said, fixing me with her pale gaze.

Dice entered the room and stoked the fire. He wore a blue shirt, which I coveted, since the rest of us wore brown and gray.

Was Pear's question a test? Was Dice listening? I tried to imagine how he would answer. "Of course it's nice to be alive, even for a few months," I said. I wanted to be humble and open and praised. I thought of the lambs hopping around their enclosures, facing off, leaping onto their mothers' backs. When they drank, they wagged their tails. "I guess two months or eighty years, it's more or less the same kind of question."

"Wrong," said Pear. She began to oil a large metal bowl.

Dice stood and watched me. I didn't understand why they couldn't tell me clearly what they wanted from me. I was desperate to follow the rules, but it was hard to guess what was right and what was wrong.

Pear said, "It's better never to be born at all, because as soon as you're born, you begin to destroy." She formed the bread into a ball.

"Is that what you think?" I said to Dice.

"If Dice didn't think that," Pear said, "would I be able to tell you that you were wrong?" She tilted the oil around the bowl to coat it. "No, I would not." She dropped the dough into the bowl and covered it with a cloth.

Dice walked to Pear. I thought he meant to inspect the bread but he reached up and brushed flour off her face.

The next morning Dice found me while I was feeding the lambs. The lambs drank down to the dregs of the milk, their mouths fluffy with foam. I lifted the bucket, and the barn cats swarmed. He watched me pet the lambs and said, "They like you, but you know this year we're not raising any to keep?"

I hadn't known that. I thought they were all to keep. "We're selling them?" I said.

"No," he said. "Eating. Today I'll teach you how to slaughter."

"But—" And then what could I say? *I'm not here to kill things? I'm happy to kill other things that I haven't raised? I'm happy to eat things I've raised if someone else has killed them?* I wished Isaac were here to translate my feelings into the sort of indisputable, blood-less ethics of which he was so fond. Isaac knew how to reason.

I could only imagine saying: *I'm happy to proclaim my commit-ment in other ways. I'd freeze on a hill for you, I'd stand in front of a bulldozer for you, probably, but let me choose.* Queen had told me Dice wouldn't make me do anything I didn't want to do. I did not want to slaughter.

"Harmony," he said. "Do you know why your name is Har-mony?"

"Fitting in?" I said. "Oneness?"

"That's right," he said. "Oneness with everything. Selflessness."

He handed me the barn cat that had seven toes per paw. The cat hunkered against my chest. "I want to tell you about how there's no such thing as the definite self. Take our old tractor," he said. "Every bit of the engine has gradually been replaced. Is the engine still itself? Or when was the point that the engine-self gave over to its new inhabitant?"

I thought about it. "I don't know," I said.

"Each person seems to have separate memories that make them think they have continuous separate selves. But what if you lost your memory? Would it still be you? What if someone else could have all your memories? Would it be you? Would it matter?"

He paused. The cat kneaded my chest with its paws, extending and retracting its surplus of claws. I tried to think, but my mind was astonishingly blank. I didn't like to imagine being separate from my memories; without them life would be as continually baffling and new as it must be to a newborn lamb. I said, "I don't know."

"Where does that feeling of self-ness come from?" Dice said, his tone somewhere between gentle and accusatory. "Does it well up from all the bits and pieces of memory and experience that make us up like the tractor's parts? Does it arise or emerge?"

I didn't know what to say. The cat writhed out of my arms, and it seemed that half of me went with it. Dice grabbed it by its scruff and it hung limply. "You know, people fear death because they're afraid of losing self-ness, all those experiences and memories. But their experiences and memories will last in the people they were adjacent to. It is so easy to share a memory, to rewrite a memory, to think that someone else's memory is your own." I thought about that sensation of falling into the quarry the first night, when he'd told me the story. It had felt so real. I thought about Queen saying my mother had abandoned me. I thought about my memories of my father, and how I couldn't tell if they were my memories or what my mother had told me. "So what is lost? There's no real evidence for individual separate selves, there's no real evidence for it." He leaned close to me. I could smell his breath, a deep mossy smell. For a moment, his mouth seemed like the opening to a vast underground cave.

I said, at last, "But I'm separate from you." I didn't know what I meant by this. He was so good at destroying the doubting part of me and replacing it with a desperation to understand.

"You might feel that way," he said, "but the borders are fuzzy. What can't be divided, Harmony? Everything is pieces. When is the whole more than the pieces?"

And then I understood: to me, it was a question of scale. If I were the size of a microbe, a human body would seem like a huge city of individuals. On the next level, Isaac and I had wanted to travel to the Trembling Giant in Utah, which looks like an aspen forest with tens of thousands of trees but is in fact one single plant born eighty thousand years ago, connected at the roots. On the next level, maybe all humanity looked like the cooperating fungus cells, cooperating to strip, heat, and destroy the Earth.

I smiled. I didn't know if Isaac would understand this, or tear it apart with his reasonableness, but it didn't matter— "Cooperation is more important than competition," I said to Dice, his words, and he said, "Exactly."

I was relieved, forgetting, for a moment, the slaughter.

Dice picked up the largest of my lambs. He calmed her, scratching around her ears as though she were a barn cat. "Best to take them out of view of the mothers," he said. He carried her across the field to the edge of the woods, where he'd set up a pallet and hay, a steel frame and a pneumatic machine. I could barely breathe. My guts had dropped into my feet, and my hands shook.

He laid the lamb on her side and took out a long straight knife, which he handed to me. "You have to cut her cleanly," he said, "confidently, or it's inhumane." He rubbed his thumb against his lip, like he was trying to press his words in—a gesture I'd learn to recognize.

He held the lamb's head back. She bayed. She flicked her ears. Her gold eyes rolled at the winter fields.

I remembered how good I became at running and leaping and throwing myself back over the pole. Isaac had taught me to be fearless, but that day with Dice on the edge of the woods, I was not. I suppose I stood there for a minute or two, with my hands shaking, what seemed like hours as I felt his opinion of me blacken and curl into cinders. He took the knife from my hand.

Efficiently, and, it seemed, regretfully, he cut her throat, then pushed her head all the way back.

I turned away, and saw the three dogs coming up through the woods. Dice chopped off the lamb's hooves and tossed them to the dogs, then hung the carcass up on his steel rack. "The first rule of farming is 'Don't get attached,'" he said.

He brought over the machine and shoved a sharp tube that jetted air in between the lamb's muscle and skin, so that she momentarily ballooned up white and cartoonish. Then he hung the lamb up again and began to skin her. Her costume draped on the ground while he cut off her ear and carefully peeled the downy wool from her face.

Then she was pink and shiny and alarmed looking without the wool around her eyes. He slit her front, throwing her heavy stomachs and intestines to the dogs too, picking out the transparent emerald-green sac of bile and tossing it away, saving the heart and liver.

CHAPTER 8

After lunch on the day I failed Dice, Bay found me washing out manure in the cow stalls.

All winter, Bay and I had been at two ends of a propeller, spinning around the same center. He often left rooms just as I entered, and I returned the favor by sitting at the far side of the table. When I avoided him for days, he'd reward me—as I did dishes, he brushed his hand along my neck and I felt my hackles rise. My game was seeing how long I could hang on to the shivers from three seconds of contact. It was like holding a candy in my mouth and trying not to suck.

"I'm going to go Dumpster in Mars Hill," he said. "Dice wants you to come." He brushed his thumb over my hand and I burned for him.

This would be my first trip off the farm since I'd arrived. Bay opened the car for me and I sat on the seat, soft compared to everything at the farm. If this was a punishment for my inability to kill the lamb, it did not feel like one. He strode off for a minute, returned, and handed me an icicle rolled in sorghum molasses. I

licked the rich brown syrup off and held the icicle, which diminished to nothing and trickled out of my fist. As we drove, I had
the sense that life was moving too quickly for me. Bay told me
that last year a giant icicle had fallen from the barn and skewered
a lamb straight through the throat.

"Dice wanted me to kill a lamb today," I said.

Bay said nothing.

As a result of the lamb or the icicle or Bay, I shuddered. Deep
down, I liked to shudder. There was some circuit in my body and
the wires were touching. I didn't want to be like my mother and
end up in a world where I was always cautious.

The back lot of the Ingles Market shone like a mirage. I hadn't
seen pavement since September—five months before—and it was
so smooth it resembled a carpet. My feet hit the asphalt too hard.
The air smelled chemical. I didn't recognize this as the world I'd
left behind.

We filled four trash barrels with bruised produce, mushrooms
in little wooden baskets, perfectly soft mangoes, plastic cartons of
cherry tomatoes, zucchinis wrapped in plastic, bell peppers, hands
of spotty bananas. I tried to ask about whether I needed to make
amends with Dice, but Bay ignored me.

"I wish Dice trusted me more," I said. We had begun to load
our barrels into the trunk, heaving them up, when he finally spoke.

"Trust?" Bay said, and turned his big face toward me, which
was fringed with power and light like a crude drawing of the sun.
"That's on you, babe. I'm leaving tomorrow to find us new family,"
he said. "Reliable family." He was provoking me, of course.

"For the next protest?"

"Maybe," he said. "Maybe just for the spring."

"How long will you be gone?"

He put his hand on my neck and I tilted my head back. He said, "A week or two." He dropped his hand. I didn't want to ask him to touch me. I wanted to be wanted.

"Let me tell you a story," said Bay. "You know how there used to be giant mammals, mastodons and ground sloths, in America?"

"I guess," I said.

"Humans killed them all off, and they killed off their predators too, saber-tooth tigers and enormous birds. Used to be a bird with a twenty-three-foot wingspan. Too big to get itself in the air by flapping. You know how that kind of bird had to start flying?" He stretched out his long arms.

"How?"

"It had to jump off cliffs and coast," he said, flapping his arms. Like jumping into the quarry, I thought, or jumping over the bar. I hoped no one was watching. Bay looked like someone you'd call the cops on. "There's still one kind of those birds left in America, the biggest flying bird in America. The California condor. How did the condors survive into the Anthropocene?"

"I don't know," I said.

"They eat whales," he said. "They fucking eat whales, and other sea animals that wash up on the shore. You feel me?"

"I think so," I said. With Bay words were only one level, the lowest level, and then there was the higher level, the animal level, of gestures and touch, of forgotten and unspoken instincts.

"Don't think we haven't noticed you half-assing things."

I shook my head. I'd been working every waking moment. I

slept only a few hours a night. I ate blue heron. My hands were calloused from the shovels and rakes; my big heavy boots had given me hot water-filled blisters. I had to massage my wrists every night because they ached so badly; I had to run cold water into my eyes because of the hay dust.

"Didn't try to help Pear with the bread. Didn't try to help Queen milk."

I was startled to hear Queen's name. So she'd told on me. And they were right. I had not helped with everything. The work was never finished.

My arms shook and I pressed them to my sides. I flickered back to the moment in the woods, Dice telling me I'd tripped into a quarry and could avoid pain by falling apart. "I'm sorry," I said.

He smiled down at me, his bristly hair sparkling. Branches clanged against the Dumpster, the sky was winter calico, and I felt hopeful, briefly, that my mother would understand. I wanted to tell her there was no definite self—maybe she would understand, since she collected objects like they were her memory, the same way a spider uses its nest as part of its brain.

As we drove from the lot I saw kids selling pink cardboard boxes of candy. It was, unbelievably, Valentine's Day. "Hey, mister," one called to Bay as we headed out. "Something sweet for your girl?"

Bay said, "Love every day of the year, I say." He bought a box. He handed it to me, but I could not open it.

I sank down in my seat, nausea crashing over me. I couldn't open my eyes till we were halfway back up the mountain, back in the real world.

spring

CHAPTER 9

One of the last lambs of the season got stuck on the way out and died. This was in early March, when Bay was still gone, finding new family. The ewe screamed and screamed. Queen found me in the hayloft before dawn. She shook me awake and told me to get a bread knife from the kitchen.

The baby had emerged headfirst, not hooves-first, with blood-soaked wool. We couldn't pull it out.

Queen cut off the lamb's head with the bread knife and then pushed the body back inside so that she could angle its feet out and pull it away. My job was to hold the ewe's head. I couldn't let her see the dead baby. This time was easier than when Dice had asked me to slaughter a lamb the previous month. Maybe I was more open now. Queen took the two pieces of lamb outside and flung them to the dogs. We brought the ewe to the mothers' enclosure, since she had milk now. "The others will be good to her," Queen said. "Sheep mourn their dead friends." I remembered the lamb Dice had killed and wondered if her friends missed her.

She went to the cellar and skimmed two ladlefuls of cow's cream into a pot, which she heated on an ice-blue flame. I made a fire in the pit back behind the storage building and hauled some chairs from the kitchen outside.

Queen returned from the barn, the blood rusting beneath her nails. We mixed crusty honey into our cups and drank our sweet milk, which was as thick on the tongue as Elmer's glue. Dry cream, Queen called it, dense from the wintertime hay. In the spring when the grass came up the cream would turn golden yellow and we'd be swimming in its quantity, though the cows would begin excreting waste so profusely that we'd have to muck out the stable every day instead of once a week. "But then, the cream!" Queen said. "Pure sunshine."

The dawn and the hot drink put us in high spirits. From behind the storage house, we could see the long view out of the folded holler—the gentle, timeworn mountains, half a billion years old and once as tall as the Himalayas, once four miles tall in places. We saw the low blue fog soften and illuminate the slopes beyond our slopes—the Smokies. There were certain times of day or night that always felt magical to me here on the farm. Here, now, five a.m. *You can stay three days or the rest of your life.* This wasn't the kind of place you could pick up and put down. We were not allowed to have anything, not even our own memories, really. Our bodies were not ours. We lived low and close to the earth. Dice wanted our lives to be unabstract.

It was inconceivable to me now that there were places out in the world called things like "the Container Store." In fact, the name *the Container Store* struck me as so absurd I was sure

I'd made it up. The sun was coming up and for the first time in months it felt warm.

"I feel bad for the people who can't see this," I said. "Like my mom." I wanted to see what she would say, even though I knew we weren't supposed to dwell on the past.

"You know Gemini's dad actually found him in Mars Hill?" Queen said. "He had a whole search crew, they tried to grab him! But Gemini's shirt was so old they tore it right off him. They ended up with scraps in their hands. He came back up without a shirt on and we all laughed for days." I imagined my mother trying to tear off my clothes at Mars Hill. Reaching for her daughter, failing. "I thought about leaving, once," Queen said. She looked around to make sure we were alone. "That was before I knew that people who leave often die out there."

"What do you mean?" I asked.

Queen picked pieces of straw from her sweater sleeves. "Well," Queen said, "it could be that they're like cats, they leave when they know they won't last." Queen tore a piece of straw into thinner and thinner pieces, like she could get it one molecule thick, like gold leaf. "I don't know. Only one girl I knew left without asking permission."

"What happened to her?" I said. My voice came out at a treble pitch.

Queen didn't answer. "Let me ask you this—what did you tell your family when you left?" Queen said. We weren't supposed to talk about our pasts, but I'd brought up my mother to begin with.

I said, "My mom and my ex think I'm in college. In Virginia."

"College!" Queen laughed. My mother was likely awake in

Durham now, probably eating Grape-Nuts, and probably imagining me drifting through a dining hall or bending my head over
a book in a carrel. No, of course by now she'd know I wasn't in
college. She might have called, asking about a bill, and someone
would have told her, *No, a student by that name did not ever arrive
for the fall semester.* She might think I was dead or kidnapped.
Maybe she'd sent out search parties, like the one for Gemini. Or
maybe, in her resigned way, her resignation so deep it was almost
sympathy, she knew I wanted to be left alone.

"What ex?" Queen said. I wondered if my mother had told
Isaac. He too may have been looking for me. "Ex-boyfriend?" The
word *boyfriend* was as ridiculous as *the Container Store.*

"He's no one," I said. "He wanted me to get educated and
settle down."

"He wanted to marry you?" she said.

"No," I said. At the quarry, he had said he would marry me
one day. But if he'd actually asked me, I didn't know whether I
could have left. "He used to talk all the time about wanting kids,
though."

"Kids," Queen said. "That's the only rule I have trouble with."
She looked around. The family would be waking up soon.

I was distressed at this admission. I wanted Queen to be more
devoted to the rules than I was, so she could buoy me up. "We
have to subtract from the world," I said.

"Oh, sister," she said. "I know."

We sat in silence. I broke the honey grains in my teeth. The
sun pulled pink mist from the ground. Finally, she said, "Tell me
how you met him."

I wasn't supposed to wallow in the past, Bay had said, and on the first night Dice had told me to be mindful of crying over made-up stories. I let the silence stretch.

"I don't really want to talk about it," I said.

Loving Isaac transformed me. I posed for him whenever he asked. When Forest Hills Park flooded from a hurricane, I clung to a tree above the creek, in which the gray water was churning by at a thousand miles an hour. We went out searching for an albino deer, and I hung from the fence posts. He liked how I was always willing. He realized this about me before I did. I was willing.

One night he found a long strand of my hair in his collar. He pulled it out like a magician pulling ribbon from his mouth. "Could make a bird's nest from this," he said. "I wonder how this even got here." He laughed. "We haven't even kissed yet."

The *yet* was all I needed. I leaned my mouth into his. It was my first kiss, hot and salty.

I walked home from his house afterward. It was one of those spring nights when a thick fragrant mist evaporates off the road but can't quite loft into the air. The streetlights pierced the miasma like dazzling stars way out in space. The insects sang in the glistening lawns. "Do you know that suburbs are actually more biodiverse than the wilderness?" he said that night. "All kinds of animals can live here. It's a wonderland."

Pear rang the breakfast bell, an old ram bell with a terrible clang. It was long past six a.m., and Queen and I had finished our honey and cream.

"I didn't ask you about your first love," I said.

"I know," she said. She patted my arm, maybe a gesture of for-giveness, but what did she need to forgive me for? She and I had both broken a rule.

I should have pressed her on her friend who ran away. I should have asked her, *Have you ever woken from a story Dice was telling you with real bruises?* I should have asked, *What was your life be-fore, Queen? How does it feel to cut every tie? Does it hurt? Does it feel good?*

Instead I said: "Better not to dwell on the past."

The sun had drawn out the colors of early spring in the South-ern Appalachians: pale taupe, mauve, angel blue, map blue. The turkey toms and ruffed grouse were beginning to display. River otters ran through the yard, sleek as fish. Snakes and worms came out into the sun.

The woods ticked like a clock as they thawed. Ice dropping. Water falling. Leaves popping open, beat by beat. Those shiny saw-edged leaf blossoms, green as poisonous snakes. Tick, tick, tick, drop drop drop.

That night, when the thundersnow came down onto the warm re-spiring ground, billowing and melting, and the lightning darted pink into the holler, we sat in the circle of chairs and Dice told us a story. "A lesson for all the children," he said. "A lesson from the Arctic that's on its way out." The lines of our attention set him at the center of a radiating star. He told the story of the *Fram*, the Norwegian ship that purposefully trapped itself in the Arctic ice, so that the explorers could float over the pole where no one had gone before. The ship took three years to work its way free, and the explorers ate their dogs, killed each other's favorite dogs out of mercy.

He said, "I've been there on that ice, it cracks like gunshots, it opens up into deep blue slits. Once the snow gave way beneath my friend, and he fell hundreds of feet into the shadows." We were perfectly quiet. "We had a whole search crew, they tried to grab him. But his shirt was so old they tore it right off him. They ended up with scraps in their hands." I felt a shiver of unease. Queen had used the same words to talk about Gemini. *Tore it right off. Scraps in their hands.* Had Dice heard us? I tried to catch Queen's eye. "The ice clenched him so tight, by the time I pulled him up, both his arms were broken." Dice whistled softly and I could feel the Arctic air, air that had never been breathed. He said, "The ice weighs down on itself as it gathers, and deep down, you can find a thousand years of ice and air no longer than your arm."

After Dice's story Queen came with me to check once more on the little lambs, and on the bereft ewe.

"Dice tried to get me to slaughter a lamb and I couldn't do it," I said.

She nodded. "Remember that you have to make an authentic effort."

"Do you think," I said, "that he overheard us talking this morning? When you told me about Gemini? When you told me about how they tore his shirt off?" I tried to remember. "When you told me you wish there were kids around?"

She smiled. "What good does it do, Harmony," she said, "to talk about it now?"

"I was nervous," I said.

"You talk too much," she said. This hurt me. She talked, too. She looked at me carefully, assessing. "Oh, Harmony," she said.

I said, "Was it hard, the first time you slaughtered?"

"No," she said. "But it wasn't here. I was on drugs and they told me to kill the guy I was traveling with. So I tried to kill him. I thought he'd been transformed into a deer. I killed the deer."

I stared at her, trying to work out what she was saying. She stroked the vertical line up her throat.

She said, "I was sure glad when I noticed that it was a deer's head in my arms and not his. Ha!" She patted my arm. Her hand was warm as usual but now I felt her milkmaid strength.

I remembered her hauling away the heron. I wanted her to say, *I never confuse animals and people anymore,* or *Dice taught me nonviolence,* or *You and I are very different, Harmony, and you don't have to worry about killing a person instead of an animal,* but instead she just said, "There's no such thing as the definite self."

CHAPTER 10

March was the month of mud. The ocean reached out a giant widespread hand, clutched our hillside all winter, and then, in springtime, released its grip, dragging our earth back to the ocean. The streams flooded and turned lowlands into swamps. I could hear the rivers rushing all night. The mud in the courtyard in front of the barn sucked my boots off. The mud in the woods by the stream knocked me over.

The earth looked like chocolate cake, black and spongy. With frozen-cold hands and tough gray gloves covered in heavy earth, we raised hoop houses for our seedlings. We hoisted translucent plastic sheets over half-circle hoops, then tucked an insulating blanket over our seedlings, knowing, without really feeling, that spring would come, and then summer. We walked the line of the electric fence and threw away the branches that grounded the current. Then we turned the line on so hot it sparked, and let the cows out.

I didn't have to sit around wondering what I was feeling: everything *hurt* so much. I worked harder than I ever had, driving myself on, like Dice drove his Suffolk mares to plow the field—on and on all day. The horses became docile when they were tired, and I did, too; by dinner my mind was white with the pleasure of sitting still. I swore I would never again be told I was half-assing. My hands got hard. My shoulders and arms got bulkier. My skin got blotchy from the sun. By March I hadn't seen my own face in a mirror for six months. So I squatted by a puddle, my face dark and waving against the light sky, to see how strange I looked. I looked like a mountain person. I was a mountain person.

But sometimes the whoosh of breath in the long house reminded me of the sound of the freeway by my mother's house. In heavy post-labor sleep I'd find myself back home again, crawling over the kitchen floor's sandy linoleum—my earliest memory. In the mintlike tingling of the springtime backwoods dawn, I'd think of my old popcorn ceiling, the drywall that couldn't even hold a nail.

I herded the sheep over the changing terrain. The springtime ground was porous, trickling from many hidden holes. The brambly new woods were as wet as a shower. During the day I watched my flock nosing around the brown hillsides, nuzzling the dead grass, and I thought, Soon there will be so much grass the sheep won't know what to do with themselves.

The first needles of grass began to come up in the sunny spots, neon green against the soil, and then in one week the hills changed color. The daytime sky lost its wintry paleness and, in collaboration with the sun, went violet at the apex. Then we had quinces, and then we had rhubarb, which we prepared with a crumble, and we brought the tables outside and ate in the courtyard, the moths troubling our lantern light.

One evening during the singing Pear said, "Maybe you'd like to lead, Harmony." And then I stood in the center of the hollow square. I called "The Grieved Soul." This was the song Bay had taught me in the car when he'd driven me to the farm.

> *What is this that casts thee down?*
> *Who are those that grieve thee?*
> *Speak and let the worst be known,*
> *Speaking may relieve thee.*

I realized that the leader, supervising the voices blasting in from all sides, also got the best spot in the audience, which was exactly like subsistence farming. *The worker reaps the best rewards.*

The snow melted as it fell, and that was the end of the snow, and March. One morning we spotted a yellow mountain lion in the courtyard. Redwing blackbirds appeared, and peonies, colts-foot, bloodroot, yellowroot, and pussy willows flowered. The stream swelled even more, and churned up a mist all around it. The vultures were mating.

After breakfast one morning, Dice said to Sara, "Will you help move this one out of the hayloft? Give her a bunk. Bay's bringing a new couple in tomorrow."

"What?" I said. "You want me in the house?"

"Yes, Harmony," he said. "You won't be the baby anymore."

It was April. Seven months. I was no longer new.

"Any bunk will do," he said to Sara.

I moved my nightgown—and it wasn't even really mine—from the barn to one of the bedrooms. Sara showed me the wicker baskets under the beds where everyone kept clothes. "No possessions," she said.

"I wish I could stay in the hayloft," I said. I had come to like that rare time of privacy.

Sara sized me up. I could see the blue veins at her temples and near her ears. She was perfect for Dice, a transparent person. I knew exactly what she was thinking: my complaint would count as *half-assing*. "I'll ask Dice for a prayer tonight," she said. "Then you'll feel better."

That evening, Dice told us to push the meeting room chairs against the wall. "By special request from Sara," he said, "we will pray." The family murmured excitedly, exchanging smiles. We linked hands and spread out into a circle.

Dice said, "What should we pray for?"

"Love!" Sara called.

"Love," Dice said. "Draw love through you and upward." He breathed in deeply. "Love," he said again. Another deep breath, and this time the family joined in. Breath, then *love*, breath, then *love*.

"If you're not rolling with it, you're rolling under it," Dice shouted.

The room seemed to belly like the rainbow parachute we'd played with in elementary school. The whole class would swing the parachute up, then rush to sit underneath it, and in our swiftly collapsing chamber, we'd look around the circle at each other's faces, made strange by the shifting polychrome shadows, till our ceiling sighed down onto our heads.

"Love." I had only just begun to think about love—about Bay, of course, Bay pulling my hair down by the fire and pressing his mouth on mine—when the pace picked up. I couldn't catch my breath. It was like being caught beneath a train. It chugged over me. *Love! Love! Love!* Light sparked in my head, like the flashes thrown off by static. I blinked desperately. Several people collapsed, and I did too, against the fragrant bright floor. The dizziness, the love, it overtook me.

I didn't remember getting into bed. In the morning, the family rose in nightgowns and one-piece long johns. To my love-addled eyes, they looked like angels. In silent grace, they engaged in the act of dressing. At breakfast, everyone seemed kinder and gentler than ever. People who had never spoken to me—people with names like Osha, Terra, Ursina, Cuke—touched my hands. I felt that whatever the lesson was, I'd learned it, because I'd thrown my body into it.

Bay returned, as we'd expected, bringing a new couple to join us. I was in the stables and he came to find me.

"Did you miss me?" I said.

"Sure," he said, the word Isaac used to use, not the same as *yes*. But I knew he had no other reason to be in the stables. He helped me carry pails of water to the troughs in the smaller pens where the hose didn't reach. He took two minutes for what took me twenty. He understood the processes of stars, trees, and animals, and the way to wring out a living from the dirt, and this understanding was what I loved. He was a part of the landscape, simple and protean.

"Why did you bring back a couple?" I asked. "I thought couples weren't allowed."

"They wanted to come." He shrugged. "At least, the guy did." I felt a quick lap of anger. I wanted the same rules for everyone.

The sheep, returned from their milking, baaed. As Bay tied back the gates of the pens, my flock rushed forward, bells jingling, into the courtyard, where they began to crop the fresh grass, watching me sidelong with their gold eyes.

"Come with me, Bay," I said. "You and me and the sheep." If a couple was allowed, I could show my interest.

"You've got it," he said.

"I know I've *got it*," I said, and flushed.

"Some other day," he said.

I turned my back on Bay and I walked west to the fresh pastures. The sheep ran to me, no longer needing any coaxing. I saw the new couple come out of the long house to watch. I felt proud. "C'mon, sheep!" I called to the dawdlers, and they coursed forward to catch me. We brushed through the tall grasses, stirring up butterflies and grasshoppers.

I came home for lunch. Now two people followed me on the meal line. An April meal, foraged: ramps, young poke salad, nettles, morels. And Dumpstered: passion fruits, bananas, clementines, so out of place with their aromas from other biospheres. Queen talked to the newcomers about reinforcing the storage house. "We tend to get around to reinforcing things only when they are about to collapse," she said. "Dice says we need to make room in the storage house for supplies for our next action. We might go to the headquarters of this coal company and put on a show for them . . ."

I hadn't heard anything about this. I wondered if I was going to be excluded from the next action too. Maybe because I couldn't kill the lamb: maybe that had been my test. Maybe because, like Bay had said, everyone thought I was half-assing. Maybe Dice had overheard Queen and me talking about the fake world. I slipped into a seat next to Queen and introduced myself. "I'm Harmony," I said.

Neither of them laughed at my name, even though I was still growing into it.

The woman smiled. "I'm Lindsay. This is Roger."

They weren't supposed to tell us their fake-world names.

Lindsay's face, and Roger's, looked creamy and bright—clean faces, I realized with a start, used to sunblock. I guessed Lindsay was wealthy, maybe because of her Blundstones, or her slippery attitude. After lunch, Queen and I showed them the barn. "How lovely," Lindsay said when presented with the pigs, whose faces were covered in purple yogurt. She suppressed her distaste for our lives, politely.

We climbed up to the hayloft. "This," Queen said, gesturing to the hay-flecked beige mattress, "is where y'all get to sleep!"

Roger smiled. Lindsay raised her eyebrows.

"We'll put some sheets on it, of course," I said. Though I didn't love Lindsay, I wanted her to love us, to confirm that the family was perfect. I remembered the power coming off the family at breakfast my first day. We lived the right way on the earth, we were essential. I wanted her to see it.

Lindsay nodded. "But I'm just wondering—are there other options?"

"All the newcomers stay here," I said. I smiled through my annoyance. I remembered Sara asking me if I was cold my first day. How foolish I had been to complain. How foolish Lindsay was to complain now.

Queen stood back, to see how I handled things, I guessed. I tried to imagine what Pear would say, what Sara would say. "Try opening your mind . . . ," I said, trailing off, searching for words that would convince her. "I mean, lots of things here will seem different, but that's intentional . . ."

"Lindsay, it's all right," Queen said, finally. "You can sleep in the dining room, in front of the fireplace. How does that sound?"

Lindsay thanked her but not as vigorously as she should have. "There'll be a place for Roger there too?"

"If he'd like," Queen said.

I'd never seen anyone sleep in the dining room before.

After dinner, Sara and Queen set up a mattress on the large clean stones in front of the fireplace. But Roger asked to return to the loft. He beamed as Gemini handed him a pillowcase to bring out to the barn.

The next day Sara told me to bring Lindsay out with the sheep. "She just barged into Dice's room," Sara said, rubbing the back of her head. "We want her out of the house for the day, so she won't go wandering around." For the first time, I felt she was including me in secret knowledge. Maybe she had noticed how I was trying harder. Maybe she felt she could trust me, finally, by comparison to the newcomers—maybe I was a step closer to coming to the next action.

"I heard there might be another protest soon," I said. I was testing my luck. "Can I come this time?"

She regarded me, unsurprised. "Patience, Harmony."

I felt my face get hot with shame. I didn't know what else I could do to prove myself. It was unwelcome to wish, for a moment, for the clarity of high-jumping, the pole rising up inch by inch to meet my flailing heels.

"Go on," Sara said. "Go take Lindsay out with the sheep."

As soon as I lifted my hand, the sheep turned toward me to head their well-worn way uphill. Lindsay had to jog to catch up with us.

She asked breathlessly, "Do they always follow so well?"

"They know me," I said. "If you tried, they'd probably all scatter."

"How far are we taking them?"

"Miles, probably."

"Do you listen to music when you go out?"

"Never," I said. Though I'd hum the shape-note songs.

"I didn't think so," she said. "So what do you think about?"

What did I think about? I didn't think, exactly. I walked. I listened. The warblers, the noisy goatsuckers with their many-noted call, and tyrant flycatchers with their peewee sounds. The faraway yells from the forest as the men felled another tree, the occasional whir of the lumber mill. Thoughts would come in imprecise and indefinable forms. I'd feel old beliefs shifting in my mind, like strange fish deep in the ocean, unable to find the light.

None of this could happen with Lindsay around. I let her question hang in the air. When my frustration became unbearable, I said, "Well, what are *you* thinking about?"

"Can I be honest with you?"

"Certainly," I said, ready to find more reasons to dislike her.

"I'm trying to imagine what life here is really like."

I flashed to the love prayer, the way we all breathed together. Now that I'd felt that faintness once, it remained near to the surface—at any moment, I felt I might fall to the ground.

"You know, all of you. What's up with all of you?"

I said, "Did you know sheep miss each other when they're apart?" Queen had told me this.

Lindsay was silent. "What's your real name, again?" she said.

"Harmony," I said.

"What was your name before?"

I paused. "I can't remember," I said. That was what Bay had told me, when I asked all those months ago.

"Harmony," she said. "I guess I can see it." I felt warmth spreading through me.

I decided to tell her about the school-bus-sized bird that could only get itself into the air by jumping off cliffs. I told her that the monarchs took an odd long path over Lake Superior and it was because they were avoiding a mountain that disappeared millions of years ago. These stories of Dice's helped me stay awake to the strangeness of nature.

I forged recklessly ahead, exposing more and more of myself. I told her I sometimes felt connected to all nature, I could look at a heron or a lamb and feel truly that there was no definite self. I explained that this idea about the definite self reminded me of the bubble room at the children's museum in my hometown. My mother would trap me in a gleaming fragile column of soap bubble—dunking a hula hoop, which was rigged to a pulley system, in a soap, then raising the hoop by the pulley quickly, but not too quickly, up over my body. For one magical moment I would stand there encased, the colors twirling and dawdling across the bubble's tenuous membrane. When I kept Dice in mind I could see how my own point of view was a brief, fragile separation.

"There was a bubble machine like that in my hometown museum, too," Lindsay said. She smelled so clean. I felt blinded by how little she smelled.

We looked for a moment at the view, the far blue ridges truncated by nearby hills. I felt a drumbeat of fear. I could almost see the terrible future Dice had described. I could see the hills beset by swarms of invading insects. I could see the megafauna dying off, every biome overrun by the vining, strangling pioneers, the animals of the world growing more desperate. The world was changing. But if we tried hard enough, if I tried hard enough, the family could keep this one place whole.

"How long are you planning on staying?" Lindsay said.

"Staying?" I said. "My three days are long over." Looking at her, I felt a muffled yearning for the feeling of my long hair falling over my shoulders.

"What?" she said.

"It's three days or the rest of your life," I said. "No one told you that?"

"No," she said.

"Well," I said, "now you know."

She reached for a flower near my hip and plucked it out of the ground. "You just seem like you have a lot going for you," she said. "You know, out there." She was staring at the scar on my palm, from the splinter when I first met Bay. I turned my hand so she couldn't keep looking.

"You don't know what I was like out there," I said. Even as I spoke, I knew my answer was the wrong one. What I should have said was that I always wanted a purpose and now I had one.

"It's so dirty," she continued, as if I hadn't spoken. "There's blood all over the kitchen and out here I keep stepping on bones." Her nails were painted black, as though she'd knocked every last one with a hammer until she had darkened the nailbeds.

"Dice says it's only in this century that people have become obsessed with 'cleanliness,' which was conveniently defined for them by the soap industry."

"Where are you from?" She had changed the subject. I wondered if that was her way of admitting defeat.

I knew that responding wasn't wise. But this was the problem with me—I always wanted to please, to smooth things over; an inheritance from my mother. It was nice, every so often, to talk about the past. "Durham."

"Yeah, me too," she said, smiling. "I thought you looked familiar."

"What high school did you go to?" I said.

"I was about to ask you," she said.

I named my high school before I considered whether it was wise.

She said she knew all kinds of people who went there, and listed names I didn't know. Then she said, "Isaac. Isaac the painter."

"He's a photographer," I said.

"Oh, right, of course!" she said, smiling brightly. "Photographer, I meant. He's a friend of mine."

I examined her, trying to place her in the squat, in the kitchen's light, which was lacey from the dried flowers, on the corduroy couch or the porch swing, in front of the centaurs or lenticular Madonnas. We stared at each other, one of those long cat stares, renegotiating our power. I may have left him, but he was not hers. He was mine. In that moment, I needed Lindsay to understand, even as I knew I was revealing too much. "I dated him," I said. "For years."

"Berie?"

"Don't say that name," I said.

"Isaac said you'd gone to Virginia."

I imagined her wrapping her black-tipped fingers around Isaac's arm, Isaac's neck. The two of them in his narrow room with the gardenias and the trains going by in the woods.

"I didn't," I said.

"Come back with me," she said. "You've been brainwashed." Fear blew away my sadness. I'd exposed myself.

She could tell Isaac where I was. And he could tell my mother. Then they'd wrest me from the only place I'd ever been happy. My countdown clock had started.

"What a decision," Lindsay said. Looking back, it didn't feel like a decision. It felt more like fate. Bay had been waiting for me by the bus stop, the lights in the tunnel pointing at his head.

The following morning, Lindsay was gone—she'd walked down to the road before anyone got up. Sara found her tracks through the dew, slick and dark.

CHAPTER 11

Roger looked so upset at breakfast that Bay took him back to the hayloft, with its rustling emptiness and slatted light. I wondered what they would talk about, how Bay would reassure him. I wished I could have spoken to Lindsay one more time—if only I could have explained myself better. If only she could have witnessed one singing, the power and knowledge in those old tunes, *I'm glad that I was born to die.* If only she could have seen the family after the action and understood how committed they were to the Earth. If only Dice had taken her on a walk and explained how we lived without hypocrisy.

I pictured her on the bus back to Durham, the same bus I'd been planning to take before Bay had found me. The bus wound its way out of the mountains, past Christmas tree farms and apple orchards, past broiler farms and broken-down furniture factories, into the Piedmont, the Cape Fear river basin, tobacco country, my old home—the journey I would never take again.

Instead, I stood on the lunch line in boots I couldn't even claim as mine. Ahead of me, two Ashers—a woman and man—

bent their heads together. "Lindsay went to the hayloft last night," the man whispered.

The woman shook her head. I strained to listen.

"She found another woman there."

The woman turned and caught my eye. I didn't feel bad for Roger. I knew that soon he would see Lindsay as I saw Isaac— he never understood me, he didn't believe I knew where I was headed, so I had rightly left him behind; now I knew my life had been building toward the family and toward Dice, the vivid, the essential. Lindsay was someone he needed to let go. The more he could cut away, the better.

I found Queen in the dairy. I needed to tell her about my conversation with Lindsay. I needed Queen to say that it would be all right, that Lindsay would mind her own business, that she wouldn't rat me out to Isaac, that he wouldn't tell my mother, and that even if he did, there would be no way for her to find me.

She was wiping down the cheese board, pushing the whey from the press into the bucket on the floor. Later this would go to the pigs.

"Roger was with someone in the hayloft," I said. "A woman, I mean." Queen shook the last of the whey into the bucket. I didn't care about the hayloft. It was my opening move, so I could shift into the heart of the matter, which was Lindsay. "Lindsay left, you know," I said. "I guess it makes sense now."

Queen gathered up a few empty baskets and tossed them roughly in the sink. I wanted to tell her to be careful. "People shouldn't be discussing things like that." She turned both taps on as far as they would go, and the water thundered.

I wanted Queen to suggest we find a way to stop Lindsay on her way back to Durham. She usually liked to talk, to speculate and scheme. "You're wasting the hot water," I said, closing the taps.

She ignored me. Instead, she shifted the baskets around as though they weren't yet clean.

"Come on," I said, pushing her toward intimacy. "You have to admit that it was brazen of him to hook up with someone on his second night." I took a mop to help her with the floor, which was covered in bits of cheese and salt and manure tracked in from the barn. "Like Dice says, utopias often break down because of love problems."

"Please," Queen said, turning to me, and her eyes shone. "Like you follow that rule. I know you want Bay." Her words hit like a slap. "It wasn't just someone," Queen continued. "It was me. Dice made me." I stood there stunned as she knelt and swept up the curds and leaves and straw from the floor with her hands.

"Made you?" I said. Queen had said Dice never made anyone do what they didn't want to do. At that time I still thought there was a demarcation between wanting and not wanting. I hadn't yet realized that in our world—a world with no definite selves, where the family's needs came before everything else—Dice could tell you what you wanted.

She was crying. "I don't need any more help, Harmony," she said.

As I returned to the long house, I glanced through the window. She was kneeling on the floor, staring at her hands. I thought that she was trying to keep the dirt from falling out. Later I realized she might have been praying.

*   *   *

Roger had decided to stay. He became family. Dice introduced him at breakfast. "Rainer is a good one," Dice said, with his hand on Roger's shoulder. Roger gazed up at him, mouth open. Then, with all of us watching, he lifted Dice's hand and kissed it. The family murmured in approval. I wished I'd thought to kiss Dice's hand when I'd arrived.

So Roger was Rainer. I thought about Queen climbing the ladder to the hayloft, her lantern's light coursing over the beams. I wondered if she pretended to be willing.

Was it clear that she was not there on her own account? Maybe she was silent, maybe her urgency took him by surprise. Maybe he didn't notice anything was wrong, maybe he ignored how wrong it felt.

It was almost May, so we dug in the fields, the whole family together, as Dice requested. We dug because tilling killed the salamanders.

Dice was the strongest. He didn't take breaks like we did. He said he'd done this kind of work long enough that he didn't need to. He pulled up ten times the amount of earth I could in one shovelful. When we went in to prepare dinner, he stayed out in the field. I was proud of him for his relentlessness.

We transplanted the kale and onions and peas and cauliflower and tiny lettuces from the hoop house, and once Dice was sure there would be no frost, we moved the tomatoes and sweet potatoes. We seeded the beans and pumpkins and melons directly into the soil. We planted blood-red corn.

Soon milkweed sprouted everywhere. We weeded with knives, stabbing deep into the ground and pulling out roots.

Spring was all-consuming, spring was desperate. I didn't have time to worry about Lindsay; I almost forgot she had ever visited the Ash Family farm. The weather changed, so warm the carrot tops rocketed up in two days. The Clark's Heavenly Blue morning glories on the fences around the orchard bloomed, large ultramarine blossoms with white throats.

The men had finished reinforcing the storage house. They drove to town in the school bus and returned with boxes of bar soap. I wondered if it was Dumpstered; we didn't buy fake-world soap. Instead, we washed with cow-fat soap from our cows, once they couldn't give milk anymore.

Dice switched the May plaque for the June. Our crabapples and blue flag irises bloomed. The common wealth. The cabbages headed up. We planted hot wax peppers. We planted okra, and it kept growing.

The strawberries lolled on their vines, pulling their red out of the dark soil, somehow. The dino kale spread its frazzled leaves.

We harvested broccoli and radishes of all colors: purple, pink, red, white. We planted dill around the brassica beds to repel cabbage moths. In June we harvested all of the garlic. We planted legumes in the holes the garlic had vacated, to bring back the soil.

Bay soon left again to find new family. He left without saying goodbye.

*   *   *

A month and a half after Rainer's arrival, after dinner, I found Queen out behind the dairy. We began to climb the hill together. Her eyes were rimmed red, opaline with tears. "Sit with me," she said. I was pleased that, as I sought her out, she sought me. We sat on the rocks in the sloping meadow. The sun had set but the rocks were still warm. She said, "I have to tell you something." I stared at her tattoo, the black longitudinal stripe from her chin down her throat to her sternum. "I'm late," she said.

"Oh," I said. Her head fell forward onto her chest. The grasses hissed and whooshed like the ocean. "Very late?" I said. She nodded.

"Does Rainer know?"

"Just you," she said.

Everything lay on a simple spectrum of royal blue or darker, as though seen through blue glass. In the far woods, the stream was strangely bright. The evening star burned above Queen's head.

"Would you keep it if they let you?"

"Yes," Queen said. "But I can't. We need to subtract from the world, not add to it. I understand why, the world's no good. That's why so many women here have neutered themselves."

I hadn't known that either. The idea struck fear into me. But then I reminded myself that the family was final, and the finality was what I liked about it. I had to be consistent.

"I need to tell Pear, but I don't know what she'll say. I don't want to have my parts tied," said Queen. "But I know I'll be living here forever. What am I holding on to?"

She took my hand.

"I'll help you," I said.

Neither of us knew anything about forever. We were children.

It was bedtime. The sky, which should have been black by then, remained luminous blue. A white light moved along the edge of the sky—not a planet or a shooting star, as Dice would have wanted, but a helicopter. "Search and rescue," Queen said. For a moment I wondered if Lindsay could have sent it.

Maybe they would leave us for lost—this would be the best outcome, I reminded myself. The helicopter floated on. Queen and I headed down the slope to the long house, whose windows were orange and welcoming.

CHAPTER 12

Queen and I passed each other at breakfast and lunch. She avoided my eyes, which reminded me of the shy way sheep pretend they're not paying attention when you herd them. I spent the afternoon herding; she was in the dairy. We didn't have a private time to talk. Her avoidance structured the day like a middle school crush; I daydreamed about her and stumbled over the fields, I walked the sheep to the lake, and I stripped and lay in the warm and cool layers of the water. I planned what I would say to her. I'd tell her to keep the baby. Maybe Dice would change his mind.

I found Queen that evening, as I ushered the sheep into the barn and she emerged from the dairy. "I told Pear," she whispered, although there was no one to hear us. "She's going to make me a tea tomorrow that will throw the baby out."

"You once told me you wanted kids," I said with a sad rush of relief. I shooed the last lambs, large now, into their enclosure. Outside the barn, the late sun made everything green and gold, but inside, night had already fallen.

"The family is more important," Queen said. Her eyes were

puffy, from crying, I suspected. Although I did not believe that this was what she wanted, I thought if she stayed on the farm she'd realize it was for the best. The family's values would smooth over the loss, and make it as small and silly as my loss of my mother and Isaac. "I don't think I'd be a good mom," she said. But this was different from not wanting a baby. For her sake, I pretended it was the same.

Pear found Queen and me in the barn the next day after lunch, in the short end of the L where the grain platforms opened to a view of the old buggies and wagon wheels far below. "Well, Queenie, you know why I'm here," she said.

"Should I go?" I said.

"No sense pretending the two of you don't talk," Pear said. "The walls have eyes, you know."

This, too, was a relief, in a way. It was nice to live in a world without secrets. "Does Dice know?" I said.

Pear nodded. I glanced at Queen.

"Is Dice mad?" I said to Pear, asking for Queen's sake.

I'd never asked Dice what happened when a family member broke a rule. I wondered whether his displeasure was deterrent enough, so no punishment ever occurred. The rules were built for us, like a passive-solar house is built to stay cool in summer and warm in winter; we were oriented correctly, so it was not hard for us to function as the builder intended.

"You were helping the family," Pear said. "Accidents happen. What matters more is what you do next."

"You don't think Queen should go to the doctor?" I said. I didn't dare ask about health insurance. I doubted Dice even paid taxes.

"We can't be numbered," said Pear. Dice had explained that people are scarier when the size and structure of their cooperation is unknown: worse than a thousand at midday is a small group coming at you in the dark.

"So what would you do if someone got very sick?" I said.

"We cure ourselves," said Pear. "Or if our time has come, we die."

"Has anyone died?" I said.

"People die every second, Harmony," Pear said. "Come on, now."

We followed her into the second bedroom of the long house. Pear opened up a trapdoor in the thickly painted ceiling. From a top bunk, we hoisted ourselves through, me behind Pear and Queen behind me. I didn't want to look back at Queen; I feared she would change her mind.

We searched the attic with flashlights. The unfamiliar space felt magical after months, and anticipated years, of the same few rooms. I found old cowbells, some as large as my head, as though made for prehistorically large animals. A butter churn from a century ago, a blue-painted horizontal wooden box that could be spun with a crank. Inside it still smelled sweetly of cream. Old skins, a collection of blue and speckled eggs. A broken primitive audio recording—a cylinder, curved black waxy shards, layered like a beetle shell. A bonnet filled with flies. Bearskin boots with pointed toes.

My mother would have loved this space. She loved all kinds of things, the gifts in her shop, the trinkets in my bedroom, the diamonds. She would have loved the bells and the butter churn. With so many old things sticking up from the floor or hanging from the ceiling, and our flashlights beaming through the motes, sweeping tidily past the cluttered walls, I felt momentarily weightless, as though the long house were barrel-rolling in deep space.

Pear rummaged ahead. Even though people didn't talk much about their pasts—another rule, I reminded myself—I'd been learning in passing what lives people had led before the family. Gemini, the patrolman who handled the dogs, had worked in an industrial chicken slaughterhouse. Sara had been a runaway since high school. Pear had been a college student, like I could have been, and then she'd been a kindergarten teacher. "Found it," she said, and I turned to see her lift a clay pot and blow the dust off its top.

"What's that?" Queen said.

"A pot to hold the brew," said Pear. She was smiling as though she'd forgotten its purpose. It was squat, with intricate black and red engravings.

"Is the brew safe?" Queen said.

"Gentler than anything out there," Pear said. She waved her hand at the window, toward the fake world. Queen nodded. I didn't believe it—there was no simple type of abortion, I thought.

We followed Pear back into the kitchen, where she began to gather dried herbs from the pantry. She disappeared into Dice's room and returned with a velvet cushion, which she placed on a kitchen chair. "For you, my dear," she said to Queen. I noticed the starbursts of shattered veins in Pear's cheeks, just below the ruddy surface. She was old. Maybe sixty. The oldest in the family, by far. Queen sat on the cushion. She looked like she was waiting for a present. "Good girl," Pear said.

She spooned pennyroyal and tansy into a glass canning jar, then covered them with boiling water. With her bread maker's broad fingernail, she broke the wax seal on a little brown glass bottle of tincture, which, she said, was made of the dusky leaflets of blue cohosh, plucked from shady coves, and soaked in moonshine for a month in the dark.

While the tea steeped, Pear talked. She told Queen to ask for the spirit child's permission to proceed. "And you have to finish it," Pear said. "It'll be another cup every six hours for a week."

The tea smelled like a scorched and wetted forest, burnt and murky. Queen took a gulp, then paused.

"I can't," she said.

"Let's sing something," Pear said. I imagined her in the classroom, in the center of a ring of kindergartners. My heart went out to her, her clumsiness, her sympathy. "What's your favorite song?"

We sang "Mutual Love," and our voices sounded wan. *But now I am a soldier, my captain's gone before. He's given me my orders, and bids me ne'er give o'er.* Queen broke off halfway through.

"I'll leave the cup for you," Pear said, gathering her herbs. She looked us over. "I won't tell Dice this time," she said. "But if you keep refusing, I'll have to, you know."

Queen and I sat alone, the cup abandoned. She laid her cheek on the table. Through her hacked-up hair, I could see her pink scalp. "He told me to do it," Queen said. "That's what I just don't get. Do you think they're trying to teach me a lesson?" She lifted her head. The wood grain had wrinkled her cheek.

"Get relativity," I said. The truth was that I didn't know.

Queen stood. She put her head to the door and glanced out the windows on both sides of the kitchen. Then she poured the tea down the sink. "Maybe I'll run away," she whispered. Her breath smelled sweet and spicy, like chai.

She wrapped her arms around me. I did not want to let her go, now or tomorrow or the next week or ever. I did not want to choose between Queen and the family.

That evening, Pear baked sugar-rolled butter cookies as a treat. After we turned out the lights in the barn, Queen gave her cookie to a raccoon. He ran to the night-silver creek and lowered the cookie into the water, to wash off the sugar, Queen said, but he kept washing and washing until it all dissolved and washed away.

In the morning, we wiped down the long table after breakfast in the green-hued June shade. Everyone else was out, tilling, sowing, weeding, fencing, sweeping the stables, stirring the milk, and sweating the new cheeses. Pear prepared another cup of the tea and passed it to Queen. "Try," she said.

Queen stood and again listened at the door, again peered out the windows. Then she took her cup, and, staring levelly at Pear, poured its contents down into the sink.

"Queen," I said.

"Keep your voice down," Pear said.

I stared at her. "She can't—"

"Then let it happen," Pear said, and her voice shook. "But do not get the three of us in trouble."

Queen set down her cup. "Pear," she whispered. "Thank you."

"I've done nothing," Pear said. "I've seen nothing. I leave you your tea and I go about my business." She was agitated. "Do you understand?"

But Dice would find out eventually, inevitably. And when the time came for his justice, I could already hear myself explaining I was only a witness. I didn't yet find it sinister the way my thoughts turned to self-preservation.

Pear said, "Do you understand?"

Queen nodded. She was not going to think about the incoming train until it barreled right into her.

summer

CHAPTER 13

Dice took down the June plaque and put up the July. I'd been with the family almost ten months, and I felt I belonged now, perhaps more than Queen did. She sought me out, in the barn, in the dairy, by the slow creek on the hottest summer evening, when the sheep tracked to the banks for a last drink before bed, kissing their snowy faces in the flat flow. I wondered whether it was wise to associate so much with her, but she was my best friend in the family. Sometimes I thought about her baby still growing, and what would happen when Dice found out. That thought scared me more than the idea of Lindsay telling Isaac where I was, and Isaac telling my mother.

I distracted myself with summertime and its work, which never ended.

Colors of a North Carolina mountain summer: Chartreuse (when the grass or leaves are between you and the sun). Emerald (when you are between the sun and the grass). Indigo—all kinds of high-frequency blues, the kinds that might damage your eyes. Gold and pink for the wildflowers and the sunsets. Shining brown for the forest floor and thunderstorms.

We ate lamb's-quarters, the plentiful wild volunteers. The love-in-a-mist bloomed. The cucumbers grew massive unless they were picked. The zucchinis had beautiful even spots, like butterflies. For a while, we'd go hunting for a single tomato. And then the day came that there were too many.

After a cloudburst, the plot dripped with diamonds. We harvested the tomatoes, coating our hands with itchy green juice that dried rubbery and opaque on our fingers.

The basil came out like a jungle. The more we cut the stems, the more they grew, spreading out low. We tucked basil in all the beds to freshen them. Basil in the pillowcases. When we opened the door to the bedrooms, basil air exhaled.

One morning, one of the sheep must have disturbed a copperhead. I found her prone body in the meadow as I was guiding the flock home. I'd failed to protect her. I didn't know what to do. I couldn't drag her, but I didn't want to leave her to rot. The other sheep looked at her, silent and patient as always. I remembered Queen telling me that sheep miss their dead.

I told Sara, and she said, "Gemini will gather up the bones and we'll give her a proper burial here, in the place where we bury all our departed friends."

But if there was a burial I didn't witness it.

"I think I'm starting to show," Queen said a few days later, as we sat in the far end of the hayloft, in the hot hours after lunch. We stripped rosemary off stems and piled it on the mesh dryer, just to have something to do with our hands.

I shook my head. She had gained weight but it seemed too soon—only two months since Rainer's arrival.

She lifted her shirt. Her line tattoo went all the way down her belly. She didn't look pregnant, only soft. I pushed her shirt back down; even here, in the hayloft, in the calm slatted light, I knew the walls had eyes.

"I have to thank you," Queen said. "Without you I never would have kept this baby."

But I hadn't encouraged her. "I don't know if I've been that helpful," I said. I felt she was trying to make me her ally, but I didn't want to be implicated in her deceit.

"Thank you," she said again.

I wondered whether I would have to betray her eventually. "Don't you worry about what Dice will do when he finds out?"

"I think he already knows. He knows everything," she said. "He'll either change the rule, or I'll run away." Her voice turned harsh. "Distract me," she said.

I wondered how to. Lindsay, the onrushing biodiversity collapse, how sinister the summer outdoors is, the heat climbing and climbing. I wanted to know if everyone felt a little afraid of open spaces, like I did. I wondered about how people who left the farm often died out there—Queen had said that—and about how we fought violence with violence. I wondered about the locks on the doors: Dice's bedroom door, the trapdoor in the hayloft, the door behind the pigpen. I wondered whether Dice would be reasonable, when it became impossible to ignore Queen's condition. "I have nothing to say."

She said, "Want to hear the story of the first time I ran away from home?"

Today, I felt an obligation to obey even the less important rules. "Maybe it's better not to dwell on the past," I said.

She said, "Will you run your hands through my hair?" She lay down, her head in my lap.

She began to talk about the past, and I became too curious to tell her to be quiet. She told me about leaving Charlotte when she was fifteen. She packed Chewy bars, her velour tracksuit, and her mom's picnic towel to use as a blanket. She wore jeans and a rugby shirt. She made a loop with her braided hair. "My hair used to be really long," she said, "a lifelong braid, so long I'd put it on the table while I ate."

She told me about riding away on a freight train, how her first night the men she met could only find a strand of pig-in-a-bucket cars, truck trailers set in container wells. Queen didn't want to go in those because they had huge circular holes in the bottom. There was a ledge all around the sides just wide enough to sleep on, but those holes, eight of them down the center of the metal floor, were three feet across, easy to fall through. Right after sunset, Queen heard the crash, crash, crash of all the cars linking together. The train started so slowly she barely noticed—but the holes immediately swallowed her picnic towel, her Chewy bars, her tracksuit.

She said she'd hopped the freight trains because she wanted to get as far away from home as she could, as fast as possible. I guessed she must have liked the romance of it, too. There was no point in anything, I thought, if you couldn't appreciate the romance. Romance, rule-breaking, feeling awake under the sunset, gazing at Bay's scarred arms—it was all the same. We'd both wanted a more essential life.

Queen sat up so quickly her head bumped into my chin. "Shhh . . . ," she said. She looked around, got up, and peered the length of the light-striped hayloft. The wind came through the many slats. "I thought I heard something." She made me check too.

"Maybe we should stop talking about the past," I said. I wanted to follow the rules, which meant I was a good family member. Not for the first time, I felt a little superior—I didn't want her to lead me wrong.

She sat back down next to me and took up another rosemary branch. "I stole from my mom," she said. "She was a good lady." Queen spoke lightly, as though she'd discussed this so many times it was no longer painful to her. She crushed rosemary blades in her fingers. I noticed the past tense.

"She died?"

Queen wouldn't look at me. "She took speed to stay awake. She was trying, in her own way. I was never in the car with her when she wasn't lit."

My mother, however clumsy and sad, had tried, over and over, to show me how much she cared. But I couldn't think about this too long. Besides, she loved an idea of me—not me, the bread stealer who wouldn't go to college. What Bay told me, back when I first sat in his car, looped through my mind. He said, *You who know nothing, love nothing. The more knowledge is inherent in a thing, the greater the love.* Maybe if my mother had tried to know me better, I wouldn't have left. My heart felt tight in my chest, like a walnut pressed in a nutcracker.

Queen paused before speaking again. "She died in a car accident," she said. "I was an awful daughter, anyway. I got in lots of fights. I was a troublemaker. My friends seemed to valorize suffering. They valorized difficult personalities." I knew what she meant: the squat's meetings went on for hours, starting out with bulk avocado orders or whether or not to kill mice, and ending with each person splitting into their own separate rage. "It's true that people who had never found a community often found their way to us," she said. "But you have to know, Harmony, if society isn't built for you, you are more likely to see its faults. You will inevitably see its faults. You will not see why you should preserve it."

"I always wished I could hop trains," I said, which was true.

"There are many ways to live outside society," she said. "You don't need to hop trains. I was at the end of the line and there was Bay, waiting with open arms."

I didn't know if she meant this literally. It hadn't occurred to me that I had just been one in a series of people waiting to be held in his long scarred arms.

"Bay," I said. I felt brokenhearted, or betrayed by Bay or by Queen, I wasn't sure.

"Bay," Queen said. "Seductive Bay."

"He seduced you?" I said. I thought of our kiss. I burned to know whether Queen had kissed Bay too.

"You don't own him," Queen said: she knew exactly what I was thinking. "We share everything. It is one of Dice's most important rules."

"You don't seem to respect Dice's rules all that much," I said.

She tilted her head. Her expression, something about it, filled me with dread.

"Be careful with Bay," she said.

"Why?" I said.

"He's like Dice's hands," she said.

"What do you mean?" I said. She didn't answer.

The smell of the rosemary. The whisk of the hay. We knew some of each other's secrets. I had to stop thinking that I could trust her. I said, "Don't run away."

For a moment I could see her as she was: a young woman pregnant, and scared.

CHAPTER 14

Dice found me as soon as I returned with the sheep the next morning. I felt my skin prickle. I didn't understand how he could frighten me with a smile. "I haven't seen you much recently, Harmony," Dice said. "You've been spending all your time with Queen."

"Not all of it," I said. I scrutinized his face for signs of what he knew. Did he know Queen hadn't taken the tea? Did he know Pear had allowed it to happen? But his face was perfectly vague; his eyes reminded me of those of marble statues, smooth and empty.

He said nothing more. Instead, he guided me toward the long house with his hand at the base of my spine. Even through my shirt, his fingers shocked me like the electric fence. We walked through the many bedrooms, all filled with dust-solid sunlight, and reached his room.

His room smelled a little like the yellow pine-needle soap Isaac used. But that was impossible; the family never used store supplies, fake perfumes. We made loamy white soap from animal fat. We washed to get rid of not the smell but the itchiness.

"Look," Dice said. He scooted a wooden box toward me with

his foot. There was a gray ball inside, shaking—a little screech owl. "Injured," he said, "probably concussed by a car. His wing is broken, so he might not last. But we're going to go buy him some nightcrawlers, and try." The owl looked like a kitten, with fluffy gray ears and huge yellow staring eyes that looked goofy, he held them so wide. The owl's feathers reminded me of the fine chevron pattern of hair down Queen's spine.

I said, "Wouldn't he be better off in the forest?"

"I feel a sense of responsibility," Dice said, "because he's an animal injured by a human." Dice picked the owl up around his narrow shoulders. The owl looked back and forth, wary and resigned. Dice showed me how to feel the owl's narrow ridge of breast, his downy sides, his regimented feathers. I held him and he was light as a bubble of glass.

"If he were a human injured by an animal," Dice said, "well, you know what I think." I knew. No fake-world treatments, no antibiotics, the most selfish and apocalyptic of human medicine. Dice watched me set the owl back in the box. "You want to care for Queen, but Queen doesn't deserve so much attention," Dice said. "She needs to work some things out on her own."

My face warmed. He knew, I thought. He knew everything. Suddenly, I remembered my bruises from that first night. Again, I wondered what Dice would do to a family member who broke the rules. *People die every second*, Pear had said.

We took his truck. I sank into the front seat, holding the box with the little owl in my lap. Dice was so good at telling me what I wanted—to let my hand infect, to come to an action, to heal the owl—so I might come to a point where I wanted all kinds of things without knowing why and still feel perfectly free. Dice guided the truck to the mouth of the dirt road, and I braced myself for a few miles of jostling. It was my second time leaving the family land in eight months.

"Queen seems much better now," I said, groping around to see if he was angry.

"Let's not talk about Queen's private life." He arrived at a paved road and turned. "Queen has done many bad things," he said. He let this sit. He drove with just one hand lightly at the bottom of the wheel. He rolled down the windows and the air came swirling in, over my lips, eyelids, scalp. I missed my hair. "She tried to run away, right before the direct action," he said. "She and a friend of hers. That's why we didn't bring her with us. The friend was named. . ." He trailed off.

"She said she didn't want to go hungry," I said.

"She's a terrific liar," Dice said.

I could feel my eyes twitching to keep up with the blur of trees, following, then snapping forward, over and over. I wasn't used to speed.

"Cassie," he said. "That was her friend's name."

"Where is Cassie now?" I said.

"Queen told us Cassie went to find the train, but we found her body there by the river," Dice said. My heart beat hard.

"The fake world doesn't sit right," Dice said, "after you've been in the real world. We think she wasn't paying attention. Maybe snakebite." My chest felt tight again, that nut-cracking feeling. I wondered if he was telling the truth. I told myself I'd ask Queen later. She, at least, was honest with me.

We were speeding past mailboxes, cheaply built houses, fallow fields, yellow signs warning of leaping deer, though we were in their space and not the other way around. Dice didn't have to tell me that the fake world was deadly; I could see it with my own eyes. "Poor Cassie," I said. "Poor Queen."

Dice looked over at me. "A little too generous of a spirit, Harmony," he said. "Did you know that before Queen came here, she was in jail?"

Jail didn't seem like a big deal. I could imagine her shoplifting, even robbing. *I was a troublemaker*, she'd said. "I don't want to know about Queen's past," I said. This seemed like the kind of answer that he was looking for.

"You need to know this," Dice said. "The charge was death by vehicle." The cars that passed us made a high-pitched roar as they approached. "She drove up on the sidewalk and killed her mother," he said.

"An accident?" I said.

"She says so," he said. The story had the feel of truth. I remembered Queen saying that the family was the end of the line for her. The road spun out below the tires. I felt myself slipping.

"Don't tell her you know," he said. "She'll deny it, anyway." I shook my head. My loose farm clothes seemed to be crawling with mites.

"Get relativity," he said. He placed his hand lightly on mine; it was warm and dry, like he'd been kneading bread. "I know you hurt because you thought you knew Queen, but this is a lesson for you. You don't know Queen because you don't know there is no definite self." We reached Mars Hill. I looked at the preponderance of letters. I couldn't help but read every word that passed, *Comfort Inn, Forks of Ivy Baptist Church, Waffle House, Zip N Slip Snow Tubing*. My whole time on the farm, I'd only read the songs in our songbooks and the plaques for the calendar. I stared down at the glove compartment and at my own dirty lap. "'There is no definite self. The self isn't a fixed point," Dice said, unperturbed by the chaos of town, "but more like a forest. Think of Pisgah."

I wanted to think about Queen and Cassie, about Queen and her mother, but I could not shut Dice out—his soft, urging voice, and the faint pulse of his hand on mine, signaled that I would find all the answers I needed if only I would listen. I knew that, if I wanted to stay with the family, I had to trust Dice before anyone else.

"Unquestionably the same forest, a hundred years ago and now," he said, "though its animals and trees grow and die, its waters come up from the ocean in clouds and then return to the ocean in spring rivers which carry its dirt away, and it is never seen in its entirety from any vista."

I threw all of my attention into listening. This was the second time he'd talked to me about the definite self, and now I found comfort in the idea. When I'd tried to explain it to Lindsay, something had fallen into place. In nature, everything was tendencies and groupings. In nature, as in a family, self-interested decisions and actions were destructive.

Dice said, "When you say 'I exist,' your words call into being a unity which has no permanence. As though you're gathering daisies from the hills and saying they're a bundle—but then the wind of the next moment rips them from your hand."

Only a few days in our holler were windy enough to wrest daisies from our hands, but I will never forget that terrifying force, which buffeted whole branches from our hickory to the ground and made the long house moan from all its joints, like a calving glacier.

He pulled into the little strip mall with the store labeled *Live Bait*. The shop had brown walls, loud fluorescent lights, an overwhelming mossy smell. I was back in the fake world. A few silent shoppers hung around in the aisles, looking at the thousands of different kinds of baits, hard shiny simulacra of minnows, walleyes, soft rubbery craws and worms, shining flies made of beads and tufts of feather, each hiding a pin-sharp hook.

Even through the bait odor, I could tell I reeked. We drew a few stares but I told myself the Appalachians were full of strange folk.

I rushed to the shop's bathroom, which was a terrible mistake. There were no mirrors on the farm. One of the rules. And here: my first reflection since September. I was wide necked and red, with my close-cropped hair, hairy armpits. I saw for the first time, as I patted water onto my face, a discoloration on my cheek, from the sun, I guessed, a big blotch that wouldn't wash away. No one had mentioned it to me.

Dice had exited the store. I waited as long as I could before I joined him. I wanted to forget about myself in the mirror. If I could forget, it'd be tantamount to not having broken a rule to begin with.

Dice stood on the low yellow block at the end of a parking space. His posture, his moccasins, the dirt on his skin, set him apart. I could almost see the strip mall evaporating, the concrete melting away, the old farmland, too, collapsing, back to the time when American chestnuts grew here, and bison made trails in the forest, and passenger pigeons, copper and blue, swarmed in colonies of billions, darkening the sky like a volcano and cooing like sleigh bells.

I approached him, hoping he wouldn't ask where I had gone. If Dice ever said *I know what you did*, I would confess to ten possible crimes.

He smiled at me. "Want a milk shake?" he said.

I wondered if he was trying to test me. "No," I said. Our ice cream was better. It contained only cream and honey, spun in salty ice.

We returned to the truck. The little owl was asleep in its box. "You know, Harmony, you said something wonderful," said Dice. "No to a treat. You may have just earned yourself a place at our next action. I may be able to count on you, despite your occasional lapse."

I leaned my head back, thrilled. Before I knew what I was saying, the words spilled out: "I love you, Dice."

"My sweet girl," he said. Bay had said Dice was the father of the intentional family, but he was better than any father I knew. When I was young, my mother always struggled to explain what had happened to my father. Instead, I grew up into the loss, like the turtle I'd seen in a litter awareness campaign that, as a baby, had gotten a plastic ring stuck around its middle, so that when it grew, its shell and midsection became distorted, squashed flat in the middle.

On the way back we stopped at a Dairy Queen, even though I'd refused the milk shake. Dice ordered a tall cone of paint-white ice cream. The enormous server, pillow-soft as an ice cream herself, elegantly dipped the cone into a vat of chocolate coating. I watched the chocolate freeze. Dice paid with cash, and the bills looked soft and floppy, like third-world currency.

I knew that money probably came from another family member's bank account. Dice had told me people tended to donate all they had when they arrived. I didn't like his using that money on ice cream. We were all supposed to say no to treats.

"Well, I'll have a try," I said.

"You stick to your word."

He had ice cream on his lip. I reached for his cone, licked the chocolate coat. The sugar burned at the sockets of my teeth. Dice let me without protest, which surprised me, and then when I handed the cone back, he dropped it and pressed the whole thing into the floor with his moccasin. The look on his face was placid but the gesture was so violent, so wrathful, that I felt sweat rise on my back, my shoulders, my face.

"Sir," said the server. He ignored her, so I did too.

All the long way home in the truck, Dice let me stew in my own juices. The longer I was silent, the more I felt I couldn't speak— a paralyzed feeling from my past, like waiting to tell my mother about the college acceptance letter I did not want. I'd ruined our whole excursion. Maybe I'd ruined my chance at attending the next direct action.

But as we pulled into the courtyard, where the three guard dogs wrestled below the enormous hickory, I felt better again. The healthiest foods, I knew, were the ones that stewed in their isolation, like sauerkraut. In isolation, there's no way for disease to grow.

I followed Dice to prepare the worms for the little owl. I sat on his floor and clamped the nightcrawlers down with clothespins. The owl snapped one up in his beak, then hunkered down in his box again.

"Go get Rainer," Dice said. He always knew how hard to push. He'd told me about Queen and Cassie, and then interrupted my thoughts with talk about daisies and the definite self. He'd told me all the rules, then let me bathe in lavender.

"Why?" I asked.

"Your next lesson," he said. I looked up at him. I knew I was frightened because my hands were shaking.

Dice led Rainer and me around to the sloping pen where the few remaining lambs sunned themselves and played, scampering sideways and tossing their heads. They were almost full-size now.

"Choose one, Harmony," Dice said. I knew right away what he wanted. It was my second chance for slaughtering.

I chose a chubby lamb, a boy with a big round belly. Dice led us to the pallet, the frame, the pneumatic machine—they used to be right by the edge of the woods but now they were deeper in. Dice roped the lamb to a sapling. The insects roared in the afternoon, and the love-prayer feeling rose up in me like a tide, and I blinked hard to try to stay in my head, seeing through my own eyes.

Dice said, "You know why I picked you two?"

I supposed the real answer was that Rainer and I had each played a part in Queen's pregnancy. This was our punishment. But with Dice there was always a lesson; I loved that about him. "So we can learn about life and death?" I said.

"Because both of you are weak. Rainer especially," Dice said. I had never heard Dice be so cruel.

"What a fool," Dice said. "Look at him." His voice rose, his neck corded. "*Look at him!*" I was horrified to see tears in Rainer's eyes.

He put his arm around Rainer. "*Wouldn't you say*"—he was loud again, his voice ringing and metallic—"that no one outside the family cares about your well-being?"

"No one outside the family cares about my well-being," Rainer repeated.

"Not your parents? Not Lindsay?" said Dice.

"No," Rainer said.

"It's nothing to be ashamed of," said Dice, gentle again. "In fact, you should be proud. We will love you like no one else can." I loved how Dice took care. His words were even more soothing after he'd been so unkind. Rainer reminded me of a nervous horse caught in the traces; Dice rescued him and calmed him.

Dice told Rainer to sit down on the pallet. Rainer sat. Dice took me deeper into the forest. "You see, no one cares about him, or will notice his disappearance," said Dice.

Dice handed me a knife, a Ka-Bar. I tilted the blade and looked at the forest reflected in it, smeared together.

Dice left me there. Soon he brought Rainer back behind the trees. "Do you trust me?" said Dice.

Rainer nodded.

"Do you trust Harmony?" said Dice.

Again, Rainer nodded. I had the knife in my hand and felt the world curving around me as though through a fish-eye lens.

"Harmony and I want what's best for you," said Dice, and in an instant he drew my right hand and knife up along Rainer's hard-beating neck.

"Control over life and death allows us to move past them," said Dice.

In that moment, I had no idea what he meant. Yet I knew I wanted to learn the truth about the world, and I expected to struggle to get there. And I felt Dice's body against me; I knew he wanted something and then I wanted it too.

I could have cut Rainer's throat. But I didn't.

It would have been so easy—a moment of fearlessness; like Isaac had taught me, you only need a moment. At times I convinced myself that I had carried it out, so that when I saw Rainer at dinner, it seemed like he was haunting me.

But that day, I lowered the knife. Dice whispered in my ear, "Good girl, Harmony." I wasn't sure why this made me good, though I hoped it meant I had earned a reward. An ice cream cone, a role in the next protest, a night alone with Bay by the fire, with his lips on mine.

Dice gestured to the lamb. "You're ready, Harmony," he said, and it was true; my heart juddered as if I were approaching a jump. The knife moved with a frictionless snickering sound. We hung the lamb up and puffed off his skin and slit down his front and threw the useless parts to the dogs.

Dice took my hands and used the hem of his blue shirt to blot them. I could see his hard stomach, its tangle of hair. "Nature is this way, too," he said.

Rainer hadn't moved. He gazed out at the forest and I could only see the back of his head. I walked around him to see if he was crying and I was startled to see he was smiling.

"Should we head back?" Rainer asked.

I felt sorry for him now. I'd held a knife to his neck. I'd never felt so much power, which meant I'd never felt so much mercy.

"Okay," I said. We walked through the tomato patch. Mindless of spiders, I plucked sungolds for both of us, and fireworked them in my mouth.

I could hear owls, but not mine, and a million insects. Insects don't have hearts and blood like ours, just a general, sloshing fluid held inside their carapaces that churns back and forth, back and forth.

CHAPTER 15

I still didn't know whether I'd be invited to the next action. I planned to ask when the moment was right. In the meantime, I devoted myself to work. The leeks sent forth their feathery pastel-purple flowers. I found an arrowhead or perhaps a spear point in the peas. So many green beans per plant, hiding. To harvest them, I sat cross-legged and scooted through the rows. The beans we missed grew monstrously long. Sometimes I forgot that it was Dice who had brought us together. I thought that it was just our love of nature that grew the family, like plums from a bough.

The black beans in maroon pods grew up among the sunflowers. We'd harvest beans in the fall, split the pods, and dry the beans inside, to eat all winter. Beans like those, Cherokee Trail of Tears black beans, needed a hundred days without a frost to reach maturity.

We found melons lurking among their giant velvety leaves. Moon and Stars melons, dark green with pale spots of varying sizes.

The corn was tall. We could already dig up the first potatoes.

In the dairy, Queen made cheese every day. We worked side by side, but we hadn't spoken since that day in the hayloft. I wished I could ask her about how Cassie died. I wished I could ask her why they tried to run away. But I couldn't get the words out. I kept seeing her car crashing into her mother. I wondered how she felt about it now, almost a mother herself.

I helped with the milking, pouring foamy sheep milk from stainless pails through a filter into the big milk jugs that we stored overnight in the trough.

We ate ricotta at every breakfast, and *primo sale*, and the shelves in the cellar groaned under the heavy new wheels. On very hot days, I volunteered to spend all eight hours in the cool, musty cellar, in the dim, washing rinds with skin-pricklingly salty water. I'd emerge dizzy at lunch and at dusk.

Instead of Queen, I placed my care on the little owl. Every day Dice would invite me to his room after breakfast and we'd pin down worms for the owl to eat. But his wing still jutted out; he didn't seem to be healing.

One day, a little while after our trip to town, Dice said, "Open the window. See if he wants to leave."

"I'm sure he can't fly," I said.

"Can't heal something that doesn't want to heal," Dice said.

So I pushed up the sash. I picked up the owl's box and set him on the windowsill so he could step out if he wanted, but he just gazed into the greenery, holding his broken wing stiffly away from his body.

"Very well," Dice said. "Let's try a different kind of cure." Dice left the room, probably to fetch a remedy from Pear's cabinet.

I looked at Dice's rose-colored love seat, the tatty lace in his windows, the row of bones—phalanges or spine bones—on his bookshelf. I walked over to his bed and touched his sheets. I bent to sniff his pillow, that wild pine scent. I ran my hand over his nightstand, its worn paint like suede. I held my breath and opened the little drawer. Inside were four bars of yellow soap. Isaac's soap. Fake-world soap. The sight of it broke my heart. I shut the drawer. We had everything we needed here, I knew. Yet I'd fallen for it: I loved the way he smelled.

"Harmony," Dice said. He'd snuck in behind me, on his moccasins. I had no idea whether he'd seen me opening his nightstand. As though to draw our attention away, the owl extended his unbroken wing like a paper fan. Dice sighed. "I can't fix him if you won't tell me what's wrong," Dice said.

"What's wrong?" I said. My heart was beating hard enough for him to hear it.

"Yes," Dice said.

I felt sick. "What's with the soap?" I said. "Isn't that against the rules?" I wondered if I'd caught him in a lie. I hated the idea of catching him at something. He was supposed to be better than all of us.

I opened the nightstand drawer again.

"Oh," he said. He picked up a bar and weighed it in his hand, turned it back and forth. He wasn't embarrassed or angry and I felt off balance.

He handed me the bar. "I like the way it smells," he said, simply.

He turned back to the owl. He trickled some plant essence from the dropper of a dark brown bottle on the owl's wing. He

murmured, in his beautiful tenor singing voice. "I think he's better now," he said.

He held out his forearm and the owl stepped one claw, then
the other, onto it. The owl tucked his crooked wing against his
body. If I hadn't seen it, I wouldn't have believed it.

"Point out the window," Dice said.

I pointed.

In a surge of air, the owl winged straight out.

Then I didn't mind the soap or the rule-breaking, the crushed
ice cream, the trouble about Cassie. Dice performed miracles,
Queen had said, and now I'd seen it was true. Dice was above
our rules.

Queen didn't come to dinner that night. July dinner: snap beans,
garlic toast, honeysuckle-flower ice cream.

I went out looking for her. Under the skyscraper hickory.
In the storage house, wide wood rooms mostly empty now. In
the dairy, where the fresh cheeses slumped on the sill, glittering with frosty salt. In the pitch-black cellar, in the pigpen, the
sheep's beds, the henhouses, the horse and cow stables, calling. I
called up the trapdoors. She's dead, I thought. What was the bone
room like, anyway? Maybe she had been bitten by a copperhead.
Or maybe she'd tried to run away. Maybe the white dogs had
caught and shredded her. Maybe she'd gone as far as the freight
yard, maybe she'd died there, like Cassie. Or maybe Dice had decided to punish her, maybe he'd locked her somewhere where we

wouldn't be able to hear her pounding. I knew there were locked places in the barn.

I wished we had cell phones, a wish that hadn't flown into my head in months.

I found her in the loose-floored hayloft. I rushed forward, relieved for only a second. She looked blue-green, sweat-soaked. A terrible smell, roadkill, high meat, reached me and made me retch. And then I noticed the ground beneath her was slick with blood.

"Harmony," she said. "I'm dying."

I knew that people and sheep who expect to die often do.

"Nonsense," I said. I suppose I thought we'd fix it, put it back. "I think we've got to get you to town, though."

"They'll kill me if I leave," she said.

"No, they won't," I said. I knew from our trip to the bait shop that I was right: Dice believed in second chances.

"Oh, I should have run away as soon as I was late," she said.

I needed to find Pear. "I'll be right back," I said.

I jumped over the ramp onto the hayloft. I ran through the trapdoor into the cow enclosure. The cows seemed huge in the dark, like aurochs. I ran back to the house, where the singing was just beginning, and I pulled Pear outside.

"Herbal remedies," said Pear. "Blue cohosh—"

"Pear, this is a case for a hospital," I said frantically.

"No case," Pear said agonizingly slowly, "is a case for a hospital." I didn't know why she was being so difficult until I looked up and saw Dice's shadow in the window.

Later, during hot nights in the long house, I'd wonder if the miscarriage wasn't a coincidence. But for now I felt only the oblit-erating roar of what our songbook called great tribulation.

Pear cut the baby away with the sheep shears. She called Dice to carry Queen through the twilight to his room. When his door closed, Pear almost bit my ear, whispering. "Take my car," she said. She pressed keys into my hand. Her eyes blinked out of time with each other as she spoke. "Go to the pharmacy. I don't care how you do it, ask for antibiotics, ask for help with a miscarriage."

My heart was in my throat. I could only follow orders; I didn't consider the consequences. I didn't consider whether Dice would be angry. I found Pear's old maroon car, which had been parked by the humanure pile so long I didn't know whether it still worked. I surprised myself by remembering to adjust the mirror, remem-bering how to shift the seat forward. It had been less than a year since I'd last driven. But it seemed wrong how well I remembered.

And then I was down the bumpy path at full speed, launch-ing off the gravel, my headlights rollicking through the trees. I turned left, as I remembered Bay and Dice had. Pear's car had a clock. It was 7:03. I wondered if I'd find an open pharmacy at this time of day.

I drove eighty miles per hour, veering so quickly around turns the car seemed to go up on two wheels. I would not hit a deer. I would not be stopped by the police. I was driving for Queen's life, and for my own: I had to get back before anyone noticed. The world was bending to me. I pulled up to the Ingles pharmacy, the same Ingles where I'd gone Dumpstering with Bay.

The pharmacist wore a white lab coat. She had powder-blue nails and a soft, pink face. She looked nervous. I was glad she was a woman. Her name tag said *Annie*.

"Please, I have a question," I said. I tried to imagine what Dice or Bay would say. But I felt winged, godlike, deranged with urgency. This woman, Annie, would not be able to stop me from taking what I needed.

"Something like fever, green face, bleeding, and miscarriage— what would you prescribe for that?"

Each word I added seemed to alarm her more. She backed away from the counter. "A doctor," she said.

"Please, *Annie*. I need the medicine." My voice kept getting softer and softer, dying in my throat.

"I'll get my manager," she said.

Begging was not working. But what else could I do? What else did I know? How had Bay done it, offering me chocolate, call-ing me Greyhound girl, showing me that he understood me like no one else ever had? I remembered how he made me feel. And then I thought: This might be the most exciting thing that ever happens to Annie. I told myself to stop shaking. "Don't do that, Annie." I touched the back of her hand, fine velvet. "Didn't you take an oath to do no harm?"

"Pharmacists have a different oath," she said.

"We live so far out in the mountains. She can't come to town," I said. I thought about what I looked like to her: a strong girl with close-shorn white-blond hair, those white-blond eyelashes like a fringe of icicles. The big sun spot on my cheek. My ochre shirt and shorts, my big heavy boots. I must have seemed so wild. Her hand, which had the softness of the owl's feathered chest, moved slightly under mine. "You'll never see me again. No one will ever know."

She looked up at a closed-circuit TV. We were both on it. I saw the bulk of my shoulders. I saw my close short white-blond hair.

"Keep your voice down," she said.

I remembered Bay loading my bags on the bus and telling me to catch them in Durham.

"Fever and what else," she said. She was speaking simply. She straightened a stack of papers. She was putting on an act for the cameras.

I described the blood, the smell. The cord that Pear cut. She went back to her bright shelves of bottles.

I wondered if Queen was dead by now. I wondered if I'd ever expected her to die in the first place.

I looked around the Ingles. So many *things*. Hand cream. Painkillers. Blue gel insoles, DEET, melting breath mints. Greeting cards. It was easy to pick out the ones my mother would have liked. The birthday card with the flocked, embossed teddy bear. The sympathy card with lilac-colored glitter.

The girl passed me three rattling orange bottles. "This is what they'd do in the hospital, three antibiotics. Morning and evening." She did not smile.

"I can't pay."

"She should really have an IV and some tests," she said. "Septic shock in particular." She looked at me carefully. "Make sure she's eating well-cooked food," she said.

I put my big calloused hand back on hers. Her hands were indoor hands, pale and soft and shaky. In this one moment, I was the lightning and she was the rod. Then she pulled away. She told me to have a nice evening.

It was past lights out when I got home. It's strange to remember I never considered driving off toward anywhere else. I'd come to the family in search of a more essential life, and this night, the flight to town and back, the out-of-body urgency, was another sign that Dice could offer exactly what I sought. Before Dice, I never could have convinced a pharmacist to give me free drugs. I never could have bent someone else to my will.

Four times, I missed the turnoff for the dirt road, turning at the Exxon too far west and the Burger King too far east. This comforted me. Even if Lindsay and Isaac tried, I thought, they would not be able to find me. We were so far off the grid.

I parked Pear's car by the outhouse. As I began the uphill walk to the long house, I considered how to get the orange bottles to Pear. I didn't want to knock on Dice's door. I stood there a moment, imagining Queen in a blur of possible states, bleeding, dying, sleeping, on the other side. I knocked. It was Maybell who opened the door a crack.

"How's Queen?" I said, scrambling.

"Our life is ever on the wing," said Maybell. A line from the songbook.

"Oh, for heaven's sake," Pear said, opening the door wider. "Excuse me. Harmony said she would help me with the bread,"

Pear said offhandedly, a weak explanation, I thought. Maybell inspected me with sour eyes.

In the kitchen, Pear squinted at the pills and nodded. She twisted the cap off one, took a pill, and then inserted it into the heel of her bread. "Don't tell anyone," she said. "You know that already." What would Dice do if he found the pills? At that time, I most feared a scolding—in my heart I did not expect any other kind of punishment. Yet even a scolding frightened me. Words seemed to have a different weight here. I'd fallen during the love prayer: I could no longer trust my body.

That evening I lay awake in a top bunk, on one of the three mattresses made from corn husks. I strained to hear anything from Dice's room, where Queen lay, but the sound of the cicadas and katydids and frogs covered everything. To me their sound, vast and tuneless, was the sound of the cooperating bacteria that Dice said were four billion years old. *When we're as old as bacteria . . . we will be as radically interdependent as they are.* Queen's antibiotics were distorting the bacteria's evolution, helping create resistant diseases humanity was not prepared for.

I wondered if Dice would have let Queen die. I wondered if he wanted her to die, the way I wondered about Cassie.

For a moment I fell into fear. There was one time I'd high-jumped wrong and fallen on my head, and all I remembered was the endless fall into what boxers called the black lights. That was what my fear felt like, endless: I wondered if Dice would have let it happen, if he'd wanted it to happen, if he'd caused it to happen.

I realized with a start that they were willing to sacrifice one for the good of the family. Well, they'd been suggesting this all along. But what was more important to me: Queen or the family? Both, I thought. And then, wickedly: The family.

The next night, Dice told a story. When he stepped into the center, we were happy. It had been a long time since the last story.

Sometimes during ice ages, Dice said, the glaciers get big enough to bounce back so much sunlight that the Earth gets colder and colder in a runaway feedback so that the Earth freezes over, glaciers all the way to the equator. And the Earth sits in this state for millions of years. The man who first conceived of this theory, the Snowball Earth phenomenon, thought that it could never have really happened on Earth because the ice would be so stable that there would be no way to escape the permanent freeze. But he forgot about volcanoes—which warm the air with gases, a little each year. And then they cause a tipping point, and the whole Earth melts, starting at the equator and spreading fast, a second runaway feedback, and on come the rivers and streams and brand-new animals lumbering across the truly immaculate warm landscape.

The consensus is that this has really happened on Earth. The Atlantic too has shut and opened three times in Earth's history, from continental drift. "The Earth is very, very old—why do we forget this?" Dice said. "The Appalachians are older than the ocean." He said, "Once, there were palm trees and crocodiles in the Arctic, and no ice. The whole world was swampy and covered in ferns, and horses diminished to house-cat size." He stood still in the dim light. "That's where we're headed," he said. I felt he was speaking directly to me, reminding me that in the fullness of time, just like the Earth went from cold to hot and back again, peace and Armageddon would follow each other endlessly, and my concerns were so trivial they were insane.

CHAPTER 16

Queen healed slowly, as far as I knew. She was hidden in Dice's room, behind a locked door. While she healed, the paulownia trees flocked the forest in lilac. The indigo buntings made families.

Two weeks later, she returned to the dinner table, where she ate her toast the way she liked it, upside down, with the butter on her tongue. Everyone welcomed her. Her hair seemed longer, almost bob length, and I was jealous. Dice said, "She's a good one. Got through a hard round of the summer flu." Dice knew the truth, and so did Pear and I, but the real story had not gotten out. Not even Rainer seemed to know.

After dinner, Pear called "O'Leary" for Queen.

And will the Judge descend,
And must the dead arise;
And not a single soul escape
His all-discerning eyes?

As I gathered up the oblong songbooks, Queen put her hand on my shoulder. "Let me say good night to the sheep with you," she said.

I had missed her. I had so many questions I'd been saving up: About what had become of Cassie. Dead in an accident? About whether Queen had killed her mother. Was it an accident? About her baby. Tucked in the bone room, *the place where we bury our departed friends*, as Sara had said? And maybe now was the time to answer the question I was afraid someone would ask, eventually. How much had I revealed to Lindsay?

We walked past the sheep, gray smudges on the black hay. I felt we were negotiating in silence, figuring out who ought to speak first. We walked past the dark hillocks of cows, the sighing horses, the mother pig and fourteen piglets. Then she said, "I wish I was allowed to be sad."

I didn't like this kind of conversation. We were not supposed to wish things were different. We were supposed to know our ways were right, by instinct, the way animals know things.

"Of course you can be sad," I said, which was true—be sad about the sixth extinction, be sad about human nature, just don't be sad about the baby.

I shouldn't have had to tell her this. She knew. She knew the baby was never hers. She knew there was no definite self, and so the baby would emerge elsewhere, like Gemini's lead bullets, melted and re-formed, melted and re-formed from the same stuff into different shapes. Queen could look for her baby in the woods and find it, in the horses and find it, in the berries and find it. His spirit could range everywhere, and could be found reflected in everything, which was true of every person who has ever died.

I stopped. "Go on ahead," I said. She clasped my hand a moment, but I pulled away. Dice had answers for everything, and the answers were truer, on the whole, than the ones I got in the fake world. There was something wrong with the fake world as it was—the thin-walled houses built with no attention to the sun; the knickknack store with levitating globes and pig-shaped flashlights for people who didn't know what to buy each other, the people who believed that buying things was an expression of love.

Queen continued walking. When I saw her far off in the woods picking up a fir branch and cradling it, I tried to push my sadness down deep. I tried to think this was as it should be, and I tried to ignore the fact that a fir branch is not a baby at all.

I started to walk toward her, not yet decided about whether to comfort her, when I saw, with a shock, two unfamiliar men at the edge of the creek. In the dimness, I could not see their faces, but I could tell from their stocky shapes that they were not Ashers. I crept behind them. One of them stumbled, flicked on a flashlight, and just as quickly flicked it off again. I remembered Sara telling me—*We see them around the land sometimes. Dressed like scientists. Looking in our rivers. Digging in the woods.*

The next day, Pear sent Queen back to work. "The butter's been acid since you've been sick," she said to Queen. "I'll come check on you later." I followed Queen before anyone could tell me not to. I needed to ask if she had seen these men, too.

Queen and I collected the butter clumps from the barrel churn and kneaded out the last of the sour liquid, a job I always botched.

"How was your walk?" I asked Queen.

"Lonely," she said.

"But did you see anything?" I said. "There were strangers by the creek."

"Probably the people who want to kick us out. Developers," she said. "Someday, they're going to figure out a way to get him in trouble."

"No," I said. "We're going to fight them off." I raised my voice, trying to remind her, involve her. "Cooperation will win. All of nature is on our side."

"I wish I could see the family like you do," she said, partition-ing out the butter.

"You have to try to be more open," I said.

"Sort of hard when you've lost your baby," she said.

I wish this hadn't made me angry. But I was angry: she seemed weak and I was, in those days, only interested in strength. "Queen, tell me the truth," I said. I hadn't gotten any answers from her yesterday. I couldn't count on Bay, who was gone half the time. I needed to know if Dice would lie to me. If he was that far above the rules. "Did you run over your own mother with a car?" My heart was beating so hard I felt like it was dragging me back and forth.

"That," she said, "is a crazy question."

"Dice told me that you did." She wouldn't meet my eye.

"Did he, now?" she said. "Jesus." She took her time maneuver-ing her sphere of butter, which hadn't melted on her cool hands.

She pushed her hair back and butter glistened on her cheek like varnish. "He only told you that to turn you against me," she said. "Punishing me, I guess. He hasn't liked me since Cassie and I tried to run away."

"And why was it," I started, panicky that someone could hear, "that you and Cassie tried?"

Queen paused. I could hear a sheep's call, and I felt all-consuming tenderness. Oh, I loved the family, the land. Nothing she could say would make sense. My heart was against her.

"She wanted to bring it all down," Queen said. "Dice has done things that just aren't right, that's what she said. He's negligent, she said, he doesn't care about people." Queen took out the roll of wax paper and started cutting it, sliding open scissors down into the shining paper, which made a sound like a gasp. "That scared me." Queen smiled. "I only got as far as the road, but you know how dirty we always are. We're so easy for the dogs to track. Cassie got a bit farther." She stacked her paper rectangles and began folding up a piece of butter.

"What happened next?" I asked despite myself. I did not want an answer.

I watched Queen shape the butter, then fold up the paper edges into perfect corners. Her hands reminded me of my mother's hands: she had been so good at wrapping presents at the knickknack store. She'd been so good at curling up the ribbons against the scissors into masses of shiny ringlets.

Queen was silent for a long time.

I wanted to tell her to stay silent. Every surface in the dairy was steel or porcelain, and our voices echoed without fading, as though Dice could come by in an hour and put his hand to his ear and listen in. "What has Dice done?" I breathed, but I half-knew—my knife on Rainer's throat, so we would learn control over life and death. Selflessness in humans never comes from nowhere. But the selflessness, whatever its cause, was why the family was better than everything else.

"Cassie would've brought the authorities up here," Queen said, "but Bay found her first." She started on a new lump, kneading.

I remembered Dice's telling me they'd found Cassie's body. "Dice said she died from a snakebite," I said. I heard footsteps across the courtyard, but no one appeared.

"Something like that," Queen said. But I remembered the feeling of Bay's burning branch on my hand. "Anyway, it was my fault in the end," Queen said, "because I'm the one who told the family where Cassie went."

If there was fault, it wasn't an accident.

The door swung open. I hadn't been alert. Someone had been spying on us.

"Hello, girls," Pear said.

"Oh, Pear!" I said. "Our Queen is doing so much better."

Pear smiled at us. It was a smile of admiration or pity. Gently, she said, "I don't believe it was a snake, no," she said.

Pear leaned toward us, her eyes blinking at different intervals. I noticed how tight her mouth looked, her slight mountain-woman moustache. She'd never gotten so close to me before. She dipped a finger into the soft butter.

"More salt," she said. She left, humming loudly. Humming, I thought, so that we could hear her retreat.

Queen's face, normally so languid, was twitchy. "Do you think we can trust her?" Queen whispered.

I leaned to Queen's ear, which was charcoal-black on the inside. "Queen, don't you remember the pills she gave you?" I whispered back.

"She told me they were homeopathic tablets," Queen said.

"No," I said. "She sent me to get you antibiotics."

Queen drew her head away from me. Her eyes looked round as a pigeon's.

I was trying to reassure her, because I wanted us all to keep living on the farm together, like we were supposed to. But I realized that Queen was excited, not soothed.

"Something changed her," Queen said. "She used to be like Sara." She wrapped the butter in a series of elegant gestures. "I wonder if Pear wants to leave," Queen said. She shouldered her hair back behind her ears again and it immediately slipped back down around her cheeks. "Would you come with us, if we left?" she said.

I looked at her face and imagined clinging to the top of a boxcar as it spanned gorges, as it wended a silver way up the Rockies. I imagined losing all I'd brought through the hole in the pig in the bucket.

But I didn't want transience. I wanted community, bound tight. "Don't leave," I said.

When Queen opened the dairy door, a tiny cat ricocheted away in fear. The lightning bugs surrounded us like a storm.

* * *

In the bright fields, pulling up weeds, it was impossible to dwell on Queen's question. My body knew that what I was doing was right for the land. Who else lived like this, so purely? There was no other place like the Ash Family farm. There were guest ranches and co-ops and sects, homesteads all through Appalachia, but there could be no other place so absorbing, so thorough, that allowed us to break down the borders between self and nature, to install cooperation, not competition, as the guiding principle, something that would not change as long as we behaved as though there was no definite self.

During breaks, we lay on the porch. The whitewashed light made our dirty faces look like bronze. We snacked on sour grass and blackberries. Sometimes Queen and I snuck chocolate chips from the storage house. Bay was still gone, and my yearning for him was as clear and fast as the stream as it plunged downhill.

Ursina and Osha and Terra were in charge of constructing something for the next direct action, which they were planning for the fall, maybe October. I waited for them to ask me for help. I watched as they soaked old jars and rubbed off the labels. They grated the bar soap, filling boxes with pearly shards. I guessed they were making some kind of foam to white out windows or gum up machines. They'd blocked off a few of the barn's vacant stables. I pressed my eye to the gap in the planks and saw their towering formations of jars and soap boxes. I would be asked to join them. Besides the ice cream, I'd done everything right this summer. I worked hard. I was working hard to lose track of myself, and in the evenings under starry skies I could lean my head back and feel nature streaming through me like electricity.

One moon-bright night, Dice stepped into the circle to tell us the story of an air force pilot named William Rankin, who ejected from his failing plane into a North Carolina thunderstorm. A ten-minute skydive ended up taking forty minutes, as the storm tossed him around like a cat. He saw the lightning where it formed, its illusory size, which he said was "like blue blades several feet thick." Dice spoke slowly and I closed my eyes, floating in the storm.

He said, "Lightning may seem to be many bright yards wide, but it's really hardly thicker than a pencil."

He said sometimes we were the pilot, and sometimes we were the lightning storm.

In late July, we finally racked off our locust mead, honeysuckle mead, blackberry mead, and scuppernong wine, and still I waited to be asked to help with the action. This, I thought, would be incontrovertible proof that the family had accepted me as I accepted them, like the song in the songbook called "Mutual Love": *Now I am a soldier, my captain's gone before.*

In early August we celebrated with a harvest festival, which Dice called the poskito in honor of the Mississippian Indians. We drank mead that tasted like white wine and honey. All of us worked half-drunk from breakfast on, eating peaches till our stomachs hurt, carrying great baskets of tomatoes, squash, peppers, to the kitchen, where Pear reigned over six family members, pickling and canning, making jams and sauces, desiccating, curing, anticipating a winter that was impossible to imagine now, in the caressing heat of the dog days. The fields sloped a bit more than usual, tilt-a-whirled when I stood up with my basket full of sun-hot strawberries.

Afterward, we lay around the porch like a pack of dogs. We heard the whir of a motor, and then Bay pulled his dirty white car into the courtyard. Those of us who were awake hooted. I noticed his beautiful blue clothes, blue shirt, blue pants, not yet turned to the ochre median of our farm apparel. He'd been gone two months, expecting to find a new brother, but he returned alone. I watched him embrace Sara and Gemini.

I had started to forget Bay. The way the scars on his arms gleamed. I wanted to lie next to Bay in a moment when he was not searching, leading, working. I wanted to lie next to Bay in a moment when he was still.

So it happened that I ran to him as he walked to the beehives. I threw my arms around his neck. He kissed my sunburned forehead. "Half the family is looking," he said. "Wait till this evening." I snuck a glance at Dice. Couples weren't allowed, but Dice permitted the sharing of minds and bodies, Bay had told me at the bus stop on Tunnel Road. I did not sense how convenient it was for Dice, my tendency to believe I could find freedom in another person.

I watched Bay. He knew how to handle bees and did not wear protection.

"They'll sting you anyway, if they want to," he said. His flat smile cleaved me like an axe.

He tilted up the lid of the first hive and squeezed in the silky grayish smoke from his herb-stuffed bellows. The bees flattened and slowed their bunched, frenetic pattern.

"Sleep, little bees," he said. The smoke smelled like woody

spearmint. He removed a honeycomb in its rectangle frame and knocked the bees onto the ground, where they crawled over each other in a pile. Bay told me that bees will find their hive if you move it a mile, but never if you move it six inches.

The burning herbs made my throat catch. I felt deliciously swollen, waterlogged, like I might cry.

The afternoon was glaring gold, the mountains violet. Heavy happiness came down and trapped us in its wax. The family was radiant, graceful, slowly rising and stretching, cradling armfuls of wildflowers. The sky and ground glittered and refracted light. We stripped off our salty clothes and cooled ourselves in the creek.

When the sun began to set, the sky too clear to be beautiful, the strip of light just above the earth a cloudless green, I felt already spent from the mead, even though the party hadn't begun. On the banks of the creek, Dice made a fire by rubbing a dowel and a block, exhaling softly onto his glowing kindling. Beginners often blew too hard at that step. The kindling smoked, like it'd gone out, but Dice sat back with satisfaction, and then the kindling popped into flames.

Bay built the big fire, brushing past me, on purpose, I thought. I followed his every movement. We roasted sausages on sticks, grilled big fatty pork chops on a piece of slate with eggplants crowded around to suck up the drippings. We ate Cherokee hominy boiled with ashes, smother-fried squirrels, dandelions in vinegar, borscht, okra, Thelma Sanders squash, cake with fresh peaches. Everyone was laughing and the sparks from the bonfire spent ages wafting upward. We sang unusual songs: "In the Pines," "Conflict," "Amboy."

Queen and I drank with our arms around each other. Sara and others danced, clapping and stamping. In the darkness, my happiness took on larger, more mysterious forms. I felt buoyed up, like a paper lantern that rises only on the strength of the candle inside it. Queen hugged me and gave me a smacking kiss. But Bay beckoned me to follow him down to the edge of the forest. I broke away. I didn't know I wouldn't see Queen again for a long time.

How did he do it? I was standing, listening to the oceanlike sound of many turning leaves, and then I was on the ground. He knocked me over. His face rose over me, even darker than the blue ridges. He breathed down onto me, like I was a bee in a beehive. He smelled like alfalfa, sweet, chaffy.

I was drunk and my head reeled backward. I reached out to touch him. He shook my hand impatiently off his face. He put two rough fingers into my mouth. Isaac had never done anything like that. Bay was certain of everything, like he could read my mind, and there was no space for shame. He held my legs down.

So this is what it's like to be *smoked*, I thought. Or, more than that—this is what it's like to be watered. I was a plant, a weed, and he was the rainstorm. How terrible when the rain won't stop. When it begins to wash all the soil away. How helpless the weed and how terrible the rain, the big dark sky coming closer and closer until it shatters into drops. Why say stop? I lay like a thistle with its home dirt washed away, my roots out, nakeder than naked.

CHAPTER 17

I woke up with a headache. I could still taste the mead in my cheeks. I remembered the night before with a jolt of emotion; I couldn't tell whether it was happiness or shame. The sun boiled on my eyelids, and when I finally opened my eyes the fields looked as insubstantial as air. My family lay scattered around the beetle-black spent bonfire, spread-eagled or curled up on the cow-cropped slopes. All the months I'd lived on the farm, we had never slept late like this.

The short shadows under the trees indicated that it was almost noon. Still, the animals weren't braying—someone had milked them. I squinted, looking for Queen. I couldn't see her, or Bay. I rose unsteadily, a whoosh in my ears as though all the liquid in me had plummeted to my feet. I walked up to the long house.

Dice stood on the porch. White light bounced off the painted wood all around him, blinding me. "Harmony," he said. "We were just about to come find you."

I didn't worry I was in trouble because of what I had done with

Bay. *He's like Dice's hands,* Queen had said. Instead I feared that Lindsay had come back, or sent someone to rescue me. I feared Pear and Queen had produced the antibiotics and blamed me.

Dice said nothing more. He held open the screen door to the dining room.

Sitting around the table were Bay, Sara, and Maybell, the one with teeth that were chipped into points.

"Harmony," said Sara, "we've called you here because something terrible has happened."

From her tone, which was grief-torn, my mind leapt to even worse possibilities. Maybe someone had died. I was standing up unstably and I noticed the strange grip of gravity on me, like I was a pin up on its sharp end.

"Queen has left us," Sara continued.

"What do you mean?"

"In Pear's car." I wondered if she'd stolen it. Or if Pear had sent her away, as she'd sent me.

"On an errand?"

"No, she left," said Sara sharply. "You need to tell us about where she might have gone."

I couldn't tell what I felt—frustration, rage, those chaotic feelings that precede pain. A branch whammed against the windowpane, shaking off leaves with every thud. *Gone, gone, gone.* I thought that I might keel over. I hadn't known when Queen was planning to depart, or if she'd even really planned to go. All she'd said was, *Would you come with us, if we left?* I knew Queen had felt unsafe. I knew she'd wanted to leave.

Maybell spoke in a shrill voice like a killdeer. "We found a pill bottle down by the outhouse, near Pear's parking spot. That must have been Queen's. Can you tell us where she got it?"

"No," I lied, wishing I had some hair to hide behind.

Dice said, "Bullshit." He rose to his feet.

I flushed. I glanced at Bay again. I could feel the weight of him on me still, from the night before.

Sara's tone softened. "Harmony, we're just trying to figure out if you know where she was going."

I thought about how Queen told on Cassie. Cassie, now in the family's bone room, slowly decomposing, so her bones could be milled up into phosphorus for the garden. My head was thudding with the beat of the angry branch. "I loved Queen and I didn't want her to leave," I added, feeling more confident now that I knew what they wanted from me. "As for the pills—I don't know. Ask Pear."

Everyone in the room sighed. I hadn't realized they'd all been holding their breaths.

"We have," Sara said, "Pear told us you had nothing to do with any of this."

I smiled, almost accidentally.

Sara said, "According to Pear, this was between her and Queen."

"Right," I said.

"Pear said you might try to protect your friend, but you really had no idea what was going on."

"Right," I said again. The lie now felt truer than the truth. I became aware of the force of my fear as it started to fade.

"Remember this," Sara said. "Queen has chosen to leave. She

is no longer family. She is no longer your friend." She made me repeat this over and over again. If you say it, you think it, and if you think it, you'll believe it, but I only realized that later.

After lunch, I joined the family in our everyday chores. We had to clean the sheep's stables, clean the cows' and horses' stables, clean the chicken houses, feed and water the chickens, make the cheese and the butter, clean the dairy, move the electric fence, check the flock, and weed, weed, weed. No one mentioned Queen. Pear was nowhere to be found. But I was no longer frightened. They had questioned me, and they had let me go.

Bay doled out more tasks. He saved my assignment for last. "Feed the chickens," he said. He cuffed me on the neck. "Fatten them up."

I chopped up the Dumpstered Red Delicious apples, unpeeled brown bananas, and stabbed the chunks of fruit onto the nails along the walls of their coops, all the while thinking about Queen. All kinds of terrible things happened in the fake world, and she had gone out alone. I pictured the fake world as Snowball Earth, desolate, inhospitable, so very lonely.

Now that Queen was gone, I wondered about her dark, doubting heart. I imagined her life devoid of accountability, a life dedicated only to herself, back to the trains, stealing, not making. I pitied her. No one person mattered as much as the group. I knew that now as sure as I knew that cream can pick up any flavor—it could pick up the flavor of sweat, even. I felt that the prelude to my time as an Asher was over; now the real work could begin.

The lights were on in the long house. I was so tired I sagged. I wanted to eat basil-flavored cream for dinner.

When I entered the meeting room, the tables were not set for dinner. The full family, including those I'd barely spoken with, twenty-three people, sat in a ring. Two stools were placed in the center. Pear sat on one; the other was empty. A hiss went up all around.

"Harmony," said Sara. "Into the center, please." I sat, rigid with fear. Pear sat next to me, slumped and spineless.

Sara began gently, "This is not a punishment, but a gift. A rebirth of our trust for you."

So this was the rebirth. Queen had mentioned it the first morning we milked together. I desperately tried to remember what she'd said. *It's a ceremony,* she'd said. It hadn't sounded like a punishment.

"You were Queen's best friend," she said, and I understood the family was making an example of me. Queen was gone, and since there was no definite self, I'd reasoned that all of us were equally at fault. But that was not, as far as I could tell, the way the family was thinking of it. I tried to be open to the gift, as Sara had called it. But I was afraid.

Here was my punishment, finally, for all those conversations with Queen, and for the pregnancy, and for the pills, maybe, too.

Bay sat next to Osha, a girl I didn't know well. She had red apple cheeks and a broad nose and up-pointing hair and a mischievous look. When Bay leaned over to whisper in her ear, I felt white rage.

Sara sketched out what would follow—I was not to talk, only to listen. As for the rest of the family, they could say whatever they wanted to me or to Pear. Sara said, "After the rebirth you have to earn our trust again, like when you just arrived."

I said, "Do you mean"—I paused, surprised how hollow my voice sounded, like I couldn't get the air out—"that you don't trust me?"

Someone laughed. I turned, inspecting the family's faces, but they looked neither sympathetic nor cruel, but blank. They surrounded me like the frames of a kinetoscope, all nearly identical. I already had tears in my eyes. Sara extended her arm to the family, palm up. "All right," she said. "Go ahead."

"Pear," Bip said, "you never lend a hand. Many times I've been carrying a heavy basket or pail, and you just look at me and walk right by. Is it because you're too old?" The group murmured in agreement. I felt pleasure hearing Pear criticized, instead of me.

A long silence, during which I almost calmed down, and then Bip's voice again: "Harmony, you never left your past behind," he said. "Often I hear you talking about the past." I was open; Dice had opened me up, and I was horrified by Bip's words.

As I sat there, I imagined Queen standing on top of a silver-topped train crawling through the red Southwest.

Sara pulled the cord for the center bulb, and the light flickered on, off, on. Everyone's high-noon face: Bright forehead. Shadowed eyes. I imagined myself into another place: wandering through my childhood yard with a prism over my eyes. Its bifurcated effects, depending on how I rotated it: a mirror that showed the sky on one side, and on the other, a blurry rainbow.

"Why are you here, Harmony?" said Luxor. "Are you here—to enjoy yourself?"

Yes, I thought, and to have friends, to not have to face the world alone. To know my position with certainty, to live a wild essential life. To stand behind the curtain and see nature's hidden workings, the slow and confident engineering of the plants, the subjectivity of animals. Luxor's tone was contemptuous. "Are you here to volunteer like a tourist? To pass the time? To fall in love?"

Bay spoke next. "Harmony, you're too focused on your desires," he said. He was talking about last night, I was sure. Instead, he said: "I've seen you eyeing the chocolate chips. You should treat food more like medicine, less like something to crave."

Maybell said to me, "You segregated yourself off from the group, consorting only with the people you think of as your special friends."

"You cared too much about that owl." Who said this? Bip, who had never seen me with the owl. "You have to take your love and spread it around."

Osha said, "You only want to go with the sheep. You're too lazy to learn other jobs."

Dice hung back in the shadows. The family attacked me more than they attacked Pear. But she had broken more rules. She was the one who sent me for Queen's medicine. She was the one who told Queen that Cassie had the right idea.

Thirty minutes, or an hour, went by. I had lost track of time. Long-legged insects stumbled across the walls. Out in the fields, the crickets harped. Dice had said these crickets first showed up on Earth around the time the whiskery, warm, strange lizards began to be identifiable as mammals. My eyes were starting to close when Sara spoke again. "Harmony," she said, "though you've been here nearly a year, we don't feel we can trust you."

The energy in the room renewed. People began again, more broadly. "You haven't taken Dice's lessons to heart." I stared at my boots, which were clotted with manure. I noticed, as time went by in leaps and dollops, how shaky I was. With every breath, my chest seemed to expand to the ceiling and fall into the floor.

I glanced at Pear. She looked so old.

Eventually, silence settled over the room. I felt carried along by the torrential noises of the nighttime bugs. I remembered how Queen said that there were pears as big as footballs with skin so soft your fingers would sink into them, which was how I'd felt the day before with Bay when he washed over me like the river, which Sara once told me the Cherokees called the *long man*. I remembered when Bay stabbed the tree, how I shouted, then how he burned my hand and kissed me. I remembered the hurt made the softness all the lovelier.

Hours and hours seemed to have passed when Dice finally stood. He walked to the center, so near to us I could smell his piney soap. "It is so important to follow rules." His voice was calming. He sounded almost like he was singing. "We cannot help you if you don't follow rules. We cannot love you if you don't follow rules." The family watched him as he circled, their heads swiveling in unison. "Our troubles and our trials here will only make us stronger there." These were lyrics from "Sacred Harp."

I let myself fall into his voice. I let myself lose track of the world. I let myself forget that even Dice didn't always follow the rules.

I felt pure and peaceful as I listened. I was sliding down from the sky with lightning around me, and I could see it was no thicker than a pencil, though it seemed as wide as horses. Dice was stroking his lip with his thumb, and I knew exactly what he wanted me to do. He would not punish Pear himself. That was my job. That was what would please him. I felt all the hair on my head and neck strain up like the room was filled with static.

I turned to Pear. My hands shook—the fearless feeling. The buzzing in my head got so loud I felt fly-struck like the sheep.

I felt myself lunge at her. My body moved but my mind was calm, watching as she fell to the floor under me. Here was the floor, the oak's golden grain was around us like a current, the calendar of all the years it had lived, and my hand pushed into the softness under Pear's chin. I know I bit her because her neck was bleeding. Hands hauled me back into the room's dark periphery. I wiped my hand across my mouth and found the red.

The hands moving me away felt good, like they were stretching me out after the high jump when my body fell onto my head and knocked me out in a curious way, when I was awake and could not move, and I could hear but not feel the hands slapping my face, and an assortment of track fathers carried me off the blue mat. Isaac sat with me in the ambulance, slapping my face and saying, "Stay with me, Berie," which was hilarious. Then at the hospital I could not remember what month it was but I knew it was spring.

I rested in the shadows, abandoned now, and I clasped my shaking hands. I watched several people heave Pear up, and she leaned on them, limping away from the circle of light, holding her neck. I sat up against the wall; my breath came out of my mouth, choking.

Dice walked toward me. His face was so weathered I could not read it. I'd been so certain I'd done what he wanted. Maybe I'd done it the wrong way, too hard. I wondered if I'd really hurt her. I didn't want to get in trouble; I noticed, unable even to disapprove of myself, that I cared more about getting in trouble than whether I'd really hurt her.

Dice knelt beside me. He put his hand at the back of my skull and angled my face toward him. "You're a good girl," he said.

CHAPTER 18

That night, I lay in a bottom bunk, watching the mattress above me bow as someone turned. I could not remember biting Pear; I only remembered her throat, soft like risen cream. I'd done it, hadn't I.

Dice had said I was a good girl, and I told myself to believe him, to give myself that gift of certainty. But tonight, nothing felt certain. I remembered lying on a couch all day in Isaac's squat, the light of the glowing coils in the space heaters he had to use, because they couldn't ask the landlord to turn on the heat. I remembered my mother bringing home gifts from her knickknack store, the "Solar Queen" plastic figurine, which wore a pink plastic skirt suit, with a little hand always elegantly waving as long as the sun shone. But I couldn't remember feeling happy with Isaac, or happy with my mother, or interested, or excited. All the Durham memories were empty. I felt as though they had happened to someone else. Dice had said my hand would cast out the splinter if I let it. I wished my mind too could take these foreign objects and cast them out.

The next day started dim and remained that way, cloudy and dreadful to behold. I was going to take my love and spread it around, I was going to get to know everyone. At breakfast, I noticed the family seemed sparse. Pear didn't appear, and neither did Dice, Rainer, and Gemini, our guardian.

Bay sat next to me at breakfast. "Let me make you something good," he said. He spread cottage cheese and honey for me on Bip's bread, which was falling apart, because Bip hadn't had time to knead all twenty loaves fully—Pear wasn't around to help him.

"Where is everyone?" I said.

"The men went out to find Queen," Bay said.

I thought about Queen driving Pear's car down through the black woods after the harvest festival. I imagined the dogs following the car, following her sweet spicy breath that reminded me of chai. I missed her. But I didn't know whether I wanted her to come back.

"Did Pear go with them?" I asked Bay, as heavy crumbs plunked onto my plate.

"She went to the medicinal plant nursery on the family's behalf."

I set my tea down and looked at my hands. They didn't look like hands that could throw a person to the floor. I couldn't imagine how I had done it. Dice had been the lightning and I had been the rod. I knew what that meant now. I was the tool. I wasn't to blame.

I pastured the sheep, mucked out the stable, then helped Sara string up runner beans to dry. We'd revitalize them in winter stews.

We sat in the kitchen, baskets of beans all around us. She kept inhaling as though to say something, but nothing came of it.

If Queen had been there, we might have kneaded butter or watched the sunset from the warm boulder above the long house. We would have planned to ride the horses bareback to the waterfall, where I'd never been. She'd told me there was a place where you could stand right and see the rainbow all around you in every direction.

I kept trying with Sara. I desperately wanted to ask if the rebirth meant I couldn't participate in the upcoming action. But I was too nervous to ask and hear her say no. Instead, I said, "What do you like about the fall?"

"I like being near Dice," she said. And then a long pause.

"Well," I said, "at least it's nice to sit down to work."

"I wouldn't if I didn't have to," she said. She showed me the big gash she had on her thigh, the result of a kick from a nervous, mastitis-infected heifer. "A weeping wound," she called it. I got those words stuck in my head. *Weeping wound.*

"I wish Pear were here to fix that up for you," I said. Sara gave me a hard look and turned away.

After lunch, Sunny came toward me. "Harmony, come help me get dinner," he said. He had a bony, angled face, sharp cheeks, sharp chin. I thought he meant to town, and my heart began to beat. "Roadkill," he explained.

We took a green wheelbarrow and walked forty-five minutes down the gravel path to the chalk-blue road. The air nipped at my bare neck.

We continued a few miles down the road. A car passed every

ten minutes, headlights making the dark afternoon look even darker.

"There!" I said, pointing out some animal remnant squashed flat on the dotted yellow line. Sunny and I approached.

"Poor varmint," said Sunny. "A sorry sight." The animal had been gray, maybe a cat or a raccoon. It looked like we'd have to peel it off the asphalt with a spatula. "There'll be better ones."

The sun sank below the cloud cover, lighting up the whole sky a monstrous orange-brown. As we crested a hill, Sunny spotted a dead deer on the road's shoulder. He bent down low over the creature, showed me the fleas still hopping on her fur.

"We always look for fleas. Fleas are for the living. They won't stick around on a long-dead corpse."

Blood rimmed the deer's mouth, but still I was afraid that we would wake her as we hauled her into our barrow. We took turns pushing her back up the hill, back toward the woods.

"Sunny," I said, "do you think they'll find Queen?"

"Hope so."

I wanted her back, for selfish reasons. But I wasn't sure if I wanted them to find her. If she was alive, I wasn't sure what they would do to her. If she was dead . . . I didn't want Queen to die out there, because she was maladapted for that environment or because—but surely Dice didn't kill fugitives. If they never found her, at least I could imagine she'd found a life she liked. "I heard," I said, testing, "that people who leave often die out there."

Sunny gave me no sign. "The fake world is dangerous," he said.

"Sunny," I said, "what happened to Pear? I mean, after . . ." I didn't want to say *after I attacked her.*

"You know."

"Gathering herbs," I said, "I heard."

He was silent a long while. I worried I'd pushed too hard. I worried he wouldn't respond at all. I kept reminding myself to stop caring so much about outcomes. *Get relativity.*

"She died, Harmony."

I felt sweat prickle all my skin at once.

Sunny said, "She was bleeding in her head, we didn't realize." I imagined her in Dice's room after the rebirth, gasping. "It was an accident, Harmony." He stopped the wheelbarrow, took my shoulders, and turned me toward him. "Dice said it was an accident."

I hadn't intended to cry, but he spoke so softly that now I felt I had to. He reached out his arms to me. We embraced, and I was crying so hard I worried I wouldn't be able to stop myself. I was a weeping wound.

I'd meant to attack her, but I hadn't meant to kill her. She could have been saved at the hospital, but I tried to forget that. Maybe she had known all along what would happen, but I tried to forget that too.

Gently, so gently I barely noticed, like when your arms wrap around you before you even notice that you're cold, another thought came to my mind. I wondered if I'd been trapped. I imagined darting back to the road, leaping in front of a car, pinwheeling my arms, begging for a ride—but I couldn't go. I'd killed someone in front of twenty-three witnesses. If I stayed with the family, then Pear's death would always be an accident. Dice called it an accident, and so it would be true. I laughed once—"Ha!" Sunny turned to me as though he knew exactly why.

fall

CHAPTER 19

The cold blew in that night. We gathered on the porch in the crystalline early-fall morning. The little pool of water where the kitchen sink drained was so blue it looked like paint. Bay's car was gone now, too—Bay's car was gone, Pear's car was gone, Dice's truck was gone.

Sara and Sunny described the tasks for the day. "Haying time," Sara said. "Who wants to come?" No one volunteered at first, so I raised my hand, thinking of my rebirth. The family members nodded congenially at me, though just two days ago they'd torn me apart.

I raked while Sunny drove the mower that cut down the spindly stalks of alfalfa, timothy, and orchard grass, which grew all over the slopes. We let the hay dry in the fields, then the next day we raked it into long snaking piles, windrows. We pitchforked the windrows up onto the horse-drawn wagon. The horses brought the wagon up to the highest part of the barn, up the ramp that couldn't support a tractor, and then we forked the hay down to the loft in loose piles.

The raking—that was the hell, hot, strenuous, and dusty, endless. I couldn't, hard as I tried, become a mountain lion or a sheep and focus only on my purpose. Most modern farms had a mechanical swather to do the job, and a tedder to turn the hay for drying, but we couldn't afford those luxuries. Pear was dead, and Queen was gone, and *no thank you, I have already been saved.*

I wished I could wheel time backward, before the rebirth, before the miscarriage, Rainer and Queen falling away from each other, Queen stepping down the ladder, ungritting her teeth. Before Rainer and Lindsay came, back to the winter, when all I worried about was when Bay would touch me again.

I thought I could see the family clearly now, see the good and bad. The bad was that Pear had died, though there was no definite self, I knew. And the good was everything else. The good was nighttime breath in the long house like frothing waves, the nicotiana, pawpaws, and cardoons, the moths fluffing themselves dry of dishwater, the fugueing tunes and fire on cold nights, the slamming rain and Earth history and huge plates of ice we found in the winter with silvery leaf impressions frozen into them. The good was the mountain lion with leaf-green eyes shouldering through the woods, even though they were supposed to be extinct. The good was the little owl who'd hurtled out the window.

And besides, down in the deep, I knew that I was trapped. Trapped good and proper. If death was the worst outcome, well, that was true for everyone on Earth; weren't we all trapped? *Get relativity.* We raked the hay. We forked the piles into the wagon. We drove the hay up the highest ramp of the barn, forked it down.

The barn's top levels filled to the rafters with hay, which smelled like a lover's hair—Bay's in particular. When the wind blew in, the chaff rose in a flickering mass. We worked until we could hardly stand. I wondered if my exhaustion would satisfy the family.

After two weeks—we were into September now; someone had switched the plaque in the holder—Dice and Rainer and Gemini returned, early in the morning. The dogs preceded them, beastly white.

Gemini drove Pear's maroon car, the car Queen had taken. The sight of it set my head ringing.

Dice and Rainer exited the truck. They beckoned for help unloading their boxes of Dumpstered produce, and I grabbed a basket and followed Sara toward them to pick out fruit for the chickens. If they asked me why, I would say I was trying to volunteer more for tasks. But I was just desperate to hear news of Queen.

Dice put his hand on Sara's neck and pulled her against him, then released.

"Where is she?" Sara asked.

He shook his head. "We followed her to Marshall, then found just the car."

Queen was fine. She was safe. I reminded myself that this was the best outcome—Queen alive and elsewhere, no longer available to tempt me into disloyalty. But I missed her.

That night, we circled the chairs for a story. Dice said that the permafrost in Siberia was melting and around graveyards the thawing corpses were infecting people with anthrax and smallpox. And once the permafrost melted all the way, whoosh, up into the air all that carbon would go, carbon equal in quantity to another industrial revolution. People kept finding animals in the permafrost, mastodons and steppe bison and cave lion cubs, ancient horses, rhinos, mammoths, their meat fresh enough to eat, their blood still liquid in their veins.

Something terrible was lurching out there in the dark, blundering its way closer. Dread, that was the feeling of haying time. Dice said, "Siberia will melt. The rain forests will burn down. The oceans will stop mixing. And the wars will start."

The next afternoon, Dice caught up with us in the hayfields. One by one we stopped raking. Everyone smiled closed-lipped smiles. He told us to gather what was dry, then beckoned to me. I stepped forward, immediately nervous.

"Go find the sheep, Harmony."

I dropped my rake. Here was a chance to prove myself.

"Rainer couldn't find them," he warned. He picked up my rake and began tightening the windrow. He knew exactly how to roll and lift the hay for the pitchfork. He made everything look easy.

"I'll manage," I said.

He nodded, and I headed off to the distant pastures. I'd been walking only a few minutes, scrambling over gulches to the sheep's little coves, when I noticed the thunderhead, dark brown and sharp at the edges, mounting in the west. I hoped the others would save all the hay we'd cut. A wind thrashed the branches. I saw the lightning like spider legs stalking over the ridge.

The clouds smeared into the ground as though by a giant's thumb, and I'd just begun to wonder about the rain when it filled my eyes and ears and trickled down my back, filling my pants, filling my shoes. The air was bright and crackling, all the dark branches were lashing sideways, and the hill was smoothed by a cape of water, which made a *woooo* noise like a ghost. I stumbled blindly upward. I felt as though the rain were stripping away my definite self, layer by layer, till I was just a thread of heat.

Buckled over, I sought the ridge. I saw at once the long thin arm of lightning point down and touch a pine on the ridge, as if to say, HERE! The pine exploded, blasting off its robe of bark, and the raindrops squiggled through the air like sparks.

The cloudburst strode onward. The rain turned to a bright purple mist, which soon subsided into steam. The sun rendered the water out of the land like fat from meat. Little streams crisscrossed the hills. I approached the tree, stepping over peels of bark. The tree would die in a day or two. I shook in my sodden clothes.

I doubted I could find the sheep now. I leaned over with my hands on my knees and gathered my nerves. My body was rubbery. I kept walking. I walked for an hour through the mud. *Why are you here, Harmony?* someone had asked during my rebirth. *Are you here—to enjoy yourself? . . . To pass the time? To fall in love?* I walked until I slipped on the hillside and fell hard, gashing my tongue on my teeth. My eyes stung. But I could tell that very deep down I liked it, the same way I loved jumping and falling, and Bay's burn on my hand. I didn't have to wonder if I could feel more. I felt everything.

When I approached the courtyard, I heard the sheep bells. Had they returned home in the storm? I entered the stable and they ran toward me. Their wool was dry. I spat hot blood from my mouth.

Had Rainer found them? Had Dice tricked me? I rushed to the long house to find out. On the porch, Dice and Sara sat on rockers. They were laughing, and they seemed to be laughing at me, and for the first time I noticed that all of Sara's molars were black holes.

CHAPTER 20

In late September, the first frosts laced our tired-out garden. I'd been with the family a year. At a breakfast, I heard Rainer ask Maybell about the action next month, something to do with the coal company clearing off all the mountaintops. My heart began to beat. I wanted so badly to be involved. "Bay will bring us a new brother first, to help out while we're gone," she said.

"Let me come," Rainer said. I was sure she'd say no. He was newer than I was.

"It will be smaller than the last one," she said. She smiled and touched his ear. "We'll ask Dice." They saw me staring and turned away.

Bay was due back soon. I had hoped that by now—a year in— I'd be trusted with showing a newcomer around, but I knew that after the rebirth I had to start from zero again. This time, Osha was in charge. She had a broad, ruddy Scandinavian face, flyaway hair, and energy for even the most onerous tasks. She was like Sara, invulnerable.

Bay's car returned in late morning. I was on the porch, fixing a hole in the knee of my canvas pants, sewing with the same viney thread that Sara and I had used to string up the beans a month ago. Osha rushed out to greet the newcomer. I heard her say, "Right on time." I kept my eyes on my sewing at first, because I wanted to seem busy.

"Here's Harmony," Osha said, "my wonderful sister."

When I looked up, my stomach dropped. It was Isaac, my ex-boyfriend. Isaac, with his hammerhead eyes. I could scarcely believe it until I saw the claw tattoo on his temple.

Lindsay, I thought. Lindsay told. Then: He's come to take me away. I wondered if he'd spoken with my mother—if she'd be coming too. I wondered what he'd do if I refused. If he'd try to get the police involved, calling it a kidnapping. Or if he'd try to number us—report us, get us for tax evasion, destroy the whole community. If investigators came they might look for Pear and link her death to me. I was a terrible liar—if they put me under oath, I did not know what I would say.

"Nice to meet you," he said. What a good idea—we'd pretend we were strangers. He stuck out his hand, and I grasped it. I knew he was feeling my calluses as I felt his silky cold palm.

I said, "Welcome." I avoided looking at his face. I looked down at his Velcro-closure tennis shoes. I looked up as Bay unfolded himself from the car and walked toward us. Bay was so rough looking, I'd forgotten; his skin was dented like a rained-on pond. I waved. He did not wave back. I could not look at Isaac.

"Nice to have you back, Bay!" I said. He raised his eyebrows and I felt silly. "Well, Osha," Bay said, ignoring me, "why don't you give our guest a tour?"

"I'll come along," I said.

"You'll stay here with your sewing," Osha said. I still could not look at Isaac. "You can show him the barn later, how about that?"

They mounted the creaky porch. Now I let myself stare, and I was carried backward, closer to everything I'd tried to forget, past Taqueria La Vaquita, its picnic tables; down Chapel Hill Road, which was once a cow path; to Wa Wa Avenue, to the bungalow's porch with its demented array of old bike parts, the swing, the cat-torn corduroy couch, where Isaac and I used to sit mostly naked in the lightning-bug evenings. There was the riotous gardenia bush, a nest of light and shadow. And behind I could almost see the train tracks slicing through the woods. And if I could see the tracks, I could see a freight train, and maybe Queen blowing by in a hammock in a boxcar. There was the life Berie would have been living, if she hadn't come here and disappeared. A sob that seemed to have started a year ago began to rise up.

Isaac carried nothing but a plastic bag. I recognized its logo, a gridded arrangement of red concentric circles—Target, the store was called; I hadn't thought about it in so long. We used to buy homewares at Target, rainbow measuring cups in collapsible silicone, baking pans with lids for the fridge, a brush for slicking egg wash onto loaves of bread. The brush fit into the category of unwashable kitchen tools, like a waffle iron, like a cast-iron pan, where you have to give up on your trust of soap. Like the clothes that say "spot-clean only." How can you trust a thing that you can't put in a washing machine? I used to wonder.

I could have left the clothes I wore now at the bottom of a river for days, and they'd have come out and still been all right.

These phenomenally hard-wearing clothes that did not belong to me.

After the interminable morning and a lunch of beet thinnings and peppers, Osha permitted me to accompany Isaac to the barn. When we were out of eyeshot, I almost relaxed.

"Berie," he said. It had been a year since anyone had called me that, and the name diminished me—the college-bound disappointment to her mother, the girl who lived a compromised life on the grid.

He smiled, with teeth. My Durham life was roaring back at me. I felt queasy, like when you stand at Kitty Hawk long enough that you, not the ocean, seem to be gliding forward and back. I didn't want to slip back into my old self, the self that lived in half measures.

Because it seemed like the most normal thing to do, but not because I wanted to, I gave him a tight hug. Both of us had more meat on our bones than we had had in Durham. I was stronger. And he was more filled-in, grown-up. I allowed him to kiss my cheek.

"Short hair!" he said.

"They made me cut it," I said, taking his hand and rubbing it over my buzz cut. "I wanted to cut it," I added.

"I like it," he said. He smelled like pine soap. Like Dice. The strangest thing, I realized, was seeing his face move, how the smile made his upturned nose a little wider, how his cheeks rumpled and then flattened, how his eyebrows jumped while he talked, as though from exertion. I'd forgotten these things. "What are they calling you? Harmony?" he laughed. All these months, even without a photograph, I'd been imagining his face in one position, static and serious. His front tooth was chipped; had it always been?

"Come on, Zacky," I said, trying to remember how we used to talk. I wanted to say, *They named me as they saw me. I'm different from the uncertain girl you knew in Durham.* But I was tongue-tied, and nervous that Osha might be watching, or Sara, or Bay, or worst of all, Dice.

"Zacky?" he said. "That's a new one."

I pulled down the ladder to the hayloft, now piled to the rafters, three stories' high, with fragrant hay. Isaac exclaimed and threw himself onto the foot of a hay pile. "Ow!" he said, leaping up. I'd once found hay prickly too.

"How did you get here?" I asked. I kept as quiet as I could.

"Easy enough," Isaac said. "Lindsay told me you were with a group called the Ash Family. She said, 'They took my boyfriend.'"

"It didn't happen that way at all. See, Roger—well, now we call him Rainer—"

"Lindsay is clueless," he said. "I get why Roger would leave her." He picked hay off his pristine hoodie. "She opened my darkroom door." But I didn't want to imagine her coming to his darkroom at all.

He said once he was in Asheville, he asked around for someone named Bay. He'd stayed at a squat till Bay came around.

"That's a lot of trouble to come out here," I said.

"Not so bad," he said. He was playing it off lightly. "I thought," he said, "I thought it'd be good for my photography, to see the mountains. I had some free time."

He was lying. I pictured myself hunkering down, rooting into the Asher soil. He wouldn't pull me out—not now, when I was just beginning to grow. I couldn't let Isaac shrink me back down to Durham's scale and contain me in his little room among gardenia flowers that creased and browned immediately after getting plucked.

"Did you bring your camera?"

He took a plastic disposable out of his Target bag and wound the clicking wheel.

"Put that away," I said. "Keep it in your bag."

"Can't I take a photo of you?"

"We don't like tourists," I said.

He gave me a long look, head to feet. I felt itchy, embarrassed. I thought about the spot on my face from the sun, and how broad I was, how calloused my hands, the bruises and cuts and burns all over from my many interactions with sheep and pine needles and large pans of frying greens, gates and fences, brambles. Isaac frowned—did he pity me?—and all my hard-won self-sufficiency seemed to drain away. "There are a few other reasons that I came," he said.

I shrugged. "And I take it you didn't tell Bay you knew me?" I said.

"Lindsay told me not to." He put his face in my shoulder. I shuddered; I couldn't stop thinking of danger, danger. "I like Bay," Isaac said. "He gets me."

I remembered sitting with Bay at the bus stop. Bay got everyone, I thought. "He's amazing," I said. "But wait till you meet Dice."

He said, "After Lindsay told me about you, I went to see your mom."

"You went to my house?" A year into our dating, Isaac first met my mother. He already didn't like her. He thought she was a fool for loving novelties. At the time I enjoyed all his criticisms of her frivolity. But then, when they met, he surprised me by putting in effort. Isaac brought Bo-Berry biscuits and they sat in the kitchen, laughing till they cried.

He was with me when we found the broken-down shotgun in her drawer. Isaac seemed even nicer to her after that.

Isaac was so likeable. My mother wouldn't like Bay, I reminded myself. She wouldn't like Dice.

Isaac said, "I went to the knickknack store."

"And what did you tell her?"

"I said you were living in a community in the mountains."

My tongue felt dry. "And what did she think?"

"She wasn't happy, Berie. What did you expect?"

The blood buzzed in my head. "I don't know," I said. "Sometimes you just have to go." I thought, If he takes me, I'll run. I'll hitchhike back here.

"She knows that more than anyone," he said. This surprised me. But here was how the years would roll on: I wouldn't come home, and my mother would start to think that this had been my plan all along, this never-returning. All kinds of people had gently estranged relatives. She lived in the fake world, selling things no one needed, horse string lights, light-up globes, solar-powered light-up houses, ceiling-galaxy projectors, the three-inch levitating globe. Every morning when she got to work she'd flip fifty switches till the whole store glowed around her. Then she'd stand behind the counter, oversized in a cap-sleeve dress, like a figurine in a Christmas diorama. That was happiness, to her. She was part of the system that was killing off all the wilderness in the world. That was her life. It wouldn't be mine.

Isaac said, "She told me to come find you. She'd been looking for you. She needed to get a message to you. But we couldn't figure out your address. She called your college and they said they'd never heard of you."

I flushed. "I thought it was your decision to come see me."

"Listen," Isaac said. "I know that you don't want a scolding, no matter how much you deserve one." I liked him better when he was mean like this, because it was easier to remember why I'd left him.

"I'm my own person," I said, in what I hoped was an even, rational tone. "I can decide my own life."

He put his hands up. "She wanted me to give you this." He took out from his kangaroo pocket a pink piglet flashlight, with two ultrabright blue LEDs in its snout. It made a little snorting noise when its lights turned on. "Might come in handy," he said. The pig stood obediently in my palm. "Do you think we can talk more tonight?" he said.

"Maybe," I said.

"I really missed you," Isaac said. He smelled so strongly of a time before this one that it knocked the breath out of me.

"You didn't," I said. I thought back to our conversations, that insult, *stagnating*.

He said, "I'm lost without you."

I laughed. It was easy to remember our compatibility. We'd liked to tease each other.

I told him what Sara had told me: this was state-of-the-art in the 1890s, the largest barn of its era in the Appalachians, and so rare—most of the old farming structures around were the windy, tilting ones for tobacco leaves, nigh impossible to convert for animals. I showed him the mattress for newcomers.

He set down his things, then lay on the mattress. He wore a Sherpa-lined denim hoodie, athletic shorts, and those Velcro shoes. He sat up and carefully plucked the bits of hay off his hoodie. Of course, he didn't care for nature the way I did. I'd separated the bucks in the forest and wept into the mauve leaves, and he only wished he'd been there to take a photo.

"Come here," he said.

I went. I always liked to be told what to do, though Dice knew how to make use of that much better than Isaac did. I sat down next to him on the mattress. I didn't have much hair but he managed to tuck what hair I had behind my ear. I put my head on his shoulder. I didn't feel like a girl who knew how to slaughter lambs, and I certainly didn't feel like a girl who had seen her friend's dead baby, a girl who had slammed an old woman to the floor and killed her.

"My girl," he said.

"No," I said. "Here we don't have possessions." I felt him breathing. "I don't know if you heard," I said, "but you can stay three days or the rest of your life."

We sat there for a long time. The hayloft was as full as it would ever be. I remembered the snow blowing in the long house while we sang last winter. How frightening nature was, in the end. How the melt uncovers what you buried. How the stream finds the bones and carries them out to the light.

CHAPTER 21

The light changed to afternoon's gold, and we came to our senses—better not to linger. I told Isaac to leave his camera in the hayloft, but I brought the piglet flashlight with me. "I think Osha should be the one showing you around," I said. We looked for her in the stables and the storage house. Isaac quickly tired of the search. "What's the matter?" he said. "Aren't you allowed to do what you want?" He tilted his head at me, taunting. He knew there were rules. What he didn't know, as I did now, were the consequences.

Instead, I said: "Of course I can." So we made ourselves liver-mush sandwiches. We turned the cheeses in the cellar, and then we peeled carrots and snapped beans in the kitchen. Osha came in with a basket of mushrooms and didn't try to separate us. She sent us to find the sheep. As I strode through the meadows, the sun combed by the dying grass, I turned back and saw him with his camera up to his face.

"You have to hide that camera," I said.

"Just pretend you didn't see it," he said. He stooped and photographed me through the grass. I tried to be mad, but I loved being Isaac's model, being seen by him. I felt something unfamiliar and I knew it was the simple form of happiness. Unlike with Dice and Bay, I knew just the right way to please him. We walked on through the evening, which was crazed with saturated light. *Love! Love! Love!* I couldn't let Isaac take me away from all this. And especially now, as I was trying to gain back their trust. But I also cared what Isaac thought of me, of us, of Dice. I was not in the habit of splitting myself in two. I'd devoted all my time to *oneness.*

So I tried to show Isaac what I loved about the place. I told Isaac about sheep. I told him how one of the sheep got killed by a copperhead, and the others missed her. I thought of Queen and Pear. "They know grief," I said. Isaac nodded politely at the story, like a foreigner who doesn't understand the language. We came up over the ridge and found the flock basking in the sun.

Isaac spoke to them like you'd speak to drunk friends. "Come on now, guys. Heads up." He wasn't particularly fond of animals. This made me feel stronger than him. I'd pulled out eighty lambs. I'd thrown maggots out of sheep's feet with pungent oil, I'd clipped their wool and bandaged their cuts with cobwebs. I was proud of who I was on the farm. I wanted Isaac to understand how this, too, was happiness.

"You two seem to have hit it off quite nicely," Osha said as we set the table for dinner. I squinted at her, unsure if she'd guessed our secret. "Oh yeah, well," I said. "Durham—we know some of the same people." I felt like I'd already revealed too much. I wondered what punishment I'd face if Dice learned that Isaac was a fake-world friend of mine. But as long as I let Dice blaze through me like a current, I told myself, as long as I let him direct me, I'd be all right, I'd protect myself by doing exactly what he wanted.

Osha set down the gray crockery. "Do you think he'll stay on?" I followed with the forks and spoons. They were prison-issue, the kind you can bend in half. "He seems like he's here for a laugh," she said.

I was defensive. "In what way?"

"Some people come looking for a family. Some come just to imagine what it'd be like if they were different. You know, mooning around."

"Isaac is a very serious person. He's very antiauthoritarian," I said. "So, you know—" And I stopped short. Dice was an authority. So was hating authority a good or bad trait in an Asher? I shook my head to clear it.

"Yes," said Osha gently. "Rebels often do well here."

We continued around the table in silence. I asked, "Should I try to convince him to stay?"

"You should be as kind and welcoming as you always are."

For dinner we ate green tomatoes and pestilent cabbages, lye hominy soaked in yesterday's ashes, and pawpaws for dessert. We formed our chairs into the hollow square for the shape-note singing.

We sang 162, "Plenary," which was the same tune as "Auld Lang Syne" but made strange with wide-open harmonies.

Hark! From the tombs a doleful sound
Mine ears attend the cry

Ye living men come view the ground
Where you must shortly lie.

Rainer led, rubbing his eyes and holding his forehead, awkward. I didn't feel envious of him anymore—imagining the family
as we appeared to Isaac, I was proud of him, proud of everyone,
in love with our communion. Isaac and I sat side by side, and the
family sang loud enough to knock our hair back, loud enough to
startle birds from the trees.

I imagined Isaac staying. Trading in his clothes for ours. Getting his sheep-shear haircut. Learning how to make leather or
drive the tractor or melt down old bullets and re-form them. But
Isaac had never been particularly interested in animals or nature
or climate change. He liked art-making, he wanted to travel and
see the world. He liked his definite self, his point of view: that was
why we'd broken up. I knew he would not stay. The fake world was
built for people like him, not people like me.

The next day, Isaac arrived at breakfast looking exhausted. "I kept
dreaming about vultures," he said.

I let Osha and others entertain him with stories about pan-
thers and swarming bees. He leaned his head on his hand and
winced at his bitter tea. I felt sorry for him. In Durham, he'd appeared to be a radical. Strange to realize I'd surpassed him there.

Sara told Isaac and me to go scoop out the four-person
outhouse down below the long house, down where Pear used to
park her car. I found Isaac some work boots to replace his shoes,

and he complained that they were too stiff. The outhouse was a rickety shack with six wooden steps leading up to the four stalls. An old flag, originally the North Carolina one, flapped over the front entrance; a breeze blew it northward all day and night. The pit below was deep but still needed emptying once a year. Someone had to wheel its contents down to the humanure pile, leave it to the microorganisms for another year, then spread it through the garden, to make the tomatoes glow.

We pinned mint in our hair to repel gnats. We needed some muscle to open up the ground-level door. The smell made us both retch. We stabbed our heavy shovels into the mass, slopped it into our manure barrow. But after a minute we noticed something strange: below the top layer, which still looked and smelled like human waste, the mound was crumbly and black like flowerpot soil. I never realized how quickly waste decomposes. In the fake world, we either whisked it through the plumbing or stepped around it on the street, but if we just left it a week, waste would return to the earth. The cleaner things seem, the dirtier they are. The dirtier things seem, the cleaner they are. "It's not bad," Isaac said. He was learning the Ash Family's lessons, the red-lens-blue-lens, the tiny globe caught between magnets.

We spent two hours on the task, making hardly any progress, and Isaac's hands blistered, and our boots caked over. Isaac wanted to return to the house for a shower, but I told him we should shower later. I didn't want him to confront our one-shower-a-week policy.

"Well, let's at least do something else," Isaac said stiffly. He suggested a walk.

"Let's check with Osha," I said.

"Come on, they'll never miss us," Isaac said.

I looked up at him. He leaned on his shovel. He looked weary and smiled hopefully. I liked being the one to decide whether to be severe or take pity.

"Okay," I said. "Remember, three days. You have to leave tomorrow."

He nodded. "Bay told me too. I didn't know it was a serious thing."

"Oh, it's serious," I said.

He looked like he was about to speak, but he said nothing. He struggled to take off the boots, trying to avoid dirtying his hands or his socks. He looked relieved to reattach his Velcro shoes. I didn't bother to tell him they weren't suitable footwear for a hike.

We set out uphill over the cropped fields. Speedy clouds covered and uncovered the sun.

"So," he said as the farm fell away behind us. "What's up with Dice?"

I didn't like his tone. "What do you mean?"

"How'd he end up here?" Isaac drew out his camera again and wound the clicking wheel. He pointed it down into the holler and snapped. "He told me he'd been stabbed six times and shot twice." We walked into the densely scrubby woods over the ridge.

I'd never heard Dice say that. I had no way to tell if this was true. "He's been through a lot. He used to work at a coal-fired power plant, so he started this—community"—I didn't want to say *family*; I imagined Isaac's raised eyebrows—"to redeem himself."

We emerged from the blindingly tangled woods onto a large,

parklike bald. Its grasses trembled. I showed Isaac the spot where I'd one night seen a group of mushrooms glowing green with fox fire. "Dice used to cut the tops off of mountains," I said.

Isaac changed the subject, which mystified me. I'd been ready to tell him about Snowball Earth and the first protest, the pipe arms, the bucket baths. Instead, he asked why I didn't go to Richmond, as I'd planned. He was trying to corner me, I felt. He said, "Tell me how you got here. Where'd you meet Bay?"

"I was at the airport," I said, "and I just couldn't get on the plane."

"But won't you get bored here? You can't even read books, right?" We walked over mossy rotting logs and rocks with coppery lichen lace. Isaac's Velcro shoes were dirty now.

"We can. We just choose not to."

"Will you have a family here?"

"This *is* my family."

"I mean, will you have children here? You used to want them."

But he'd always been the one who wanted kids. I made an effort to smile at him. He was attempting to dominate me even out here in the sacred backwoods. We reentered the forest at the edge of the bald. The weather was different in the woods—cold and damp. As we pushed past the rhododendrons, they shook water onto us. Rhododendrons had crept down south during the last glacial maximum. But this wasn't their favorite territory. As the planet warmed, they were shuffling north again.

"Sure," I said, "I mean, maybe. I haven't decided." I could hear the creek. I remembered Queen splashing out of it, holding the dead heron in her arms.

"You're allowed to decide?" His lips were chapped and white. He was cold. I could have handed him my sweater the way Sara had handed me hers. "Osha told me no one here ever has kids. It's part of the culture of the place, she said."

"Well . . . ," I said. Isaac was testing me. "Well, that's because we're trying to restore the world, not just maintain it—we don't want to add to the population."

"It seems like there are a lot of rules."

"Rules from the people who live here," I said, quoting Dice. I heard a crunching deep in the hemlock-dark woods. "Wait— shhhh," I said, and grabbed Isaac's hand, which was freezing. I was crouching. I squinted, peering into the tangled shadows. What was I so worried about? We'd been on-message—I rifled back through our conversation. Had Isaac implied that we'd known each other in Durham?

Isaac interrupted my panic by laughing. He pulled his hand away. "Look at that beautiful dog!" he said. One of the huge white dogs was trotting toward us, its loose mouth seeming to smile. "I have never seen a dog like that."

"They kill wolves."

"Do they?" he said, scratching the dog's ears.

I said, "Didn't you see all the warning signs for dogs when you were coming up?"

The dog sat back and looked at me. Its eyes held none of the herbivore calm of the sheep's. I felt as though the dog's eyes connected directly to Dice's. My heart sped up.

A moment later, Dice came up in the woods behind. He moved very quietly.

"Good thing Belu came by, right?" he said, putting his wiry arm around Isaac. "Twenty years ago when I used to be a tracker for the national parks, I found a boy who died just a few feet off the trail," Dice said. "He was lost for just an hour, probably, when he got hypothermia. It was a rainy day, not any colder than today." Dice lifted up Isaac's pastel-blue hand and shook it up and down as though to warm it. Isaac's wrist went limp, and his whole posture changed; he leaned over, looking up at Dice.

Dice said, "Confusion sets in fast, and then your skin feels too hot, and you rip off your own clothes." He kept his eyes on Isaac's face. They were the same height, but Dice had all the energy. Dice said, "Lucky I found him. The longer someone's lost, the longer they stay lost. Every year an inch of dirt settles on them. Twelve years, a foot of dirt. But often enough the bears eat the remains, and all you can find are boot grommets." Dice dropped Isaac's hand. Isaac straightened. "You hear me?" Dice said. "If you want bones to fertilize your garden, you have to keep them."

Isaac stared at him. His mouth was slightly open. He pressed his hands against his cheeks.

Dice said, "You may be wondering how we found him. The rain washed the scent away. You have to follow the pattern of broken branches. Follow the white breaks. That's how I found you. I can tell you're a lefty."

Isaac rubbed his forehead. "I would love to learn that," he said, finally.

"Stay on," Dice said. "I can sense the connection you've formed with Harmony. Though she's doing Osha's job," he said, smiling at me in a way that made me feel panicked.

"Actually, I was wondering," Isaac said. "I'd like to stay a few extra days, if that's okay. Maybe a week? This three-day thing isn't really long enough for me to get a good sense." Isaac gave me a quick smile.

But I wanted to grab him and clap my hand against his mouth. *You can't disrespect Dice*, I wanted to hiss. Dice waited a long time before responding, and in the silence, my head whirred.

Finally, Dice said, "You know our convention."

Isaac said, "Three days, or the rest of your life."

"We have to abide by that," Dice said. "I'm sure you understand."

Isaac said, "I thought that here, since it's a free place, away from society, people could be *free* to arrive or depart how they wanted to." He was making things worse for himself.

Dice allowed another long, confidence-sapping pause. "Freedom," he said. He gestured for us to follow him uphill. We came out onto the bald. The weather had changed again. Clouds brushed the treetops. A group of birds shot up like fireworks before they explode. Dice sat on a log and pulled Isaac in next to him.

"Bay told me you used to go to protests. And now you're a college student?" Isaac nodded helplessly.

"But as I see it," Dice said, "the man in the plane about to drop the atomic bomb has two ways to protest." Dice took Isaac's hand and palpated it. "He can either refuse to drop the bomb, in which case the officer can move him out of the way and seat a new bombardier who is willing"—Isaac's large guppy eyes were focused on Dice—"or, he can sabotage."

"Yes," Isaac said.

"He can drop the bomb over the sea, over the forest."

"Sabotage."

"Exactly," Dice said. "See if you can't stretch your mind a little. What is freedom, do you think? Is it moving aside or making something new? Don't you see why we have to be so careful with our processes, our structures? You can stay three days, or the rest of your life."

I wanted Dice to stop touching Isaac.

"In just a few days," Dice said, "we're going out to an action. We need trustworthy people to stay at the farm. So you will decide tomorrow." He set down Isaac's hand. I remembered how Dice had treated Rainer so cruelly in the forest. For all of us he had a different way. My first night, Dice had let me tell stories and cry, all alone in the garden.

Dice glanced over at me. "Anything to add, Harmony?"

"Am I coming on the action?" I said.

"No," he said. "Remember, the people who stay behind are just as important." My face warmed. This kindness from him was everything to me. I'd try asking again later.

I was about to say *get relativity* when Dice noticed something. "On your face," Dice said to Isaac. "Turn your head." Dice pushed back the hair at Isaac's temple. "A talon," he said. "How funny. Harmony has two just like that, on her back."

I wondered when it was that Dice had seen me naked.

"I noticed that too," I said. "So funny." I felt queasy with fear.

Dice whistled, and all three dogs came crashing out of the forest.

"Why don't you two talk about your talons," he said, standing. "And what odd luck that is." He looked us both up and down. "Come back soon, boy," he said. "Osha needs you."

He headed into the forest. The three dogs examined us, then turned to follow. I waited until I couldn't hear their feet on the leaves.

"Come on," I said, standing over Isaac. I took his hands, warmer now, and heaved him up.

"What would you do," he said, "if I wanted to stay?" He began to walk so slowly my legs ached to keep pace.

"You can't stay," I said. "Dice knows we know each other now. The claws."

"Why does that matter?"

I didn't answer. To calm myself I pressed my hands together the way Dice had pressed on Isaac's.

We hiked downhill and spotted the flock of sheep on a knob, idling in the grass. A little farther, and the holler came into view, folding serenely around the barn, the long house, and the storage house, the hickory, the kitchen garden. In all the hazy peaks beyond our house, we couldn't see another dwelling. But I knew that the housing developments were marching over the hills. Isaac said, "Don't you miss civilization?"

"We're civilized," I said.

"I mean, don't you miss grocery stores, choices, that kind of thing?"

"No." I felt danger in Isaac's question, his searching, searching, searching.

But I did miss some things about civilization. I missed the kind of girl who'd tie a black grosgrain ribbon around her ponytail. I missed video tutorials for fishtail braids, milkmaid braids, Heidi braids, and braids stuffed with daisies. I missed the store at the mall that made cookie cakes, Mrs. Fields, the smell of stiff teal frosting, the different smell of gel-like frosting.

I missed seeing a police officer with a forearm tattoo that said, *Dying to be loved*. I missed under-cabinet lighting, putting damp towels on the hot car seat after the pool and drying in ten seconds, double-chocolate Milanos, the TV reporters getting blown sideways like the first airplanes while covering hurricanes at Kitty Hawk, gummy hard-to-wash deodorant in my armpits, tiny leg hairs in the bathtub, wigs pinned to the walls as décor like busted lapdogs, the kind of jewelry that makes your skin green and metallic smelling, a song from the past that said, "If being afraid is a crime, we hang side by side."

I missed entering rooms filled with Isaac's friends, rooms filled with smoke and people who overthought everything. "Nobody knows the nature of traps better than one who sits in a trap his whole life long": poetry even I could understand.

If I went back I'd have to apologize, I'd have to explain why I'd left. People would think I was silly. But here, I could forget what century I lived in. I could forget what country. I could forget who I was. I didn't matter. All that mattered was what I did—guiding the sheep home, mixing in the rennet with the milk.

Sara and Gemini led Isaac to the loft at bedtime. I was searching out a bunk when Dice pulled me into the meeting room. He had a strong grip on my wrist that sent thrills skittering up and down my back.

"Harmony," Dice said. "Will you go make sure the new boy is comfortable? Bring him some water, some cake?"

"He's got some water. I gave him a jar."

"Harmony," Dice said, as though I hadn't spoken. "Will you go make sure the new boy is comfortable?"

"Yes," I said. Avoiding Dice, I dropped the pig flashlight into my work boot and tipped it forward so it slid to the toe, hidden. I put on a pair of clogs, grabbed an electric lantern. But I was halfway to the barn before I realized Dice might have been asking me to do something for him.

"Yoohoo!" I shouted from the cows' stable, so Isaac would know to expect me. The electric lantern cast enormous, snaggletoothed patterns on the slats. I found him huddled up under the dirty-as-bark comforter, only his face out in the air. He said he was scared to death in the barn, which resounded with animal breaths and the occasional sleepy bellow. He thought he could hear bats or flapping around the hayloft.

I got under the blanket with him and thought briefly, agonizingly, of Queen. Dice must have sent her out on a nighttime mission like this. They must have lain on this same mattress.

I set the lantern behind our heads, and I could see Isaac's cheek, his cowlick-spread hair. I lay as far from him as I could. I felt him shivering in the mattress springs. He'd traveled out here, squatted and searched for Bay, just for me. I had to remind myself that I didn't want him anymore.

Isaac broke the spell. "Can I see your tattoos?"

I remembered how faithful Isaac had been, to get the claw on his temple, last spring when we still thought we'd always be together. I thought about pulling my musty shirt up and turning my back to him so that he could get close and scrutinize my shoulders in the lantern light. "Of course not," I said.

"I want to make sure it's really you," he said.

I wanted to cry. I said nothing.

He said, "Aren't you going to ask me what I think of all this?"

"I don't really care what you think," I said.

"I live on my own now," he said. "It's better, really, than the squat. And I can afford to. I've been doing event photography."

I'd told him while we were dating that I wished he would sell his photos. I wanted him to support himself with his art. And Isaac had scolded me for the suggestion—he didn't want to sell out and subject his work to the marketplace. "Wow," I said. "Event photography. I'm sure all your friends are so proud." I was remembering how he'd burned me, choosing college as though he could change the system from the inside. He'd abandoned me in my search for a more essential life.

He gave a short laugh. "Be happy for me, Berie."

With each *Berie*, he knocked me down another inch.

We lay and let nature roar over us for a while. I could hear a slight whistle from his nose, and loudest of all, my own awkward swallowing. "How is it really going?" he said.

I'd told Lindsay about Arctic explorers, butterflies, and the school-bus-sized raptor. I thought about telling Isaac the same. But he didn't like associations and groupings, the oblique Dice style; he preferred forthrightness. So I talked about the way we wanted for nothing—"The only troubles we have are the ones we create for ourselves," I said, thinking about Queen's face when Pear had busted in on us that night in the dairy. "I'm telling you," I said to Isaac, "we are self-contained. We are independent." I thought about nursing lambs and singing under the stars. Bathing in the creek. The cold fresh smell when spring came up. The fertilizer-irrigation tank. The sungolds. I once asked Dice, *Is the Ash Family a utopia?*, and he said, *We're much too careful for that*, but he was not quite right. To Isaac, I said, "There is a way to live in harmony with the Earth."

I noticed that he did not seem to be paying attention. "Come on, now, Isaac," I said, feeling sheepish.

"You sound happy here." He paused for so long I thought he'd fallen asleep. "But I think you could be happy in Durham, too."

I shook my head.

"You're fooling yourself if you think you'll be able to stick it out here." He was looking up at the barn's shadowed rafters. "You're not a commune person."

I felt a quick hot anger. He couldn't know. I didn't have a definite self.

"You could take what you've learned here," he said, "and I'd help you, we could buy a little house with a sleeping porch, I've been looking around for us, a porch and a garden, you'd see. I'd take your photo, and you could grow us some strawberries, we could plant another gardenia, we could drive out to see Blackbeard, we could see where they wrote Croatoan on the tree . . ."

"I'm tired," I said, though I was listening carefully.

"With my photography, we could afford . . ."

I knew the walls had eyes, but I lacked the willpower to end the conversation. I imagined leisure, the warm summer concrete, block parties with luminaries, my hand out the car window buffeted by the rushing air. Maybe I could find an essential life in Durham too.

"I'm sorry I left you," he said, though hadn't I left him? "I want you back."

I looked at the side of his face, colorless in the electric lantern light. I knew I should say *I won't come*, but I couldn't form the words. He looked straight up into the smoky dark.

"I'd ask you to marry me," he said.

"Because that worked out so well for my mom," I said.

"I mean, marry me," he said. He must have gotten warmer because now I could see his breath flowing from his mouth.

I didn't like the direction we were going in. I didn't like the happiness I suddenly felt—how my heart beat, how I smiled, covering my face with my hands so he wouldn't see.

"Berie," he said, into my ear. "She forgives you. She wanted me to tell you that."

But she was disappointment, layered and layered, like polar ice, where one arm's length is a thousand years of snowfall. She didn't know how to forgive. "But the necklace," I said, sitting up. "Can she forgive me for making her sell the necklace?"

He smiled for the first time. "She put the money in the bank for when you want it. If you come home, we'll all go on a trip together. We talked for a long time. We could go to Morocco. She'd love the markets."

She'd never left North Carolina before. I hadn't thought she was capable of leaving. I lay back, whomp, into the spiny hay.

"She still has the earrings, you know." He touched my cheek

gently and withdrew. No one on the farm—not Dice, not Bay—was this gentle. And then he said something that surprised me. "Can you forgive us?" he said. "Forgive me."

I felt Isaac was promising something more than a return to the old ways—something new and better. I'd left impetuously, proud and uncertain. Suddenly I was overcome with doubt.

He spoke very softly. "I'm thinking about how I'd love to kiss you. I've been waiting to say it all day."

He leaned toward me. His mouth—a shock how soft and lovely, I knew it so well, like I'd traveled back in time; I'd never expected to find my way back here. As long as we kissed, the world with him accordioned out from us, and I could see my mother waving amid her lights, Durham's brick tobacco castles, the Eno, the quarry, and Isaac's room—once he'd covered his windows with black paper and punched a hole in the center sheet, and the light forced its way through the hole and cast, on the opposite wall, the perfect image of the gardenia bush and the woods beyond, upside down and wavering. I imagined traveling with Isaac and my mother to places the Ash Family had renounced forever—flying and landing in the red desert. I imagined marrying Isaac, how I'd carry poppies, though their petals fell so quickly. I imagined growing old with him. And then I remembered Pear, who didn't have a chance because of what I had done. I couldn't leave. The family could testify against me; there were twenty-three witnesses. I remembered how the family haunted the people who left, and how the people who left often died. Dice could follow the white breaks. The woods keened. All my fears came swirling in like snow.

Isaac pushed up my shirt. He thought our encounter was going well. I felt heart-shattering pity for him. I could not feel him, I was absent now, and it had never been clearer to me that there was no definite self. When I thought of making a life with him, I only felt loss—loss, even, of the pain of work, and the fear, and Dice's all-seeing juice-colored eyes. The family cared about me more than anyone ever had, and they proved it with the way they constrained me, trapped me. They could not bear to see me go.

I didn't want Isaac, did I? I wanted the pure, essential world. If I could be with Dice, I could lose track of myself, I could understand the thrill of seeing a branch in the shadowed woods move and transform into the antlers of a buck, I could understand why the last garnet sun, gripping the treetops, seized me with such astonishment. Why did a walk through the woods always feel like a coincidence, like just exactly what I needed? Queen would have understood. Coincidence, the loveliest gift of perception, the rhyming of it all.

I sat up over Isaac, knocked his hand away—I felt desperate to explain myself to him, to make him understand. I thought frantically. "You might think you love me," I said, "but there's no such thing as a definite self, you see." I stared down at his face, wan in the fake lantern light. "It's very important that you understand this. The self is an illusion. We're all just shifting groups of memory and personality, but you can't hammer down a self in all of that."

"Shhhh," he said. I tried again.

"Listen. If I took all my memories out, and put them in, I

don't know, a tree, and put my personality in the tree, would the tree be me?"

"It wouldn't, Berie."

"Yes," I said helplessly. It all made more sense when Dice was saying it. "So you may love your memories of me, the unity that you perceive, but there is no fixed point. I'm not really here at all. Neither are you." I believed it in my bones but Isaac's face was blank, uncomprehending.

"I know who you are," Isaac said. "I've always wanted you. Even now," he added.

"We can't be together."

"Why not?"

"Because this is my home."

"It won't always be."

"I'm sorry," I said. There had been a question open since Pear died—the question of whether I should leave, now that I saw how unyielding Dice was in his rules. A question since Queen left—since Queen lost her baby—since Queen got pregnant—and now I had answered it. There had been a question open since I let my suitcase ride to Durham without me. I couldn't comprehend what *forever* meant but I had the feeling that forever was the kind of thing that steals across you slowly, like the Trembling Giant in Utah; only when you zoom out beyond the human level can you see that it's all one tree after all. I was going to stay there forever. I never had a choice. Well, that was that.

I stood.

My lantern animated the monstrous hay shadows again. The cows were boulders in the dark, snoring and gently clanking their chains. I walked back to the long house, looking at my feet, not at the stars. I thought I heard Isaac say my name—my old name—and I stopped. Dice was looking out from his lit-up window, still as a tree. I couldn't see his shadowed face, whether his eyes were closed or open.

CHAPTER 22

It was Isaac's third day. Gray diamond frost sparkled on the yard, and it was hard to get out of bed. I dumped out my boot but the plastic piglet had vanished. I laid my cheek on the dirty floor- boards and gazed at the space below the beds. The piglet was gone.

"What are you looking for?" said Sara.

I got up quickly and banged my head. "Oh—a sock."

"But you already have both on, silly!" she said.

The days were shortening, so we had to turn on the fluorescent lights in the milking parlor. The barn was thrumming from the generator, and the air smelled like exhaust and warm animals. I thought about my mother, if she had been planning for my return. She loved to prepare, to set the table, to organize her shop be- fore it opened. I could easily remember her broad clomping walk as she went about these tasks, but when I pictured her face all I could see was Pear's slow-blinking eyes.

Isaac, still squinting with sleep, helped me pick up dusty, cool handfuls from a kiddie pool filled with corn and barley grains. We lugged buckets back and laid a long line out along the fifteen-animal grain feeder. The sheep could hear what we were up to and baaed stridently—either because their udders were full, or because they were hungry. I kept waiting for Isaac to speak. We let fifteen sheep in through a small gate, and they thrust their heads through the feeder's bars into the trough to tongue up the grain. Then we lowered a lever to lock the bars, holding the sheep in place, so we could milk them.

I went down the line, hand-milking the sheep into a stainless-steel bucket. I told Isaac that the needle of milk should hit his bucket with force, till the teat in his hand was like an empty glove.

Isaac said, "I don't like getting all up in there." I'd once felt that way. He didn't like how the udder felt like human skin, oily and fragile. We went down the line in silence. The polydactyl cat followed us, waiting for a slosh of milk over the side of the bucket.

"Have you thought any more about coming home?" he said hopefully. I wanted to cry. In the hayloft, I'd had a vision of a happy shared future, but I knew how false it was.

"Remember when you told me I was stagnating?" I said.

He said, "I didn't mean you should leave forever." I didn't like the way he smiled, as though he understood more than I did. "I asked you to marry me."

I told myself it was time to be unkind to him. "We shouldn't be together," I said. "And I'll prove it to you." I reached for him. He thought I meant to hug him. He put his arms around me, arms so thin compared to Bay's. But I was already feeling in his pocket. I found his camera, and I plunged it into my bucket of milk.

"Berie!" he said. The word rang against the milking parlor's walls.

I drew out the sopping camera, its lens glossy with milk fat. I wondered if the film was ruined. I dropped it onto the cement floor and stepped on it with my heavy boot, to make sure. The plastic cracked like bones. Now the light would get in.

"Berie," he said.

"Harmony," I said.

"You didn't have to do that," he said.

I picked up the broken camera and put it in my chore coat's pocket. We let the first fifteen ewes go, brought on the next fifteen. We poured our pails into jugs, and then poured the jugs into the copper cauldron, to start the cheese-making for the day. The air smelled sour, like turned milk. I lit the big bare gas burner. It produced a thrush of blue flames.

Isaac stirred the huge mass of milk in the cauldron—the cauldron large enough to boil a man in. I had the feeling he was still gathering his weapons, finding a way to convince me to change my mind.

"Sabotage," Isaac said. I ignored him, and he pressed on. "How can I do more sabotage in Durham?"

"You could put glue in the ATMs of the bad banks," I said. Knowledge from Dice. "But you only like peaceful protest, remember?" He shook his head.

We measured the milk's temperature. I added the little spoonful of rennet, taken from the stomach of a baby calf Queen had slaughtered. This used to be her job. In a few hours all that milk would congeal into white custard. Then I'd cut the curds, scoop them into molds, steam out the liquid. When the cheese was ready, Isaac would be gone.

"Let's set a time for me to come back to Asheville, then," said Isaac. "You're allowed to go out whenever you want, right?"

"Of course," I lied. *Allowed to.* I hoped the racket from the generator was loud enough to prevent my voice from carrying.

"All right, well how about Valentine's Day, then? I'll bring your mom up. I promised her I'd set a time."

It was wrong to think he was deliberately hurting me. I was the one hurting him, I thought—yet I felt powerless.

"She'd never take off work and come all the way out here, just to . . ."

"Just to what, Berie?" I cringed when he said my old name. "Just to see her only daughter?"

"Keep it down."

"You keep telling me to be quiet," Isaac said.

I tried to think of a rebuttal. "Well, respect—awareness—"

"You used to be very loud, Berie," he said.

"Call me Harmony," I hissed.

"Marry me," Isaac said. "Come back to the real world."

"You know nothing about the real world," I said.

And there things ended. Josiah came in with the milk from the cows, and we took the pitchers in for breakfast.

The broken camera weighed in my pocket.

*　　*　　*

Breakfast was a languorous meal, with many crocks and trays scattered all over the scarred table. We were eating leftovers, in leftover season. This was the lull before the grind of winter. We served chicken fat and apricot jam on pancakes. We passed around the bowl of sour cream and banana mash. We ate Dumpstered ham, with a greenish, metallic tinge to it, and sweet potato puffs, fragrant with nutmeg. Isaac sat across from me, by Osha, who spoke about gullywashers she had known. In some parts of the mountains, it rained ten feet a year.

I gave Isaac a long look. I let myself feast on every detail. He had his hood up against the cold, but I could just see the toenails of his tattoo at his eyebrow. I looked at his wide, dazed eyes. I looked at the down on his knuckles. He was too soft and skinny to be an Asher. He looked like he didn't belong.

I told myself I was letting him go.

I told myself that this was only hard because it was temporary, my past jutting into my present. I told myself that over the course of years, I would forget him, and that was good and natural.

As breakfast concluded, I grabbed the compost and gestured to Isaac. "Here, I'll just show you how to add to a compost pile, if you ever want to make your own."

I was so focused on Isaac that I didn't notice Bay until I was crashing into him. I stumbled back. He steadied me with his hands. "Pedal to the metal, Harmony," Bay said. Isaac was watching.

"Hey, brother," I said, though I didn't want him to be just my brother.

Bay said, with his hands still on my shoulders, "Has Isaac treated you right?"

I glanced at Isaac, who looked small next to him. "Maybe," I said.

"I'll squash him for you," Bay said. I was delighted. Bay turned to Isaac. "Looking forward to leaving, friend?"

Isaac shrugged. "Show me the compost?" he said to me.

Bay gave me a shake, and Isaac and I walked down to the kitchen garden.

"He was standing there so that you'd bump into him," Isaac said. "What's wrong with his arms?"

"He tried to fight me," I said. "I won."

Isaac laughed uneasily.

"Sheep shears," I said. "But he got over it. We're in love now."

"You never used to be so mean," he said.

"Have you forgotten why you left me?" I said.

"Bay told me he sleeps with all the new girls."

I shrugged, feeling winded. Maybe we were both lying. I stuck my shovel into the compost pile, but Isaac, of course, merely watched.

I said, "I'm not going to meet you and my mom on Valentine's Day. I want you to understand that I'm not leaving here. I reject you and your various proposals."

Isaac looked down. His wide-set eyes had such long eyelashes, which made him seem sweet even now. He nudged a squash with his foot. "I'll see you on Valentine's Day. Let's do two p.m." He named a coffee shop on the west side of town. "You'll want to come. By February, you will."

We stood in silence by the compost heap. A pair of candy-red scarlet tanagers landed on the leaning fence. They weren't even rare; I just loved them. I wrapped my arms around myself, because my heart, like the two-inch rock protruding above the flat field, was exploding with lightning.

I couldn't restrain myself. "See those beautiful birds?" I said to Isaac. But he didn't turn.

Bay yelled down to us from the back porch. "Train's leaving," he shouted.

"Back to Babylon!" Sara said, loading Isaac up with pemmican wrapped in waxed cloth that I recognized was made from the pale blue fabric of my old Peter Pan blouse.

Isaac and I didn't hug goodbye—it wouldn't have made sense. We were acting like we barely knew each other, of course. But he shook my hand. Then he leaned in to my ear. "The film won't be ruined unless you unspool it," he said.

I watched the car pull out, and I could feel a part of myself stretching, like a fishing wire, connecting me to the car that had now vanished into the forest, to Isaac, to my mother, whom I could almost see in the kitchen, opening the statement from her new bank account, wondering if I'd come home. The fishing wire grew taut and snapped.

When Isaac left, the morning was warm, almost clammy. But midafternoon a green wind began to blow, and soon small, hard Dippin' Dots snow was flurrying in the dark places of the woods. First the snow melted, then it stuck. That was it, the greenery was done for—"You're done for!" I laughed to the deciduous trees—in two days the woods would be yellow.

CHAPTER 23

Isaac was gone, and the snow fell, and the family prepared for the action, to which I was not invited. Sara took down the September plaque and put up the October one.

I should have thrown the broken camera in the lake, but instead I wrapped it in a piece of canvas and buried it behind the storage house, near the parked school bus. I wondered how long the film would last underground, whether it might outlast me.

We took out the winter-weight sweaters and traded them around. I saw my sweater from last year, hand-knit wool with a high neck, go to Gemini, and I tried not to covet it. Instead I accepted a faux-Nordic sweater style in an acrylic blend from Dillard's.

I wondered about Isaac and Bay's drive back to town. I'd rejected Isaac's proposal. And then he'd spent hours in a car with Bay, from whom we'd been keeping secrets. I didn't know Isaac to be vindictive, but the farm could change people. Isaac could have told Bay that we'd known each other in Durham. He could have told Bay that I'd revealed where I came from to Lindsay, and that, in doing so, I'd made the family vulnerable to his search, to my mother's search. He could have talked on and on about my moment of doubt, the time-travel kiss in the hayloft. I imagined Bay's rage as he heard how blithely I'd exposed the family, how casually I'd considered leaving. I imagined Bay telling Isaac that I'd killed a woman by smashing her head on the ground. I imagined Bay threatening Isaac, describing how the family could track him, haunt him. I imagined Bay's rough face tensing, his hands, which could pull out a calf or twist a hen's neck, tightening on the wheel. The family did what it had to do to survive in peace.

I sought out Bay, hoping to reassure myself that Isaac had revealed nothing on the drive back to Asheville. I looked for Bay in the hayloft, the barn, the storage house. While everyone rested, he was milking. He knew how to do everything. I loved him for that. I asked him, "How was the car ride back, with that boy?"

"Terrific," he said loudly. "Perfect. What a guy."

I should have been suspicious then, but instead I chose to be happy.

I watched Bay milk the cow, a blue-nosed girl with Dalmatian spots. His hands were terribly strong and sure. He was always sure. And he chose me, I thought. From all the many fake-world people he could have chosen.

I said, "I heard this protest is very small."

"Only ten people," he said. "It's an action, not a protest."

"Do you think I'll be able to go next time?"

"That's not the right goal." Bay's bucket was frothy. I couldn't look away from his hands. Nothing more captivating than his knowledgeable hands. "Whenever I lose track of myself, Dice reminds me of the point of everything. Like a lightning bolt understands a rod."

"I remember you telling me that the first time," I said. I remembered the bus stop on Tunnel Road, my old clothes, my old hair, the way a new world had opened up to me. A fond, tearful feeling overwhelmed me—passing time, the raw sweetness of life, the girl I used to be, when Bay spotted me at the bus stop. Not a girl, I corrected myself, but a grouping of memories.

"Bay," I said. "I want to belong to you."

"We don't believe in possessions," he said. He was silent. He stood and slapped the cow on her rump. "I may still miss you while I'm gone."

I nodded, trying not to smile. And he grabbed the short hair at the nape of my neck, pulled my head back, lifted the pail, and tipped the milk into my mouth.

We sang that evening. I called "Ragan." I didn't need to look at the words. I hoped Dice understood what I was trying to communicate: take me with you, you can trust me.

> *Farewell, vain world, I'm going home,*
> *I belong to this band, hallelujah.*
> *My savior smiles and bids me come*
> *I belong to this band, hallelujah.*

After the last note faded, Dice made his way to the center. He said, "Tomorrow we'll aim for sabotage." The family laughed uproariously, joyously, and I did too, even though he hadn't said anything funny. He asked, "What can an action do?" He said an action can do five things: disrupt a harmful thing, send a message to the public, show our enemies that we exist, express ourselves, or let us live differently for a while. We nodded our heads and shouted *yes!* each time.

I caught up with him as he walked to his room. "Dice!" I called. He ignored me. I grabbed his blue sleeve.

He brought both his arms high above his head, as if he might try to hit me. I watched him warily, the way the little owl had watched me. But he was only stretching, getting out the crick in his neck.

"I wanted to see if I could come tomorrow," I said.

"Did that visitor boy call you by a different name?" he said.

All I could hear was my heart in my ears. "Of course not," I said.

"A fruit, was it?" he said. "Apple? Or was it Berry?"

"I don't think so," I said. Despite our matching tattoos, I felt it was impossible for them to be certain that Isaac was my friend from Durham. *Terrific*, Bay had said. *Perfect.* That had put me at ease. I'd later learn that Bay had known, and Isaac had been coerced into a confession during that car ride. And if Bay knew, Dice knew; that was how the family worked. But in the moment I was focused on lying, and felt I'd been convincing, because Dice smiled.

Dice stepped closer to me. He smelled just like Isaac. "You can't come, my dear. If you were a little more open, you would see why."

"Wait," I said. "Do you think I'll ever be open enough?"
"Someday," he said, which was all I needed.

In the morning, I woke to see Bay's car and the maroon car that had been Pear's idling in the courtyard, exhaust flaring around them.

The sky was lamb's wool colored a little pink, as though there were skin behind it. Ten family members, Rainer and Osha among them, loaded the cars with trays of glass jars. I thought the jars were filled with jam. I couldn't tell. I wondered if the jam was poisoned—what kind of sabotage they could do with it.

Thirteen of us remained, but not Dice, Bay, or Sara, so the family felt pitted. We worked and waited, and kept to ourselves. I milked the animals alone.

While family was gone, the woods went yellow—the hickories, oaks, tulip trees, basswood, birches, and beeches went yellow, and in the understory, the dogwoods, striped maples, holly, and witch hazel shone in flaming shades of red and chartreuse. On the western slopes, the green-black hemlocks and sturdy firs gathered themselves for winter. We slaughtered a hundred of our chickens. We cut their throats, let them bleed, dipped them in boiling water, then dropped them in a barrel with spikes jutting in from its sides, and hit them with a water jet so they churned in the barrel, flopping and flapping, claws chasing the bodies. A mulchy mass of wet feathers fell out at the barrel's base. We fed the chicken heads to the pigs.

I wondered whether my mother would travel somewhere with Isaac, even though I wasn't coming home.

I'd never flown. The flight to college would have been my first.

After I'd left my mother at security, after she'd handed me the photo of my father, I'd sat in a sculpted-foam chair in the waiting room at RDU. I watched the men on the tarmac gesture with their illuminated orange batons. Close by, planes took off; farther out, they landed. Though we hadn't even begun to board, I felt the altitude sealing my ears.

I followed the slow crowd off solid land and into what I thought was the plane. No, it was only a tunnel on wheels. The fluorescent lights were half-off and I felt like I was dreaming. It looked to me like a dorm room hall. I'd have to buy sheets and a blanket and maybe one of those hydra-headed lamps, all paid for with my mother's mother's necklace.

I reached the low round entrance to the plane. I touched the lustrous red and silver paint on its exterior. A flight attendant smiled and beckoned me forward.

"Excuse me," I said. I turned. *How could you be so closed-minded to something you haven't even tried?* someone might say. *What about broadening your horizons, finding yourself?* But even then I knew I wanted to narrow my horizons, to wall myself in with mountains. Even then, I knew there was no self to be found.

I dragged my carry-on behind me up the jet bridge. Isaac and I knew from hiking that the uphill is easier than the down.

Standing in the waiting room again, I called a cab. I half-ran down the airport's wide hall, and I heard my name being called, being called. I ignored it. Maybe that was the moment I became an Asher.

The driver guided his cab past La Vaquita, its plastic cow like a sentry on the roof; down Chapel Hill Road to Durham's Greyhound bus stop, where I planned to spend the night. We were near Isaac's squat, and not far from my mother's house, but I did not want to see them, their disappointment, their resignation. All around me the scenery was falling away—houses slamming back against the ground, revealing they'd only been false fronts.

The cab driver looked at me sadly, but he could not halt my terrible progress. Night bugs flew from around my feet as I walked to the bus station's ticket window. I had not been on the plane but I knew just how the flight to Virginia would have gone. I could see the pink sunset ocean tilting against the window, then flattening again, the sun splitting the plane's quiet dark, the bleary bus ride into the center of town. No one would be waiting for me—Isaac had made me feel that anyone who knew me would eventually tire of me. My life had already flashed before my eyes.

I knew more about that uncertainty than this new uncertainty I'd thrown myself into. I told the clerk at the ticket counter that I wanted to go to the mountains, and I went to Asheville by the earliest bus, and there I met Bay.

The family had been gone eight days when, in the middle of the night, someone flicked on the electric light in the bedroom. No one had ever turned on the light after bedtime, the whole time I'd been there. Something was wrong. Everything constantly went wrong:

the sheep escaped, or one of the dogs sounded the alarm about an invisible enemy. But no one ever turned on the bedroom light.

Disoriented, I closed my eyes and turned over and tried to burrow down again. I managed to sleep a little longer, until voices rose from the kitchen. Dice rushed through the bedrooms. "Maybell," he called. "Josiah. Luxor."

The people he named jolted from their bunks.

I saw Sunny sit up across from me, scratching his cheeks.

"What's going on?" he asked.

"Let's go see," I said.

Bip's voice came from a lower bunk. "If Dice didn't call you, you shouldn't." I paused, but Sunny, either because he didn't hear or because he didn't care, was clambering down from his bunk. I jumped down too. Sunny reached his hand out, and I took it.

Sunny pushed open the door to the dining room. The lights were on there, too, and Bay and Sara were back. They were wearing unfamiliar black clothes. The room smelled like burning grease. I scrambled to understand what I was seeing. Josiah was carrying two sloshing buckets of water, and two people were laid out on the table, blocked from our view. Dice and Sara dipped rags in the water and squeezed them out on the people on the table. "Hog and lard," Josiah was saying. "Honey. Bandages."

"Here," Dice said. He handed Josiah a shopping bag. The bag looked silky, opalescent—then I realized it was plastic.

Josiah pulled out rolls of gauze. "Store bought?" he said.

"All praise to that boy's money," Dice said. "Without it, we couldn't have returned."

Which boy? I thought. Isaac? Then Josiah stepped aside.

Sunny gripped my arm. The people on the table were naked and blotched bark red with blood or burns. One of them—I could tell from her hair it was Osha—had a shining, blistered scab down the side of her face, down her neck, down her shoulder.

In shock, I stepped forward, and Bay noticed me. He pushed me backward out of the doorway, shut the door, and locked it. I stood in the dark entry room with Sunny. We listened to the sounds from the dining room. The drip of water. The murmur of voices, shuffling footsteps. Someone was sobbing quietly. I wondered if it was Osha making that sound, or someone who saw her.

I turned to Sunny, bumping into his chin. I hadn't realized that he'd put his nose in my hair. He stepped back uncertainly.

"What do you think it's from?" I said.

"Town," he said.

I lay in my bunk. The light was off again. I guessed it was two or three in the morning. Through the window, I saw Bay collapse into one of the porch's rocking chairs. He rocked and the porch groaned. Above him the small clouds around the moon had a rainbow tinge. I got up out of bed, my nightgown falling down to my ankles. I stepped on the sides of my feet out to the kitchen, poked at the coals, boiled water in an enamel cup with chamomile. I crept out onto the porch. "Bay!" I said. He didn't turn. I went up to him and tapped him on the shoulder. He looked at me with eyes as bright as tracers.

"Not now, Harmony," he said. He pushed my shoulder, like you'd push on a sheep to get it through the right gate. I stumbled sideways, barely holding the cup steady. He didn't seem too angry to continue, and anyway I liked being a little breathless; the fear helped me focus.

"Take this," I said. He held the cup like he didn't know what to do with it, then he put it on the ground. "Aren't you cold?" I said.

He lifted his arms up and held them wide. Herding gesture, bird of prey gesture. Every time I saw him he was larger than before. Bay said, "What, exactly, can I help you with?"

"What happened at the action?"

He sighed, bringing his arms behind his head. "The police arrested four of us. So while we were caught up with that, Osha and Cuke went on their own. They risked their lives to take down a dragline excavator."

He leaned his head back. When he closed his eyes I let myself look at his half-ruined body. I felt the familiar surge of blood to my face—my body scolding itself for my desires. I ran my fingers down Bay's neck, lightly, like Isaac used to.

Bay said, "I should stop you," he said, "but it's nice, you know, sometimes." And for a while I just touched his face and neck, while we looked out toward the night and pretended that we didn't know what was happening. The sky still looked black to me, but the birds were singing from all the trees.

"Are they going to be okay?" I said.

"Yes," he said. "They did good work."

"Were you one of the people arrested?" I asked.

"No," he said. "I bailed them out."

"Was it expensive?" He didn't answer. "Did Isaac give you money?"

"Isaac?"

"The boy," I said. "With the messy hair. You brought him back to Asheville." A flock of small black birds moved over us, migrating, and I could see them, which meant the sky had lightened. Their wings made a whispering sound. The early hour made me feel safe, like what we were discussing was a dream and inconsequential in real life. "What am I missing?"

"You're missing a whole world," Bay said, rubbing his eyes. "Several worlds, in fact, fake, and real, and realer. The bats are in the bat world. The birds are in the bird world. There's a lot you're missing, sister."

"Did you drive him home?"

"Oh, he's home all right." Bay turned around and looked at me, and I felt sweat break out all over me. My hands got shaky, and I laced my fingers together. "I took his money," Bay said.

"How?" My mind went on its fast rambling way. Did Bay take him hostage? Threaten him? How else would Bay get money from him? Had Isaac let it slip that we knew each other? "You told me that he was perfect and terrific."

"I'm sorry about that," Bay said. "Didn't want you to do anything stupid while we were gone. Because we really love you." He paused. I knew I would spend hours thinking about this: *Because we really love you, because we really love you.* He looked out at the hickory tree. "Don't worry." I imagined the two of them in Bay's dirty car, the long snaking road past Mars Hill, past tobacco shacks, past fuchsia maple trees and brown-gold sycamores. "I just asked him for a donation. He's pretty well-to-do, believe it or not." Maybe Bay had told Isaac about the action. I could almost see Isaac nodding, excited to be a part of it. Bay was always able to get what he wanted. He let us do the work ourselves.

"He didn't seem rich," I said, trying to be casual.

He kept his head turned away from me, and I again started to stroke his neck, which, like his face, was stippled with tiny scars. "He said some funny things, Harmony. He said he knew you in Durham. Is that true?"

I stopped touching him. "No," I said.

"Another thing. Isaac said he came here to steal you away from us. Is that true?"

"No," I said. I turned to look at the hickory tree and noticed the skinny, desperate squirrels rummaging around the roots—hundreds of them.

"And so I asked him for a donation, for your sake, you know. He was willing. He wants to help you."

"No," I said again, less a negation than a prayer.

"How did he find you?" Bay said.

I remembered the hillside with Lindsay. I'd talked about my mother pulling the soap bubble over me, and she'd said, *There was a bubble machine like that in my hometown museum, too.* "He couldn't have known," I said. I reached out to touch Bay's hands, and was surprised to find that he let me.

"Come on," he said. He stood. The sky was spanned by a meat-red line. "Let's go," he said. He led me across the court-yard, back behind the storage shed. He knelt on the ground and patted the earth, like a doctor feeling for tumors. He found what he was seeking, and dug into the ground with his bare hands, scrabbling in the dirt and pulling up clods, like he'd gone insane.

Humans aren't meant to dig like dogs. He reached a piece of canvas and then I realized, with a wave of horror, what he was seeking. The canvas was stiff with mud. He pulled it up and out rolled the camera that I had interred. He, or Dice, must have watched me bury it.

Bay stood up and looked at me, just looked. I knew some terrible punishment was on the way. He would tell Dice. My apology, my regret, my horror wouldn't matter to Dice. What mattered to Dice? The family, whatever form it took; it was mutable, an energy, an idea, a wind. I'd told Lindsay. I had started this. I didn't know how I could save myself.

"I know you think you'll get some mercy because you touched my neck so nicely," he said, "but it doesn't work that way."

I fell onto my knees into the dirt. My body must have known from fairy tales that this is what you do in front of kings and executioners, you go on your knees in front of them, and beg. I looked up at Bay, who regarded me with the gentle curiosity of a birdwatcher. I could try running away. Maybe, like Queen, I would escape. Or maybe, like Cassie, I wouldn't manage to. If there was no such thing as the definite self, it would make no difference anyway.

"Don't tell Dice," I said. I kissed the tops of Bay's black boots.

He said, "He already knows. Let's go to him and see what he wants to do with you. You know what I'm saying, sister?"

I tilted my head up at him. I could feel all the gathered tears falling down my cheeks at once.

CHAPTER 24

I felt light like a kindling twig as Bay and I walked through the many rooms of bunk beds, to Dice's door. Bay carried the camera with him.

"Knock," Bay said. I knocked.

"It's Harmony," I said. "And Bay."

Silence. I examined the door, roughly painted white, with dirt deep in its grain as though it'd been forced in by an explosion. I could hear the sleepers' breathing from the bunk beds and felt so far from the family as I'd first seen it, the family that ate upside-down cake, the family that shouted *love, love, love.* I wondered if I should knock again. Next to me, Bay shifted his weight like a horse, patient. Then Dice swung the door open.

His eyes looked bloodshot. "Let's go out," he said. The room had that pine-soap smell that I found intoxicating. Josiah bent over the bed, where the two injured lay, mummified in bandages— therefore, they were still alive.

Dice led us out his side door and into the barn. A few sheep stood and wandered over to watch us but I was only thinking about the room somewhere nearby where the family buried their departed.

"Out with it," Dice said.

I glanced at Bay. Bay smiled at me. Even when his lips parted he did not reveal his teeth.

I wished I had no body because then I wouldn't have so easily revealed my fear. There was no way to lie to him. So I had to find a different way.

"I know where we can get our hands on some money," I said. Both men turned their faces toward me.

Dice said, "Say more."

"In Durham," I said. "It's something we could sell." Dice began to pace up and down by the feeder trough. He looked underweight. His legs, in particular, were textured with veins.

For a moment, I let myself imagine going home. If my mother had really forgiven me, I could tell her I was happy with the family, I could explain myself and at last be seen and understood.

"In my mother's house," I said. "In a cookie tin. She has two diamond earrings. She works all day, so we could just sneak in and out." I paused. How could I be sure she'd be working? But she was always working. "I could distract her at work." The sad rising sunlight pulsed on the floor like it was sending me a signal.

"Real diamonds?" Dice said. He had stepped quite close to me. He was smiling placidly but his eyes were tense.

"Part of a set," I said.

Dice kept his eyes on mine. Even now, I loved his attention. I'd loved it since I arrived.

"And where does she live, Harmony?" Dice said gently.

I paused. I imagined seeing once again her beige house with its bright green lawn where once the magnolia had stood. I imagined Bay and Dice arriving and finding her unexpectedly at home. What would she think of these strong dirty people? She'd fear for her life. "Don't you think I should go along?"

"If you tell me how to find these diamonds," Dice said, "and we go, and we find them, you can come out with us on an action. You can be a part of all that we do. You can help nature fight back, really fight." I pictured Osha and Cuke, their waxy horrible skin. But I wanted to be fearless and reach the marrow of life. "We'll forgive your indiscretion." He took the camera from Bay's hand. Out of his pocket, he withdrew the pig flashlight. My heart was in my throat.

Bay said, "There's so much more to know, Harmony."

I made the decision then, but it only seemed like a decision afterward. I was like the woman who hands her pocketbook to the man who never intended to rob her, or the man who dies under his bed when the funnel cloud never touches down; I'd been preparing and waiting so long that I could no longer see that I had made a decision.

I told him the address. She kept a spare key for me inside the clay terrier on the porch. "The key might not be there anymore," I said, and realized, with a pang, that it was; she probably came home each day hoping I might have returned. She kept the Colonial Girl cookie tin, with the diamonds, in the closet in her bedroom.

"Harmony," Dice said, "I trust you now. I trust you. I won't forget this. Remember the little owl?" he said. "Sometimes it takes a while to learn how to heal."

And Bay took my shoulders and walked with me into the next room. I wondered if Dice was, in his way, paying me a compliment. Maybe I was a wild animal. And someday, all he'd have to do would be to point out the window, and I would be free.

Bay said, "Diamonds, huh?" Something unfamiliar in his voice—gratitude, or sadness.

"My grandmother's."

I joined the others who had stayed behind to prepare a staggering breakfast for the family members who had returned. My brothers and sisters didn't know that Dice had welcomed me into his trust, but that morning everyone seemed particularly purposeful and beautiful, like the first day I'd arrived, working together so perfectly that they seemed like they could read each other's minds. We made cheesy grits and sour-cream porridge and pork chops and pancakes with sorghum and hickory syrup, dumplings boiled in ham water, baked garlic, pulpy cooked-down squash, bannock. So they would take my mother's earrings. I'd always disliked her obsession with objects. I only wanted them to move quickly, so she wouldn't be at home and scared.

Rainer and I sat side by side at breakfast. "How was the action?" I said.

"Before I was arrested, people came on horseback," he said, "and the police shot the horses with water cannons." He looked down at the bread on his plate as though he didn't know what it was for. "I keep thinking about Osha and Cuke," he said. "The way they smelled."

I touched his shoulder and he leaned into my hand like a cat. "Bay said they'll be all right," I said.

"I don't think so," said Rainer. He picked up a slice of bread, looked at it, and put it down again.

"Here," I said. I passed Rainer a jar of apricot jam, and he received it in trembling hands, and dropped it to the floor. He was usually so quick to help, but now he stared down at the glowering orange mess, and I ran to mop it up.

"I'm sorry," he said.

"That's all right," I said. He sat at the table holding his head in his hands. I remembered how pudgy and jovial he'd been when he arrived.

I gave hay and water to the sheep and threw down fresh straw. I napped in the hay. I noticed for the first time how the year was looping, fall memories laying over old fall memories. The hickory turned yellow and dropped its leaves. It was a day like this when Queen killed the heron.

At dinner, Dice told us about Osha and Cuke's bombing the dragline excavator. I imagined their lobbing handmade grenades into its bucket. He talked about waging war on behalf of nature. The family roared, booed, applauded, in urgent merriment. Dice let us enter his room, where Osha and Cuke sat on pink cushions, bandaged and monstrous. We approached them one by one and said thank you. The burn appeared to have eaten one of Osha's eyes. Five long tentacles of burn wrapped around Cuke's throat and jaw. They smelled like rancid burning oil. And yet they sat completely still with stiff, perfect posture that betrayed agony.

I wondered if they'd ever work again. I wondered whom he'd send out next. What if I burned up like they had? Would I put myself in danger for Dice, for the climate, for the mountains? Yes, I thought, I would. I was always willing.

We had the real solution for living with the Earth. I was only just beginning to understand how difficult the real solution could be, but that made it more true, more real, especially when I had Dice and my family to inspire me, people who lived selfless lives in the ceaseless present. Trying to live in the present is like trying to sip from a waterfall. Can you open your mouth and let the whole waterfall flood in? They would never look back on their lives and see years of sleepwalking, of petty discontentment. I wanted to be as alive as they were. I wanted to understand what life *meant*.

After visiting Osha and Cuke, we gathered again in the meeting room. I wanted to sing till my throat hurt, or hear one of Dice's stories, because stories and singing dissolved my worries, made me certain, banished the definite self.

But instead, Dice made Rainer stand up. "Rainer broke a jar," Dice said. "A jar of jam." A hiss went up around the table—sauerkraut would have been one thing, because it was easy and plentiful, but jam was precious, a basket of apricots in each pint. "I need each of you to tell him what that really means. Tell him what his error means to you." So we went around the table and each person murmured something—"That jar will never carry another harvest," "That jar served us for many years," "Rainer, you have wasted our bounty."

When it was my turn, I didn't pause. I added, "Rainer, this isn't just the jar. You need to be humble like a single tree in a forest." I had been through this too, and I had survived. Again I felt the intimacy with him I'd felt in the forest, when I could have sliced his neck. Dice must have felt this way all the time: a godlike feeling. The family nodded all along the table.

winter

CHAPTER 25

Bay left that evening. His taillights washed the bedroom in red. I
guessed he was going to Durham, because before he left, he gave
me a kiss on the ear and whispered, "See you soon." I hoped he'd
be back quickly. I imagined him pulling up to my mother's house,
making his way over her lawn. I imagined him feeling around in
the clay terrier for my key. She would be at work, she was always
at work, and I didn't need to worry. Bay would enter the house.
He'd notice the mean and poor materials, the linoleum and the
vinyl, and he'd notice the care she took with everything. If he
looked he could find out everything about her. He could find
her ribbons and papers for wrapping presents, her napkin rings
and candleholders, her clothes that were larger than life-size. He
could go to my room and find my track spikes and the photos of
me as a spinning blur and my heart-diffraction glasses, all evidence of a girl who'd wanted to break into a different world.

I imagined my mother coming home from work, afterward.
Maybe she'd set down her keys and catch the Ash Family scent
in the air: horses, frost, wood smoke. Maybe she'd see her dresses

pushed aside. She'd shake her head—I hated to imagine—she'd think she was being foolish. I wondered how often she checked the tin for the earrings. Maybe once a week, or once a day. I imagined the detectives raising Bay's fingerprints in their flour. My mother didn't have the resources to pursue an investigation, I was fairly certain. It was likely, anyway, that she would know right away it was me. She'd picture me creeping through the house. This was what made me weep: she'd know it was me—who else knew about the tin?

All I wanted was for Bay to return. Once he returned, I could settle down again, and begin the process of forgetting, which I knew was inevitable. Sometime soon I wouldn't care about the earrings, but the family and the stewardship of the mountain and Dice's truth would last forever.

We underwent a week with thunderstorms every afternoon, thunderheads mounting above the ridges, tall and dark blue blots against a raging pink sky, which swept into our holler, forcing leaves down flat and shiny on the sodden forest floor.

Bay was gone one week, two. I couldn't bear it any longer. At dinner I asked Dice, "Where is he?"

"Finding new family," he said.

"But he should go to my mother's house and get it over with," I said.

Dice smiled. "He's careful," he said. He squeezed my wrist. "Nervous heartbeat," he said. I wanted to hold fast to my concern, as though being concerned would help my mother. But my moods always changed, without my control, sad into happy into sad, tumbling in the bright stream.

*   *   *

When Osha and Cuke took off their bandages and joined us at the table, we celebrated. We roasted a whole deer. We made a cake with candles in it and sang special songs.

Osha and I mended sweaters, darning the moth holes and patching the elbows. I couldn't look at her face. I only looked at her hands.

"How are you feeling?" I said. Osha and I had not spoken since Isaac's visit.

"Frightened," she said.

"I can imagine—"

"About the environment," she said. "The end is near. Siberia will melt. The rain forests will burn down. The oceans will stop mixing. And the wars will start."

She couldn't help me with the sewing for long before she complained of a lightning headache. She went to lie down. Neither she nor Cuke worked much anymore.

That night there was the most brutal storm yet. We could hear the trees and branches writhing, the wind whipping, the wind shoving itself into the cracks of our bedrooms. No one could sleep in such a mess. I dropped down from my high bed, floorboards like ice against my socked feet, and crept to the kitchen. I found a dozen people there already, red and black in the firelight. The rain stopped: it had become snow. We hummed the Sacred Harp tunes until the fire dried our throats. This, this, this was what I had been looking for. Love, community. My worries left me, and I was limp with gratitude.

I'd fallen asleep next to Rainer and when I woke his arm was across my front, and as I blinked the rainbow-edged sleep from my eyes, Rainer's arm was for a moment Bay's arm.

It was dawn, and the dining room was bright as midday, washed in brilliance. The dirty white walls and floor looked like marble, luminous. An end-of-the-world hush had come over our holler. The snow rose all the way to the porch. Nothing moved. I thought about the bears and the squirrels, sleeping in their trees and caves. This was the real world. I lay under Rainer's arm until the first milkers dressed themselves to go to the barn.

At breakfast, Gemini made his new bullets such bright silver, they looked enameled white.

We passed the days with fall tasks—painting, mending, chopping wood. Josiah had taken over Pear's role as the medicine steward, and he went to town with Dice to buy minerals for the sheep. I took Rainer to the barn to rub his chapped hands through the sheep's greasy wool. He'd never tried milking a cow before, so I showed him, and it didn't feel like treachery against Queen—she'd left, she'd abandoned us—but when he said, "I just noticed how light your eyes are," it felt like treachery against Bay.

Bay had been gone two weeks, almost three. Osha and Cuke had disappeared. I didn't ask where they had gone, because I did not want to hear the answer. To a calmer homestead, I hoped, in a distant prairie. Maybe they had even moved to a town. They would be happier there.

I felt the swift brightness of the season. Ice silvered all the evergreens. When the ice fell, the sky threw down more.

But then we were brought low. I wasn't the first to get sick, and I wasn't the last. The first was Josiah. He must have caught the sickness in town. Now Dice had to brew the tonics and tinctures, mix the ointments and balms. But the remedies were not strong enough. Within a few days, five others were bedridden.

In the fake world this virus might have been knowable, annual, treatable. In Ashland it was a plague, the likes of which Dice had never seen. The six infected couldn't move, could barely eat the salty chicken broth that Bip simmered on the stove day and night—using up the chickens that were supposed to last till the spring. The sick shook and moaned, sweated and shivered. Their lips cracked. They vomited. They whimpered in the night. I couldn't wait for Bay to return. He'd have ideas for treatments. But the sun kept rising and setting with no sign of him, and we flew into the disease like an arrow into a target.

The family divided in two: those who tried to tend to the sick, and those who were too afraid. I was in the second group. Dice called an emergency meeting and said someone would have to take on all the duties for all the sheep and the cows. Not just herding, which could only happen in fair weather, but all the feeding, watering, lugging the grains, pitching down the hay, cleaning out the manure-heavy old straw, wheeling it away, pitching and spreading new straw, but worst of all, the milking. Some of the sheep were drying up, but not the cows.

No one wanted to volunteer, so I did, and hoped that assigning myself such a difficult task would cancel out my previous cowardice. But even the brave people were trying to protect themselves. The only one willing to touch the sick and hold them and drip cool water into their mouths with a rag was Dice, of course. Dice was our father and didn't let us down. He slept an hour a night or less, on the sickroom floor. He kept it clean, mopping with vinegar, the scent of which, to this day, brings me back to the impassive mountains.

One night, unable anymore to bear the coughing and snuffling in the long house, I took a blanket to the hayloft. And there in the darkness, I remembered: I could leave. I could walk down to the road. No one would track me, for now. But they could track me later. If I went back to Durham forever, I'd spend all my days looking over my shoulder for Sara and Bay, knowing they could pin me for Pear's death, if they wanted. And I couldn't leave for a little while, I couldn't abandon the family. I'd been waiting for a time like this—a time to be devoted and essential. In the hayloft, buried deep under the gamy blanket, I was thinking of the birds, swifts, who spend ten months at a time on the wing, sleeping, eating, mating on the wing, and then pilots catch sight of them cruising a mile high. They're hard to study because they're too good at flying, Dice had said. The natural world was full of things that made me choke up on mystery. And now I finally felt that I'd done it justice.

I wondered whether Dice would let me go to town to buy some medicine. Maybe, in this situation, it'd be okay—I knew bail and bandages were different from medicine, but those purchases had been made out of necessity, and maybe Dice felt the same way now. I could find Annie, the pharmacist, again. I thought fondly of her periwinkle scrubs and her well-rested, angelic, pink, pillowy face. Annie, she'd hand me rattling amber bottles and I'd carry them up here in my pockets.

Eight were sick, then nine. I, no longer a coward, bundled in three coats, worked for the sheep and the cows. I fed them, watered them, milked them, and cleaned their beds, and every day I left more and more tasks for the next day. The milking alone took three hours in the morning and three again at night. My hands were swollen and sore and I rubbed them with Bag Balm but still they bled. The fingers of my right hand wouldn't uncoil. I passed the week in a blaze of agony. Every minute that I was awake, I was shoveling or milking, but I couldn't go fast enough.

The sheep were crying. Several developed infections because they'd gone too long with overfull udders. Others were drying up. I loved them, but I couldn't take good care of them alone. And they trusted me so much; they were so patient. I couldn't bear to look at their long-pupiled eyes.

Twenty were sick one morning. Only Sara remained in the dairy. I milked the cows and came to the long house, exhausted. My hands could barely grip. We were running out of wood, and our generator in the creek had frozen in place. Rainer had been desperately trying to wire up the solar panels before he, too, took ill—but solar panels aren't much use in the winter mountains. We needed wood, but we didn't have the power to chop it.

Dice was alone in the kitchen. He was dipping towels in boiling water and squeezing them out, to bring to the sick. The steam was so thick in the room it was like a cumulus cloud.

"Dice," I said.

"What do you want, Harmony?" he said, not bothering to look up from his work. The steam flowed up around him and spilled across the ceiling.

I wanted him to notice how hard I'd been working. "What if I went to town to buy some kind of medicine?"

He stopped. He turned, with a hand over his heart. His eyes looked dead, because he was so tired. "It's a virus," he said. "There's nothing to do but wait."

"We're in danger," I said.

Dice stepped toward me. In a flash he reached out around me and yanked me against him. I'd noticed how thin he'd looked since the last action, but his frailty was an illusion; he'd only gotten stronger: being held against him was like being caught against a mountain laurel, all steely cords, a bramble. I writhed against him, but I could not free myself. He'd never held me this way, no one had, but it felt familiar. I seemed to remember being held this way the way an animal knows to sense a forest fire: by instinct.

"The family always survives," he whispered into my ear. "These are the rules."

He released me. I stumbled away, gasping.

Dice turned back to his work. The steam in the air between us was like words.

*   *   *

That afternoon I found I couldn't even pick up the milk pail to bring it to the dairy, where Sara was trying her best to keep up with the endless flow of milk. I was worn out. I lay on the iron-cold dung-strewn floor and cried. No one, not even Josiah, had recovered yet. The only way we could keep going like this, unless Bay returned with a crowd, was if the sick began to heal. While I sobbed on the milking parlor floor, I noticed, curiously, that no tears were coming out of my eyes.

I milked for a moment, then stopped. I needed Dice to remind me what I was supposed to be doing. Was it too soon to milk again? I'd lost track. Resolute, I left the sheep still locked into the feeder, and I left the milk pail in the middle of the floor. Four cats, bewildered by their good fortune, darted in from the corners.

I should have noticed my mind wasn't working right, but you can't notice a thing like that from the inside. I stumbled over the ice in the courtyard, slick and rippled as mucous, and forgot I was going to ask Dice for help. I made my way to the creek. The woods were high with snow now. Afternoon. The landscape was only four colors, white snow, black trees, lapis sky, and lavender shadows. The half-moon burned in the sky, and I almost thought I could see the stars piercing through.

I stomped the ice, jumping on it till it cracked with a gunshot noise, and I fell into the water. I was planning, I think, to soothe my arms by bathing them—so the swelling would diminish, so I could pick up the milk pail and hand it to Sara, so I could milk twenty-nine more sheep, and feed them, and water them, and then start with the cows again.

I had my arms thrust up to the shoulder in the quick black

water. They'd gone tingly and numb. And then the very last of my sense told me to take my arms out of the creek and walk to the long house. I headed back up, though terrific squalls fought to keep me down. I had to crawl through the courtyard, and when I reached the porch, the sky was bursting with pink stars.

The landscape was silent. A blizzard was coming, maybe.

Dice was there for some time, lifting up soup on a prison-issue spoon. I stared, mind-boggled. "What happened to the sheep?" I asked Dice, my tongue like a rock.

"They'll be all right," he said.

"No—" I said. "I left them in the feeder." I kept talking about the sheep. Dice was gone and every bed was full. Sara was here, and Gemini. Was anyone still healthy? I saw Rainer, gray colored, dropping down from his bunk like a spider.

"I'll go see the blessed sheep," he said. "Now shut up."

At least one day passed. I remember the ink-blue night flooding down the windowpanes. Then the hills were bioluminescent green with putrefying fox fire, or so they appeared—maybe it was sunlight of another day. No one brought water or broth that night or day, though many called out asking for it. One unidentifiable white morning, I thought I saw Bay gliding through the courtyard, waist-deep in snow. His car wasn't there. The forest road must have still been impassable.

He passed from my view, then entered the house. I could feel his steps reverberating in the woods all around. He entered like a blazing sun and glanced around the sickroom. Rainer's bunk was still empty. "Bay," I said. I needed to ask if he'd taken the earrings. My head was too heavy to lift up. He ignored me, or didn't hear.

He found what he was looking for and picked up a slight, silver-haired body from one of the bottom bunks. I didn't recognize the person, till he stirred, and I saw with a shock that it was Dice. Dice either grimaced or smiled, his head falling back, as Bay arranged him across his arms. Bay carried Dice away, out through the courtyard, kicking through the feet of snow, and down, out of sight.

The wind whisked the bright powder in around the windows and doors. I was down to the nub of my sense, but I knew if I didn't get water, I would surely die.

I didn't see how I could get out of the upper bunk where someone had placed me days before. I rocked myself to the edge. My arms were shaking, too weak to hold me, and I dropped to the floor with a terrible thud. The room wheeled, and I lay on the ground and crawled to the kitchen, arm over arm, like a beggar in a desert.

This was my lowest moment, but it didn't last, because I'd made my way to the cast-iron stove, which was cold. Arm over arm, I hoisted myself vertical and found on top the giant pot filled with soaking beans—the last move Dice had made before he got too sick to continue. I poked the sheet of ice on top until it broke. I dipped a cup into the smoky-colored water. I drank and drank, euphoric, and reached my hand in to eat some of the raw, sodden beans. The pipes had frozen, but I opened the window and piled the pot with snow, stocked it with dippers, and pushed it across the uneven floor back to the sickroom.

I sat for a moment, then stood; my knees felt as pliant as paper. I made my way to Dice's room. I thought he might be in there, with Bay. He hadn't locked it. It was empty, in disarray—blanket on floor, sticky brown splashes on the nightstand.

Back in the bedrooms, I gave half the room a drink, holding the dipper to parched lips. I'd helped them. Perhaps I'd saved them. This was my place. I fell asleep in the twelve inches of space below Sara's bed.

When Josiah recovered, our fortunes changed. Later on, after a singing one night, he told us about how difficult it was to choose what to do first. Water first, then heat. Most of the wood was frozen solid, but he managed to chop enough to fill the stove, and then he brought in more logs to thaw in the dining room. Then he cleaned the sickroom. There was vomit all over the floor, and leaves and branches had blown in from the winter storm. The house was barely a house anymore, but a container for nature.

Soon Dice and Bay returned. "Did you find the earrings?" I asked Bay from my bed.

He patted my head, his hand cold as tree bark. "I was out finding new family," he said. I tried to read his thatched face.

"Where did you take Dice?" I said. I'd given him my mother's address; I felt I deserved a straight answer. He knew I was saying, *You fled when we needed you.*

Bay shook his head. "Cabin nearby," he said. "Dice got mad when he woke up. It wasn't his choice." For an odd moment, I wondered if they could be blood father and son. But no fake-world kinship could provoke devotion like Bay's.

"Such a noticer," Bay said, and gave me a flicker of a smile.

I believed Bay, and it was easy to believe when Dice was offering me a rosy venison broth, when Bay was scrubbing the rooms on hands and knees, when they got the farm moving again, so that when I was well enough to get up, they let me rest for days and fed me sunny silver pie and thanked me for bringing the water.

The sheep had escaped their enclosures, so they got enough to eat, for the most part, and only eleven of them died. Some of the cows would never give milk again, but that was all right—beef for us now, and in the spring we'd let the good mothers keep their babies, as I always wanted.

Many of the chickens died for lack of water. The pigs were all right. They would inherit the earth. The cows and horses had also gotten out of their stables, and they'd all been drinking out of the same spot in the stream where I'd broken the ice.

We burned the mattresses. The maggots, which had come from nowhere to infest all the rot, slunk back to their hidey-holes in the earth. We all got to bathe in Dice's bathtub, by the stove with the tiles of billow-sailed blue ships, and we luxuriated in the grime that our bodies shed.

And Josiah had found Rainer frozen dead in the milking parlor, his clothes half-off, his boots off: hypothermia. Dice only told me this when he determined I was well enough. No one talked about it, but I knew the shepherd dogs must have mauled his corpse.

After I'd recovered, Dice summoned Bay and me to the barn. We stood pallets on their edges and laced them together to form a new enclosure for the pigs, then let them out, four curious six-hundred-pound sows with pink ears shading their faces. Dice led us back to his room, through the side door. On his bed was a long white sack, made of bedsheet, lumpy and sewn shut. It was Rainer. "Why do you want my help?" I said, squinting against the tears that burned my eyes.

"He liked you," Dice said.

Bay took his upper body, Dice his middle, and I his feet, the lightest part. We carried him out and through the courtyard and into the pig enclosure. He was ungainly, but I'd hauled many un-gainly objects on the farm—cauldrons, tables, logs. The sheet was clean but I thought I might be able to smell, despite the cold, putrefaction. I wondered if below the sheet his skin was coal col-ored, his nose rotted off. I preferred to think of him resting inside peacefully, as he was in life, freckled and redheaded and pleasant faced. We laid him down by the door in the pig enclosure, and Dice dismissed me. I didn't get to see what was inside—the bone room. I imagined that they'd dig a grave in the barn's dirt floor.

We did not mourn Rainer, since there was no such thing as the definite self and the individual members of the family did not matter as much as the whole. But as I mended I thought about him more and more. I was the one who'd sent him out. He'd been so quiet. A good hard worker. One day I'd lain under his long careless arm, and the next he had vanished. He liked the Sacred Harp song "Plenary," so I sang it in the woods, where he'd found and carried deer, uncomplaining about the heavy loads.

No one in the fake world cared for him, he'd said.

Now even if Lindsay came looking she wouldn't find him.

CHAPTER 26

Once the farm was back in order, Dice brought me to his room. Our spirits were so high those days I was not nervous at all. I could barely remember his clinging to me in the kitchen. I'd been so sick then that nothing had felt real.

Dice gestured to the velvet couch. I sat. His eyes seemed further recessed into his head, his cheeks sunken, his neck all cords, like there was a vacuum inside him trying to pull him inward. The illness had left him skeletal.

"Are you all right?" I said, before I could stop myself.

He smiled. "Don't worry about me," he said. "We found the earrings." He picked up one of the tiny bones from his bookshelf, looked at it, and placed it carefully back.

I was relieved. Now he'd know he could trust me, I thought. I'd made up for Queen and Pear and all my smaller transgressions. "Did you sell them already?"

"They were right where you said." He picked up another bone, studied it. "Your mother was there too, unfortunately."

My mind heaved in every direction.

"She didn't want to give us the earrings," he said. "As you can imagine. Even though we told her it was to support you."

"I wish you hadn't said that," I said. "What if she reports us? Why did you tell her you knew me?" I'd been searching for the right emotion and now I found it: rage, pure hot rage.

"And so there was—how can I put it—some conflict." He tilted his head. He was perfectly still. "She wouldn't help us. And she got out a gun, did you know she had one?"

The trees on the ridge were afflicted by a wind that pressed them flat. The wind rushed around the house, around the tree, and everything flowed in its wake. Dice's tone was lilting.

"We didn't have a choice, in the end."

I felt my head flowing off my shoulders like a comet, past the tree, the house, the porch, the snow.

"The fact is, you're the only one who knew about the earrings. So unfortunately, it looks like you did it. You killed your mother for some cash. Understandable; that's the problem. That's what the law will see, an understandable crime."

"What?" I said. I felt like the chicken head, gawping. "What? What? What?"

"Take out the sheep, Harmony," said Dice.

My head was a whiteout. Whiteout. "The sheep," Dice said again. He could tell he shouldn't leave me alone. He could tell he had been pushing too hard. He said in a voice so gentle he sounded like a young girl: "How about I teach you something instead?" I nodded.

We could hear Maybell and Josiah shouting cheerfully at each other as they milked the cows in the courtyard. From his nightstand, Dice withdrew a few small bottles. He held one up to the light and shook it. "Drink," he said.

It smelled sterile and went down so strong it scorched my vocal cords. "What is this?" I said, and my voice came out hoarse. Dice let the comment fade, and in the silence, I coughed.

Dice said, "I had a dream about you, Harmony." He sighed. "Where you were a giant so tall that your head parted the clouds, and you walked out of the mountains and onto the prairies, growing bigger as you went, till you met the ocean and you drank it all up, snapped up the ships and ate them up, and the rain came down around you and jingled like bells . . ."

I felt uneasy. He took the jar from me, drank, and passed it back. The brew began to hurt my teeth, as though it were sweet. Dice said, "We have to burn everything but the bridges."

"How can we do that?"

Dice said, "For biggest impact from littlest effort, you can't beat violence."

I wondered whether I was going crazy. They'd killed my mother and I was letting Dice teach me a lesson.

"You can't," he said, "just drop a match on the floor of a power plant and expect that anything will burn fast and hot enough to cause real damage. You have to direct the fire," he said. "You've made jam, bread, leather, cheese, soap—this is no different." He fetched a jug of gasoline and a stockpot, and put a hot plate on top of his stove with the ships and their sails. "No fire around gas," Dice said. While we waited for the water to boil, Dice and I shredded bars of soap into chips, using an old cheese grater.

Once the water boiled, we put another pan inside, to form a

double boiler, and Dice turned off the hot plate. He told me to fill the inner pot with gasoline. I'd experienced gasoline as a smell, a quiver in the air as it made its ghostly escape from the pump at the station. I'd experienced its relative, diesel, as a taste, sucking it out of Isaac's biofuel engine. But gas was a liquid too, pale yellow like apple juice. The color of Dice's eyes.

We heated it in the pot above the boiling water, then stirred in the white chips of soap. The gas fizzed and crackled as it ate up the soap. I'd always liked the smell of gasoline—there was something fresh and atmospheric about it. But the smell changed when the soap went in. It smelled not like death or danger or evil but like sadness—the smell of a poor home like my mother's, the smell of industrial detergents. We stirred until the mixture took on the consistency of jelly. Dice told us that the carbon in the gas might have come from the corpses of animals who died in the Jurassic or Cretaceous period, but the Appalachian mountains formed long before that, when horseshoe crabs were the closest thing to a land animal. "War fuel for the environment," Dice said. It was napalm.

By the end, because of the gasoline or the alcohol, I was having trouble standing. "You're a good girl," Dice said. He left me alone. I lay in his bed.

Night fell and I was awake, staring at the crouching shape of my mother, unwilling to move and discover that it was only a blanket on Dice's pink couch.

I thought, I'll stay here until my hair reaches my ankles. What good is hibernation if you have to wake up from it? Well, I've had it, I thought, I'm through.

The night turned into morning, and I didn't get up. I was catching up on a year of missed sleep. Dice stayed away. Someone left a tray of bread and butter on the nightstand.

I felt blighted, creaky, too warm and too cold. Even small motions required huge effort, and I found in myself a profound weakness I'd never suspected. Like a sinkhole, my ground had given way.

I spent the day staring out of Dice's window at the whiteout. I parsed the landscape for motion, but what always seemed at first to be new people arriving invariably resolved itself into birds. I could see my face in the window, the barn melting into my eyebrows, the mountains just cresting my hair, and I looked like my mother.

I told myself that by the summer, I would be happy again. I would try to be good. I would understand how to break myself open—I imagined cracking a geode, the dusky crystals inside— and let the world rush in.

Bay brought me dinner right before sunset: cold sheep ribs and whole milk. He pulled me out of bed. "Get the blood moving," he said. My head rocked. We sat side by side on Dice's velvet sofa, but I didn't turn to him. The milk was in a tin cup. The cream was yellow, the milk beneath it was blue. Sad, I was thinking, how milk is only white around the edges, where we see it, and inside it's black. "Thank you," I said.

He knocked his hand against my cheek. I felt sick looking at him. I pushed his hand away. "Did you kill her?" I tried to say. But the words came out not as words but as a hiss, a sigh. I worked my jaw like a dying fish.

"I want to make you feel better," he said.

I didn't look at him. "Did you kill her?" I tried again.

He took my face in his hand and turned it toward him. "Come on." He didn't give me a chance to pull on my sweater. Outside it was achingly cold. It was evening, murkily teal, precisely the time of day when the sky isn't light enough to silhouette the trees, and pale shapes seem to float. The long house glowed bioluminescently. We sat in the spotty snow under the hickory, where we could almost be seen.

He gazed at me from the nest of his face. I wondered if Bay had left my mother slumped by the wall or prostrate on the floor, her solar queen waving goodbye. Who had found her—found her gaping? I'd thought Bay was the solution to everything.

He touched my shoulder. I jumped away, feeling skittish as a cat. "Harmony," he said in frustration. "Don't worry." Once even a brush of his hand could send me reeling for days. I was wondering about when the sterilization hurts more than the wound, when the victory costs more than the defeat.

He got close to my ear. "She's not really gone."

"What?" I said.

His voice was sharp in my ear. "She didn't die. We didn't even see her." Then he kissed my ear.

"Why are you messing with me?" I said, and my voice broke.

"Dice was not telling the truth. I am." His breath was hot; the night was cold. "You're too sad, you're sadder than I expected." He pulled back. "Don't tell Dice I said that." I didn't know why Dice would lie to me. I was used to Bay's being Dice's hands, and it was uncomfortable to sense him venturing out alone—I didn't know where the truth was. The yard spun, and I pressed my cheeks with my hands.

"Are you okay?" Bay said, his expression faltering.

I didn't speak, because I didn't know the answer.

Bay looked around uneasily. "I mean to say"—his tone grew more confident—"there is no definite self." There was the Bay I recognized. The sure one, the one who was always loyal. The one who'd never contradict Dice.

"'Come, my soul, and let us try,'" he said, "'for a little season.'" My swollen heart darted in his direction. He belonged to the milk cow and the bees, with all that tough gentle knowledge stored up in his hands. It wasn't too late. In that moment, I chose to believe Bay. My mother was alive. Bay grabbed my hair and pulled it down, exposing my neck. I opened like a gate. I was sure he liked total surrender. It was the kind of feeling that wiped out all possibility of escape. For the first time I touched his scarred arms, and the skin was slippery and soft as liquid.

Deep winter roosted in the holler. The snow came down like white wings. The trees froze to the heartwood.

We sang "China."

Why do we mourn departing friends?
Or shake at death's alarms?

I was thinking about Valentine's Day. I could count the days from when Dice put the February plaque in place. I felt that my mother was alive—it was the torment Bay had seemed to feel when he'd diverged from Dice's story. But how did he know she had a gun? Maybe he was guessing. My mother would have known—from Isaac—that I was connected to these people. There wouldn't have been crossfire. So this meant that Dice was lying to me about my mother's being dead. Maybe he was lying, but because he had to teach me something. To teach me that if my mother had to die, so be it—that was what needed to be done to keep the family together. To teach me to stop thinking of the fake world as an option. I should let Isaac come to town and leave. I would not see him.

I was passing Dice's test. Not fleeing, but recommitting.

At night I listened to my heartbeat, which sounded like a drum way down in a mine, and I wondered if this was what it meant to be *one with nature*, a passive and ceaseless tranquility.

Dice's after-dinner stories took a winterly turn and struck deep into my winterly heart. At the bottom of the Earth in the center of Antarctica at Vostok, he said, the coldest place in the world, glaciologists were drilling an ice core, and they had to stop before they drilled as deep as they wanted to, because they found underneath all that thick ice a pristine lake the size of Lake Ontario that was filled with pure clear water that had been sealed below for millions of years. There was an island in the lake.

I felt Dice was seed-bombing me with ideas that would grow next season. I told myself that the family was enough. Dice was enough.

*   *   *

The night before Valentine's Day I lay awake for hours. When I fell into a half sleep the breathing of my family became beating wings. I rose like the heron and fell with a jerk, like when Queen shot it, resurrecting and falling again and again. Out the window the owls were swooping in and out of the barn. I remembered my mother crying in the kitchen. "Of course you didn't ask to be born," she was saying. "Of course you didn't ask to be born." I remembered the Sacred Harp song that went, "And will the judge descend, and must the dead arise?"

For the first time in my year and a half on the farm, I went out at night, creeping out of my bottom bunk, away from the heavy air and the noises of breathing like frothing waves, through two more bedrooms of the hall-less long house, and out into the courtyard, in my nightgown over my long johns. The wind caught me, and I seemed to be floating a few feet above the ground. Who was I? What was I looking for? The questions were beside the point. Dice had ripped me out of my body, reducing me to something less than an animal, less than an idea, down to just wind.

I could find Isaac and learn for certain whether my mother was dead or alive. I imagined settling into a chair across from him at the coffee shop in Asheville. Plastic and letters and money and flimsy tables, all the fake-world things. Hot cocoa in Styrofoam. There was so much Isaac didn't know, would never know, would never understand, but that was how I wanted him, wasn't it, wasn't that my revenge, because *you who know nothing, love nothing.* I could see him once more and say goodbye forever.

CHAPTER 27

It was Valentine's Day. In the night I'd planned out how I'd get to Isaac. I considered three options. One was to leave and try to hitchhike and hope no one noticed, but I dismissed that; the dogs would sound the alarm and I'd look like I was running away. Another was to volunteer for some errand. The bait shop, the hardware store, something. Maybe Dice would let me go to town alone. And the last option was to try to get Bay to drive me. I knew now that I had some power over him.

Dice sat next to me at breakfast but he did not eat. I had never seen him eating, not our buttercream cakes, not our rib stew. I followed him onto the porch after breakfast. "Dice," I said, "do you trust me?"

"Yes," he said. He looked me up and down. I felt him peering into my head, watching my plan to see Isaac unfold.

"I was hoping you'd let me drive to Mars Hill today," I said, "to run an errand." It was our first private conversation since he said my mother had died. He wanted me to believe that my mother was dead, and he wanted me to join with the protests. He always had a plan, an intention. And I loved him for it.

"An errand?" he said, peering at me. His brow was like the falcon's brow, heavy and bony to protect his eyes if he dive-bombed a rhododendron.

"A latch for the sheep gate," I said.

"Gemini can fix it," Dice said. "I don't trust you that way yet."

So I could turn to Bay. I thought about how to manage it. We'd start the hour-and-a-half drive to Asheville right at lunchtime. When Bay drove to the first Dumpster—I knew he had a whole circuit in Asheville, unlike in Mars Hill, where only the Ingles was worth scavenging—I'd cajole my way into going on a private errand. I could ask Bay if he needed me to pick anything up at a hardware store, perhaps, or if he wanted me to buy him some chocolate. Then I would walk to Isaac. I didn't have money for a bus. Maybe I was walking right into a trap. But I was getting used to walking into traps.

Eventually I'd find my way back to Bay. I'd return to some predetermined meet-up point and apologize that my errand had taken so long. I'd say I got lost, and he wouldn't be mad. We'd drive back, and I'd know for certain whether my mother was dead or alive, and once I knew that I could finally calm down and be worthy of the family, and the spring would arrive, and now that Dice trusted me I would be able to take action for the land. I imagined spiking trees, sleeping high in a tripod, smashing windows, lighting fuses, throwing bombs. I wanted all of it. I was ready for it.

*   *   *

I found Bay in the tool room in the barn, screwing a pitchfork back onto its handle.

"Can we drive into Asheville this afternoon?"

"Why would you want to do that?" I watched him sort through the screws so carefully.

"It's Valentine's Day."

He said nothing, focused on his work.

I continued, "Remember last year, how we went to the Dumpsters? That was my first time in town as a family member. It was such a special trip."

He reached out his hand and caught it in my sheared-off hair. I felt like the owl that calmed under Dice's hand. "All right," he said. "Let's go."

But I was supposed to find Isaac at two p.m. It was too early still. I wanted to leave here after lunchtime, so I'd have at least an hour with Isaac, if he came.

"I think we should leave in a few hours," I said to Bay. "You know, when we're more tired. So we can relax in the car."

"This afternoon I've got to help Gemini with some lumber project," Bay said.

"Can you wait an hour? I should milk."

Bay said, "What's up, Harmony?"

"Nothing," I said.

"Hey, Bip!" he called as Bip went to ring the breakfast bell. "Can you milk this morning?"

Bip nodded. How different the family must have felt to Bay,

who was able to boss people around. I thought how the longer I stayed with the family, the better off I'd be. In a few years I'd be like Gemini. In a dozen, I'd be like Sara.

"Can we at least eat a snack?" I said.

Bay gave me a sloppy, appeasing kiss on the cheek. "I'll buy you a nice snack," he said. "Maybe some pancakes. For my valentine." He unlocked his car.

Bay ordered French toast for me at the diner in Woodfin. I saturated the thick triangles with artificial maple syrup. I got a coffee, which I marbled with plastic thimbles of cream. I was sure I had never tasted anything so delicious. On the farm they were probably eating heavy cornmeal cakes with sorghum syrup, and tea from the land. Bay ordered eggs and toast and only ate the eggs. He wouldn't eat that fake-world bread. When I was done, I regretted that I hadn't dilly-dallied to slow our progress to town. So I ate Bay's toast as deliberately as possible.

The waitress called me sweetie. "He's been giving you enough to eat?" she said. She kept trying to catch my eye when Bay wasn't looking. The clock read only half past ten.

I went to the bathroom to gather myself, and to stall. I couldn't resist the mirror, though I knew it was a bad idea. I hadn't seen my own face since the bait shop. I looked strangely gaunt. No wonder the waitress had been so concerned. I had a line now between my eyes, and pitted cheeks, and my sunspot had darkened. My hair had grown over my ears into a shaggy bob. I splashed water on my face and slapped my cheeks. Isaac would not like the way I looked.

I rejoined Bay. He whistled as we headed to our first Dumpster in town. We pulled up to the Aldi's parking lot. The store reliably didn't spray bleach over the food waste. Bay handed me a headlamp and nodded toward the Dumpster. "I'll be the lookout," he said. Below a layer of scummy mushrooms I found bell peppers, raspberries, Butterball turkeys, and box after box of cream cheese. We piled our haul into bins in the backseat. Now I smelled terrible, along with everything else. I started to worry about how my plan could go wrong. I imagined finding Isaac and looking so dirty that he'd call the police. I slumped in the seat as we drove to Amazing Savings.

Bay looked at me. "Hey, you're the one who convinced me to go on this trip," he said.

"I don't feel well," I said. Maybe now was the time to sneak away. "Actually, I wondered if you have any errands you'd like me to run while you do the rest of the Dumpsters."

"I need you as a lookout," he said, "even if you don't want to get in."

"I'm sure there are some things you want around town." He nodded, with a slightly mocking smile, which I loved. "Can I turn on the radio?" I did, without waiting for his reply. I shifted the dial till I found a pop song. "*Do you not think so far ahead?*" a man sang in falsetto. "*'Cause I been thinkin' 'bout forever.*" I'd forgotten the sound of fake-world music—the soft electronic layers, the drums.

I glanced up at Bay to see if this was all right. He was still smiling.

"So what do you want?" I said. "Potato chips? Twix?"

"Sure, why don't you go off on your own little mission?" he said.

I couldn't tell whether he was joking. He gestured expansively at the little bungalows we were passing. Dice wouldn't permit this, I was sure of it. But I no longer knew, after our conversation about my mother, whether I could predict Bay's actions.

I watched the snowy landscape swoop by the windows. I admired the flamingos, gnomes, and plastic play castles in the yards, all vacant now, and I let myself imagine all the things inside the houses: lunch boxes and crayons, spaghetti-strap sundresses, Pop-Tarts on porch swings, and so on. All the many things to which I'd bid a permanent goodbye, without thinking it through.

"I knew you'd understand," I said, though I wasn't sure whether he understood, or whether he was yanking me around. "Now that I've been with the family so long," I said, reminding him, "sometimes I just feel like I need to get away a little, by myself."

"Not enough solitude in Ashland?"

He turned up a new road. Bay's face was marvelously cool, roaring yet expressionless like an overfull creek. Meaningless as rushing water.

"Of course, Harmony," he said. And he slammed down the brakes.

My heart split. The car that had been following behind us swerved, horn blaring. And then we were alone on the road. Everything was silent, except for the radio. I punched it off. I put my hands up to cover my face.

"I'm sorry," I said, into my hands. "I shouldn't have . . ."

"Have what?"

"Shouldn't have asked . . ."

His face was trembling. All these months I'd never gotten a good look at it. I always looked at his lips, or his neck or chest. He was giant, rough, blazing. He was not beautiful at all. When he found me, at the bus stop, had I looked at his face? If I had, would I have come with him? He had hidden himself from me all this time.

He lifted my forearm to his face and kissed it. I closed my eyes. Soon this terrible fear would pass, but for now I couldn't stop trembling. Then, scarcely after becoming aware of the soft sensation of the kiss, he circled my forearm with his hand and dug his nails in as deep as they could go. I was too surprised to cry out. When he dropped my arm, five livid crescents had begun to bleed. I clamped my thighs together to try to stop trembling.

"Ah, come on, Harmony," he said. "I kissed it first."

A few cars passed us, driving over the yellow line. My door wasn't locked. I could get out. I could stumble up to one of the silent houses and ring the bell. But he could follow me. Queen had told me family members who went into the fake world tended to die out there. I hesitated. Isaac's proposal seemed so far off now, like a dream. I might have left, but I needed to be fleeing from and fleeing toward, and I could not discern the toward.

Finally Bay put his foot on the gas. The car leapt forward, as though it too had been wounded. I felt relieved that I didn't have to decide anything anymore.

"You want the radio?" he said.

I shook my head.

"Don't be a brat," he said. He put on the same Top 40 channel, turned up the volume.

"Let's just go home," I said.

He ignored me.

"I'm sorry," I said again.

I wouldn't see Isaac again. Oh, why couldn't I just be content with what I had? I was always looking for more. Maybe I would never be satisfied. The fake world was not enough, and neither was the real world, and I didn't know what to do; I hated myself. I wanted to jump twenty feet, a hundred feet. I wanted the chestnut trees, the passenger pigeons, the Coosa and their endless palisaded gardens along the French Broad, the bonnet-headed oxen and jaguars and mastodons, I wanted to be able to cancel out my nattering consciousness and just float on air. I had to exhaust myself. I had to throw my body into something. I kept pressing the place where Bay had slashed me, to keep the pain sharp. Dice had told us that, at a certain point, superstorms off the warming sea can't keep their centers, they fall apart. We'd have more big hurricanes, but we'd never have a hurricane that took up the entire planet. Bay must have known I was the same; this mood was not stable.

We went to the Amazing Savings and then Food Lion. We took clementines, limes, cans of tuna, pork chops, Grape-Nuts, peas, mayonnaise, maple syrup, ginger, turmeric, cranberry juice, and brownie mix. Soon I felt dreamy, anaesthetized. My whole body felt weightless, like that children's game where, after you press your arms hard against the door frame, they float up of their own accord.

* * *

Bay acted like nothing had happened, until we were driving up the path through the woods, past the many *BEWARE LARGE DOGS* signs. "I won't tell Dice about your little outburst," he said.

Right now, back in Asheville, Isaac was just settling into a booth with hot cocoa and a heart-shaped cookie, turning around every time the door swung open to see if it was me. I wondered how long he'd wait before he gave up. Two hours, maybe. Then it was six hours back to Durham. I'd rejected him in Durham, and at the farm, and again now, it was done, it was final, I'd made myself clear. I would never see him again.

This was the outcome I was supposed to want. The less temptation to rejoin the fake world, the better. But it was easier to love the Ash Family as an act of defiance, an act of scorn against all who had hurt me—rather than to love the Ash Family as a last resort. I wished Rainer were here so I could ask him how he managed: he had known what it was like when no one else in the whole wide world cared if you lived or died.

spring and summer

CHAPTER 28

Lambing season was upon us, with the stresses of difficult births and bummer lambs, triplets, disinterested mothers, along with the beauty of those bat-eared babies hopping around the stables, leapfrogging onto their mothers' backs. This year I got to choose a dozen of the girls to raise, so I could let myself love them. I should have been happy.

But the spring was sad. I replayed that moment in that car with Bay over and over. I wondered if I would ever feel at rest, in the real world or in the fake world. Bay ignored me when I sat near him or when I sat far, when I touched him or talked to him or loudly joked with Gemini next to him. I wondered if he felt he'd revealed too much to me. Maybe he felt I'd led him astray. He shouldn't have confessed that my mother was alive. I reminded myself, "Get relativity." Who was I to know whether something was good or bad? By what standards did we judge? The saddest moment might be the happiest moment. The thing and its opposite are kissing cousins. When you're sure that you're right, you're most wrong.

I tried to remember how I used to deal with this kind of heart-break, out in the fake world. But here I couldn't watch television with my laptop warming my chest like a cat, couldn't get high, couldn't buy a beautiful new dress. I treated myself to everything that I wanted, cubes of butter, honey from a spoon, patty-cakes in bacon fat. I tried to cheer myself by splashing into the creek on a hot day and feeling the slow water's luminous capture. Then I remembered how Bay untied me like a knot, how his fingers stroked me until, like the glass, I was humming in one clear sound.

Every day I woke up and considered if I wanted to keep going; every day I pulled up fewer and fewer reasons, like rifling the algal floor of a depleted wishing well.

Time continued thundering forward. The water in the swollen streams came from ice packed around the roots of trees, snow in the coves and shadows. The faraway ocean sucked it all home, tugged it violently through brimming channels. And every year more of our four-mile-high mountains got dragged along with it.

The ephemerals, the trillium and bleeding hearts, lady's slippers and crested dwarf hearts, swiftly neared the twilight of their growing season, and the irises and daffodils began to rip open their bulbs. Here came the millions of black summer flies, in the milk, in the whey. When we sliced cheese for dinner, we found their corpses crouched in air-bubble caves produced by their own bacteria.

After dinner, the sheep sat in meadows whose flowers were taller than they were. The milk was at high tide. The strawberries bloomed in a matter of days. The sow swelled like a balloon and gave birth to a litter of ten. They fell out into my hand, one after another. The next day, the piglets nibbled the paws of the sleeping dogs. We dug out the garden, weeded, reaped. The more you harvest, the more you get, because plants are so indefatigable and desperate to get their seeds into the world. Every time you clip a zucchini, the zucchini plant will try again.

Dice told a story about scientists who, for all their technologies, really had no way to check if there was a meteor hiding behind the sun, heading right toward us. And why shouldn't there be? We're about due for a mass extinction.

The longest day of the year came, and our holler was hushed and sedate in the syrupy heat.

All alone, I brought the throw rope to climb the old-growth trees that stood around the stream in the next holler over, where the ground was so steep that no logger had ever come. Queen had told me that where the branches were too sparse, I could throw first a lead line with a beanbag on the end, then a length of sturdy rope, and finish with a friction knot, and in this way I could climb from canopy to canopy, not touching the ground for hours. I clung to the cool sturdy trunks of oaks and hickories, and tested my weight on the branches. Below I saw the body of a crashed plane, the burned-out structures of an old silver mine. A robin's nest with the open-beaked chicks. I saw a mother bear with two tumbling babies.

I saw Bay everywhere, but he no longer paid attention to me. I'd lost my mother, Isaac, Queen, and now I was losing Bay. I thought about how everyone who might have loved me ended up disappointed. It's all right, I tried to tell myself. Life is very long.

There's time for many waves of splitting and reconciliation—this is only the beginning with Bay, only the beginning! But I also felt that I was running out of people to lose.

On the night of the harvest festival, I saw Bay dancing with Sara. She'd made herself a crown of wildflowers on long stems.

I rocked on the porch till I felt seasick. I stared at Bay and Sara, her flower-fairy hair. I remembered last year when we'd centrifuged the honey and met down by the forest.

At a break Sara came over to me. Laughing, she said, "He asked me! He's my brother, and he's your brother. Stop sulking."

"It's all right," I managed. But he wasn't mine to give or withhold.

It's all right, I told myself. My mind, pulled along by my body, was a weak dog chained around the chest and shoulders.

The momentum of spring was over, and the year, a spun-up string, now began to untwist. I did not speak to Bay. I barely spoke at all. I didn't look up at the sky, and I didn't walk on my own through the forest, and I didn't eat glowing little plums till I burst. I sat with the sheep, stroked their warm horns. I was trying to lean into my numbness, like leaning into the wind, letting it hold me.

Into this unwinding sad summer came the uninvited guest.

After lunch one day, as we lay about on the porch, dozing, Gemini rode up on one of the dappled horses. He sprang from the saddle, and we watched him run into the house. A few minutes later, we could hear the dogs' hoarse clamor. I thought it must be Queen or Isaac, and hope speared through me.

Up limped the stranger. The family murmured in alarm. He was taller than any of us. He reminded me of beef cattle that grow grotesquely large on enriched corn. "Call off the dogs," said the stranger to Dice, who stood at the threshold, unmistakably our leader.

The man held a blue Velcro briefcase. He wore a khaki vest with bulging pockets. His chin disappeared into his neck on a long, fleshy incline.

Dice whistled and the dogs ran to him, smiling. "Why are you here?" Dice said.

"Testing the water," said the man.

"The creeks?" Dice said.

"Yes, sir," said the man.

"Are you from Delta?" Dice said. I recognized the name of the developer company.

"No, sir," said the man. "I'm testing the water." He looked up at Dice.

Dice stepped off the porch toward him. I remembered Dice as I first saw him, the prizefighter, fists up against the world. If I had been the water-testing man I would have fled. Sara and Bay edged in, and the rest of us stood and stepped off the porch, coming closer and closer the way predators do, to intimidate.

The man smiled. He had large, clean, crooked teeth. "So it seems a few of your streams are already impaired."

"Our streams," Dice said, "sustain us."

The man's chin receded farther into his neck. "I noticed a generator in one of them," he said.

"Are you a scientist?" Dice said.

"Yes," the man said, defiantly. "Sir."

"Are you researching for some kind of impact statement?" Dice said.

The man seemed to notice then how close we were around him. His eyes darted. He was looking for gaps.

"We didn't know any people lived around here," he said.

It seemed to me that a shiver of fear passed through the family. We couldn't be numbered. We couldn't be found.

"Leave," Dice said.

The man stepped backward, bumping into Sara. She smiled at him like an angel.

"Tell your boss," Dice said, "if he tries to remove us, we will destroy him." Dice reached out and took the man's hand, as he'd taken Isaac's hand. Dice stared at the man's eyes, wouldn't let him look away. "We'll ruin him," Dice said.

The man withdrew his hand. He held his hand and rubbed it, gaping wide-eyed at Dice.

"Bay, will you drive our guest down to the road?" Dice said.

"Come here," Bay said to the poor man.

In the evening, Dice told us that they'd try to get rid of us because we threatened the fake world. We were a model for a successful alternative. Maybe this man was from the FBI. Dice talked about the Green Scare, the way that environmental activists were becoming the top-priority terrorists for law enforcement agencies. "Amazing," Dice said, "that the government is more afraid of people conspiring to help trees and animals than people conspiring to kill each other." The family laughed. We were angry.

The man was, perversely, a sign of our success, Dice said. The better we got, the more the fake world would fight us.

*   *   *

That night, someone woke me. I heard the scratching sound of a match being struck. In the candlelight, Dice's face floated before me, ragged and orange. "Come with me," he whispered. He had sweat on his face. I wondered what he'd been doing in the cool night to get so hot, if he'd been running, lifting heavy objects. The flame, as though trying to please him, grew tall. He brought the candle close to my arm. I stood and my nightgown's hem brushed my ankles. I felt I was in a dream.

We got in the truck. We drove for hours and hours. I was half-asleep. The night air came in through the windows, broad music. The headlights seemed to X-ray the trees. We tore past the forests and hills, which at times broke to reveal the view of the ridges beyond the ridges beyond the ridges. A red helicopter rumbled low over us, then cut away through the forest. "Putting out a fire somewhere," Dice said.

We pulled up at a rough-hewn cabin. I knew we were not near the farm because the landscape was crossed by huge steel towers, the likes of which I'd never seen, holding aloft three long-distance power lines each.

The lines on their strutted towers were keening above the yowl of frogs and crickets. "The more humid the air," Dice said, "the more sound the electricity makes." It sounded like low-voiced men singing falsetto. "We're not in North Carolina anymore," Dice said. "This is a place that man wants to build on." He reached out and gripped my shoulder. It was too dark to see his face.

The power streamed on through the lines, wailing for the

lamps it would light, the radiators it would heat. I followed him down a dark hill. We seemed to be going so quickly, as though we were on a moving walkway through the waist-high grass.

"How long have you been with us, Harmony?"

"Almost two years," I said. I was sure he knew that. I couldn't wait for each day to pass, to add it to my total, to measure up my time here against my time in the fake world.

"Oh, it seems like so much less," he said casually. I could hear the smile in his voice. "Harmony," he said, "since that stranger came by today, I'm worried that our world is very close to ending."

"Yes," I said.

"That man," Dice said, "is a real threat. But all summer I've seen signs."

"Yes," I said. Though it was hard to recognize, in the peak of summer, how the world might be in danger. Hail had not shattered our tomatoes. Our bee colonies had not collapsed. No tornado had boiled into the holler and tipped our storage house into the ground. "I saw some men by the creek once."

"Exactly," he said. "Exactly."

We were far from the power lines now. The night was dark like velvet. All around us was the hush of the primitive world.

"Here," Dice said. We were in a treeless, tilting field. "Let's settle here." He lay down in the grass. I sat nearby. After a moment I lay down too, facing upward. And then I saw, for the first time in my life, the Milky Way. It bulged down toward me, so dense with stars it almost looked like an aurora. It sluiced all my tension away.

Next to me Dice began to speak. He said, "Here's the truth

about *get relativity*. It's not that everything is good and bad at once. It's that we can't rely on our first reactions to make that determination. We must be more discerning. It's a finer theoretical edge, do you understand? A finer cutting edge." I'd never thought about it that way. *Get relativity* as a tool not for mixing emotions together but for precisely dividing them. I loved how he was discerning; he built this world because he was able to carve right from wrong with an edge so fine I couldn't see it.

I let myself fall into his enchantment. He said universes may blossom like soap bubbles, their space-time so curved they are smaller than atoms. "I want to include you on an action," he said. He reached and stroked my brow and his touch was different from everyone else's in the world. "I want to know that you'll do exactly what we ask."

"Yes," I said.

"You're not sure," he said. He was right.

"Dice," I said. In the night, all alone, I knew I could be honest. "Is my mother really dead?"

"I believe that everyone in the fake world is as good as dead," Dice said.

"Did she die when Bay came?" I pressed.

"She did not die when Bay came," Dice said. His tone was as measured and calm as when I'd confronted him about his soap. "I said that because I love you. I want you to stay."

"You could have just told me that," I said. I wasn't angry, I was relieved. I felt like laughing.

"No," Dice said. "I know you. You need to get lost before you will listen. Don't worry, I'm smiling." He took my hand and put it on his mouth, and I felt his smile, his prickly skin, his lips, his slick teeth. He removed my hand. "She will die eventually, everyone does. And for you, the right moment for her to die was in the winter."

He explained that all moments could be lived at once, that time is not a daisy chain but a big stack, each moment stacking on top of the next. You're always watched over by your future self. So your departed, Dice said, are always with you, and a moment of love is as good as a lifetime of love. "You know, like ice cores," Dice said. "The ice cores of Lake Vostok. Deep down where the pressure is high, an arm's length could be a thousand years." And the pristine lake beneath the ice had been sealed off long before the *Argentavis magnificens*, with a wingspan nearly as long as a school bus, upwelled from the smaller birds and began to jump off cliffs to force its heavy body into flight. He subsided into silence and I felt that through my tears I could perceive every color that made up the light in the stars.

He told me to sit up and he hugged me, swaying back and forth. His body was hot as fuel and very hard. I could feel his eyelashes on the nape of my neck. I shivered, but with strength—a starting motor. Later, I'd think through his words and I would find them incomprehensible. But up in that empty field, the stars like a cataract thundering down around us, the grass blackly shimmering, all of my attention channeled toward Dice, I felt I'd found the truth of things, which was, like everything with Dice, lonely and compassionate.

"I need my sons and daughters to make sacrifices for the land, to face pain for the land," he said. "Can you face pain?"

"I think so," I said. All it takes is a moment of fearlessness. And then maybe Bay kisses you after.

"I think so, too," Dice said. "If I open your door, what will I find?" His hand on my forehead.

And there my mother was, crying.

He drew back. Had he seen her, too? "I'll teach you to make weapons," he said. "We will find the ennobling conflicts that will convey us to a better world." We walked back up the hill, the stars disappeared, dawn smoked the black sky.

Dice drove me back as the early morning burned off into the sticky midday. The drive took six hours but we were going in circles, I was almost sure—I kept seeing the Dairy Queen where Dice had pressed his cone into the floor.

After Dice parked he beckoned me to the slopes beyond the storage house. The cows were out in the field, their bells clanging at all pitches. Dice pointed to the electric fence, which rhythmically snapped with current. "Touch it," Dice said.

"Really?" Little sparks flew from where the wires connected.

"Don't think about it. You want to."

So I didn't think about it. I reached out and grabbed the wire. For a moment it was only hot, and then every muscle in my body cramped. I let go and my organs, hand, and tongue were on fire.

"Good girl," Dice said.

fall

CHAPTER 29

Dice showed me how to make slow-burning fuses of shoelaces soaked in a potassium chemical and granulated sugar. He showed me how to make tidy newspaper packets of cotton soaked in gasoline and Green Thumb fertilizer, but we didn't assemble any yet. "Cuke and Osha," he said, "misjudged this blast." We kept our wares in a flameproof metal box, the kind used for paint solvents. The whole family was seized with urgency. Dice didn't say whether we would be burning our napalm in the power plants or the dragline excavators or the banks that financed the mountaintop removal or the houses of coal CEOs, or the new exurban sprawl, the developers, or whether we'd wait for the creek-testing man to return, but we trusted he'd find the right place to strike. We were hurtling toward winter.

We stepped up our labors. It seemed like most of the family now was preparing to fight. Dice showed me a faster method to make napalm: I could just dump Styrofoam into the gas, and the gas ate it hungrily and turned to sticky sludge the color of sunshine.

Dice and Sara shared their private stash of moonshine with me—private, but not unauthorized, because now I deserved that kind of luxury. I needed new tools with which to prepare for the action. It was only rotten sorghum. The alcohol made me weak but also marvelously calm and tranquil. Maybe now, calm and quiet, dizzy and tired, bleary-eyed and able to carry out only simple, repetitive tasks—which was everything on the farm—I'd become a mountain lion, a sheep, or a leaf, and dissolved my definite self. I was a collection of memories, some mine, some Dice's, some straight from the earth and instinct.

And then Queen came home.

The Great Pyrenees dogs found her in the morning and sounded the alarm. She came riding up, sitting behind Gemini on the spotted horse. I stared at her in awe. I was a bit drunk, and so happy to see her I found myself laughing and wiping tears from my eyes. Her hair was long and wavy and suddenly I could see why Dice had named her Queen. She looked cocksure and dangerous. She dismounted and kissed the horse. I dreaded the punishment she'd be in for, returning like this. Maybe she had some bargaining chip, a whole lot of cash, the governor's head in her satchel.

Dice came out. "Well, Queen," he said. "Have you traveled far?" The air seemed to ripple off his back.

Queen said, "I have a warning." I felt she'd planned out this speech—she spoke more quickly than usual. "They're going to try to buy you out and if you don't say yes they're going to arrest you.

The builder is friends with the governor." She had lost a tooth, one of her canines.

I glanced at Dice. I was surprised how glad he looked to have her back. "I know," he said. He was so good at staying in control. "Thank you."

"So I thought, fuck this," Queen said. "I want to fight them."

"Exactly," Dice said. He looked around at the family that had gathered. "Cooperation, consistency," he said. "They won't displace us." I believed him completely.

Sara sent Queen to the dairy and me to the lower compost pile. And at lunch it became clear that they were trying to keep us apart. Queen sat next to me, then Sara called her away again.

We sang after dinner. Queen led "The Great Day."

I've a long time heard that the sun will be darkened.
That the sun will be darkened in that day.
O sinner, where will you stand in that day?

Queen sang the alto part. She was so beautiful. I knew everyone saw it too. She kept her hand high for the hold, then slashed it down to continue, and at the end of the song we broke into laughter because we'd sung it so well.

Afterward Sara sent her to the hayloft. We still hadn't had a chance to talk.

After lights-out, when the breathing in the long house had gone regular, I crept to the barn. I wore my nightgown and my boots. I stepped on the sides of my feet. No one guarded the door.

I climbed to the hayloft and found Queen. Her lantern was on. She lay open-eyed on the visitor's mattress.

She stood and embraced me. She didn't smell clean. "Just who I wanted to visit," she said.

"I wondered if I would ever see you again," I said.

"I was always planning on coming back."

"You never told me." I was breathing heavily, concerned she'd vanish before I got all my answers. "Do you think they'll manage to kick us off the land?"

"They won't have to," Queen said. I shook my head, confused. "Listen," she said. "I'm here to save you. I've been out there long enough to realize that this community is really messed up. Dice lets people die from negligence. Cassie. Where's Pear? She wasn't at the singing."

I didn't answer that. Rainer too, I thought. Osha and Cuke. I shook my head. "Queen," I said. I thought about our jelly jars of napalm. "Things have changed since you left."

She peered into my eyes, puzzled. "Speak up," she said.

I spoke slowly. "We have been preparing for a war."

She sighed. She gave me a hug—the line on her neck crushed against my face. She was a big girl, I'd forgotten, or maybe I'd shrunk. In low tones, she said, "The police are coming up."

My mind was stuck on *police*.

"I want Dice to come to justice," she said. "He's killed people. I showed them where we are on the map. The rangers will find us with helicopters. They will arrest Dice."

I shook my head. What about how saying things makes them true? "Dice told me that you ran over your mother," I said. All along, I'd thought Queen was the honest one. But I wanted to push her, to catch her in something. I had a feeling Dice was right. She'd denied it before she left, but I'd wondered. "Did you kill your mother?"

"What difference does it make?" she said.

"Tell me," I said. I had that same feeling as when I'd held the knife to Rainer's neck, when I'd talked to Annie about pills. A feeling of power. A feeling of being Dice.

"I was on drugs," she said. "But yes. I hit her with the car. I didn't mean to." She shook her head. She'd told me Dice had worked miracles—he'd gotten her off drugs. I looked at her round face, her dark line tattoo, and wondered whether the faithful Queen was still there somewhere, waiting to be called.

"He didn't abandon you," I said. "So why would you abandon him?" I imagined the helicopter landing in our kitchen garden, crushing all our winter seedlings. Heavy-booted men breaking down the long house door, finding our narrow father in his iron bed. I felt white-hot panic. "Aren't we doing the right thing for the Earth?" This was indisputable. Get relativity, stability is an illusion, there's no such thing as the definite self—in the Ash Family, we shared everything, we were all complicit, or all innocent.

"He's not a good person," she said. But I knew that he was. I knew from the mountains and the animals and the fineness of the edge of his ideas, the tools he'd given us to live rightly as so few people could.

I said, "What will happen to him?"

"You'll be fine."

"But—what if they kill him?" I imagined rifle-armed men backing Dice into a corner.

"We'll make a new home," Queen said. "We can build a farm somewhere else, if you like. Just get the people we like. And we could read books, if we wanted. Have children, if we wanted."

"No," I said.

"It's already done," she said. She sighed. "The helicopters are going to come up any time."

I left her. Down the ladder, down past the cows and horses and sheep. I saw a barn cat run, then stop, then raise its back, crest its fur, and skitter sideways into the dark. It was an omen of the end.

I moved by instinct, the way animals move. I didn't rush to put on my pants and shirt and jacket. I looked back at the hulking barn, checking for Queen. The wind arrow turned in the moonlight, muddled by the holler's confused currents. Then I knocked on Dice's window. The glass made a harsh clatter under my fist. *Tock! Tock!* Dice's light flickered on. He peered out the window and beckoned to me.

CHAPTER 30

"The police are coming," I said. The world felt turned on its ear. "Queen called in helicopters. She means to get you arrested."

He paced back and forth. I'd never seen him so agitated. If a sheep fidgeted like that, it was probably near death. "All right," he said, in a terribly restrained voice.

He slid the bookshelf to the side. The songbooks teetered and fell. He knelt and removed a piece of the floorboard. From the shadow he pulled a black iron key. He handed it to me. I was momentarily afraid to take it from him. I wondered what punishment was coming for Queen.

"It's for an old stable that once housed our goats," he said. He said I could find my way if I jumped into the pig enclosure and went into the door behind them, or through the black trapdoor from the hayloft. The trapdoor was under the visitor's mattress. "You need to get in there and clear it out," he said.

"Clear what out?" I said. I was still prepared for a scolding.

"The bone room, the bone room!" Dice said impatiently. "Go set fire to the bone room. Destroy it."

"Why?" I said.

"Don't make me say it. You know why."

"Set fire—how?" I said.

"Haven't I taught you anything?"

"Yes," I said. "You have." How to lamb, shear, milk, slaughter, and butcher. How to plant, grow, harvest, and preserve. How to make bread, make hay, make food from trash. How to trust, how to be involved in the wild parts of life. How to brew an abortion and how to brew napalm.

"It won't spread if you lay it right," he said. Did he really believe this? And then he paused. "There are bones in there," he said, "our departed friends. They protected us, but now they'll hurt us, they'll draw the evil toward us. Listen for it, Harmony."

For a second we were both silent, listening. *Woooo* went the wind in the trees. "Hear the choppers?" he said. "That's evil coming for us." My palm hurt where two years ago the splinter had stuck. The screech owls sounded like human babies; our little owl was out there somewhere, swiveling its head to try to find the sound. I would be for Dice what our songbook called a valiant soldier. *And all his valiant soldiers eternally shall live!*

And that was the last time I ever saw him.

I took an electric lantern, a jam jar of our napalm, a long fuse, and a wooden spoon. I was determined to do my job right. I ran into the pig stable but couldn't navigate between the pigs. They were enormous and asleep and snoring. I didn't want to wake them, so I went back around to the cow stable and headed up into the hayloft. The temperature had dropped, and I shivered as I stumbled through the enormous stacks. Queen was sprawled out asleep on the mattress. I didn't know how she could sleep through a night like this; now I wonder if she might have been high. I tried to pull the mattress out of the way and fell over. She woke up.

She smiled at me, sadly, knowingly. "But you will get in trouble, coming out here," she said.

"Certainly, you don't care about my getting in trouble," I said, "since you're so determined to destroy all our lives."

"Don't worry," she said. "They won't arrest you and me, we're victims, you see."

"I'm not a victim of anything," I said. "Move. I need to get to the door underneath."

"Harmony," she said, "they've forced you—"

"Come on," I said.

She got up and together we lugged the mattress away. I brushed the hay aside. Beneath was a glossy black door.

"Where are you going?"

"I wanted to check on the lambs," I said.

I opened the door and dropped my lantern down.

"At this time of year?" Queen asked.

I lowered myself down into the dark room. My feet landed with a crunch. The room was warm and smelled like vanilla. "I'll explain tomorrow," I called up to her.

My lantern cast weak light on the small room I'd never seen. It was a crypt. Bones of every description were stacked against the walls—cow horns, sheep skeletons all attached, and human skulls, too. There was Pear. I recognized her teeth.

I spooned out the clear sticky jelly. It never occurred to me to disobey. I'd made up my mind way back at the start, when Bay had burned my hand and I'd traded that pain for a kiss. Or before, when I hadn't gotten on the plane. Or before, when I didn't know if I would ever find what I was looking for. You just have to throw yourself into it.

The fuel dripped off my spoon like honey, so slow. I didn't know if I was laying the fire right, not to spread. The barn had lasted through a century of lanterns and lightning. It was a strong barn.

The room was filled with parents and children, stacked up against the walls or loose on the floors. I just had to get it all covered, quickly, quickly. I took out the long sugar fuse and put its tail on my honeyed stack of skulls. I lit the fuse and watched it crackle. But it was no good: it did not lead the fire, slowly, in the right direction. The old dust and straw on the floor whipped into flames, which shot up the walls in white-gold threads, then curtains. In no time the room was red with smoke.

I wouldn't be able to get back into the hayloft, I realized. I could see Queen standing above, a shadow waving, before the flames swallowed her up. The room rippled as though submerged in water, so I couldn't be sure of what my burning eyes were seeing. In desperation, I pushed the door open—and it was unlocked. I jumped in among the pigs. They turned toward the unexpected warmth. I leapt over them. I could feel the flames behind me. Then I started to hear the squeals.

Choking smoke followed me as I fled into the frosty night. I crawled, heart throbbing, under the hickory. It didn't seem possible that the whole barn would catch, but I heard the windows shattering under the fists of heat, and I watched as the flames reached their arms out of the sheep stables, the chicken houses, and grasped upward. The left side of the barn looked like a jack-o'-lantern, exhaling terrible windy moans and breaking into red.

The lights went on in the bedrooms of the long house. I heard shouting behind me, and wailing, and I watched as the dark shapes of people—my family—darted past me. Was it Gemini? Was it Sara? Several people rushed to open the door of the dairy and ran into the tumbling smoke. Others ran to open the large door of the stable. But I was rooted into the ground.

I watched a sheep run from the stable, its wool alight. Then another and another. They couldn't all get out. The fire roared like the ocean. Up went the chestnut planks, the sheep, the cows, the horses, the pigs, the chickens. I could hear the animals screaming and I still hear them.

The dogs barked and howled; so did the wolves and owls. All the predators, the woods themselves, were rising up in protest because they loved us, and the propellers were thudding, *chock chock chock*, I could hear them now.

I began to run toward the road. I sprinted down and down and down, fell and fell and fell. And over me flew two enormous blinking beasts, for a moment they were those ancient birds, their wing beats whipsawing the forest and sending the earth into the sky like the rapture's answer to rain.

*   *   *

The sun hadn't even started to rise when I collapsed onto the asphalt road. My white nightgown was scorched and filthy. Perhaps two hours had passed since Dice had handed me the key.

A white hatchback stopped. An old mountain woman rolled down her window, with her hair whitely falling to the base of her spine.

"Asheville?" I said.

"I can help you," she said in a quavering antebellum voice. She had warts on the water lines of her eyes. "Are you a runaway from that cult?" The word was so unfamiliar to me I thought at first she'd said *from that cold.*

"It's a family, a co-op," I said. "A homestead."

"Oh, my child." She pointed at the sky with a trembling hand, a hand not fit for farmwork. In the moonlight, I could see the dull cloud of smoke.

I entered her car, which smelled like cleaning fluids, the kinds we didn't have at the farm. "Can we stop at a pay phone?"

"A pay phone? I've got a cell." The phone was as big and flat as an index card, with a spiderweb fracture, under which the display was as clear as water, with no pixels to be seen. I dialed Isaac. His number was rooted as deep in my head as my mother's address. His phone rang through to his voicemail, his gently crackling voice. I left a message and then dialed again and he answered. Relief pumped into me like helium—I felt I was rising into the air. I told him there was a fire and the family had scattered. I didn't explain much—the woman was listening. We would meet in a park. The woman drove in silence on the empty road. I didn't wonder till later why I heard no helicopters or sirens.

By the time I reached the park all my thoughts had collapsed to a pinprick. I felt something similar to hopelessness. It was the feeling of being alone with my memories. No one now could confirm the truth, so everything I could say would be tantamount to a lie.

For now I sat in the space between what happened and what I would say about it. I reclined on a park bench.

Isaac would drive all night. I thought about the reasons people do that. To make up after an argument with a faraway lover. To make it to someone's deathbed. It was so urgent. I wished we could live all the time with the rules suspended like this: the way I'd always felt, on the farm.

In the park that night I was in no danger. Some crusties approached me, maybe in search of dope money. From behind I might have looked like any short-haired girl. But I turned and bared my teeth and they scuttled back into the dark. I couldn't think about what I'd done—any of it. There was lots to distract me—icy street lamp light fanning through landscaped trees, the wet bronze statue, the smooth noises of the cars, the fake world I had forgotten. Dawn began to raise the sky. My skin was clammy with dew. The first pigeons flopped down from their hiding places. An early jogger in a glowing yellow vest swerved around the bench, to take the wide way around. A few dog walkers came out, with their bumbling little mutts. Our white dogs would have eaten these dogs.

The sun hadn't even come out when I spotted Isaac crossing the street from his car.

He was not the same. His neck was wider, his shoulders full. He had stubble on his cheeks.

"There she is," Isaac said. "The girl who needs no help from nobody."

I thought of his giving Bay money, his kissing me in the hayloft, his inviting me home. I said nothing.

"Christ, Berie," he said. "What is this dress you're wearing? You need a shower."

"I don't."

He gave me a long look, sweet and pitiful. I stared at the ground. "You're right," he said. "I shouldn't have said that. I'm sorry."

"And I'm sorry I left you hanging last Valentine's Day," I said. "I really tried to come meet you."

"Valentine's Day?" he said. "You came to Durham?"

"No," I said, "When you were going to meet me in Asheville . . ."

"Oh, right. No, I never came. You were so mean when I left, remember?"

But I remembered his saying he'd come whether or not I wanted him to. I remembered his saying, *You'll want to come. By February, you will.* I needed someone to have that faith in me.

I said what people would come to expect me to say: "I wasn't really myself."

"You can't keep thinking that your actions have no effect on people," he said.

I'd forgotten how out in the fake world, too, everyone tells you what to think and feel.

"She can't wait to see you," he said. How beautiful the sky was, even here.

"Who," I said, hoping.

"Who else," he said. "Your mother."

"She's okay?" I said. Bay had been telling the truth, and Dice had too, in the end—and though I'd trusted them, it was still a surprise to learn that the real-world truth matched the fake-world truth. I pictured her heading to her store, flipping on all her multicolored lights, settling into her chair with her chin on her hand, smiling. She was alive. "But the earrings," I said.

"She knows it was you," Isaac said. "It's all right." He reached out and patted my neck, quick and gentle and slightly fearful, the opposite of Bay's touch.

I stopped staring at the thrilled sky. I refocused my eyes on Isaac, who looked wary. "I bet I sounded like a nutcase on the phone," I said.

He laughed. I was delighted at the sound. I let myself hope, even, that we might try to go back to how we were before, despite his uncertainty. I didn't yet know that something had broken in me. The candle might have been there, but the wick was gone.

Isaac wanted me to drive back but I couldn't even get my hands to grip the wheel. Both my eyes jerked open and shut. The sun rose very, very slowly, though we were driving toward it, east. The sky was dim for hours. I watched the digital clock in the dashboard, and it ticked forward in bursts.

Queen might have escaped the hayloft. She could ask around

after me and find me in my condominium in Durham with the paper-thin walls.

The family might have continued to exist. Dice could have gathered Ashers on another continent. Maybe the barn fire didn't spread to the long house. Maybe the police didn't arrest anyone. Or maybe the police didn't even come. Maybe the police had said to Queen, "We'll come with helicopters, we'll find the leader, we'll save the family," and then they'd sent her on her way and laughed to themselves, because the violence, the murder, the firebombs, the fear Dice cultivated and cherished, mattered so little to them. The mountains were full of people like that. Maybe if I climbed back up those sinking mountains I'd find it all just the same, the spinning windmill, the sighing cows, the men and women singing shape notes with doors open to the frigid winter.

I felt, in that cold morning in the car, that I was an hourglass that had just been flipped, and all my sands were just starting to shift downward to that strangle point. I was astonished at the functional beauty of pavement, the cars. The candy-colored signs on tall poles by the roadside. The serious people heading in all directions. Each had their own task and their own destination.

Isaac bought me a small crackling bag of gas-station chocolates. I sat in the throne of the '92 Taurus. I felt like an ancient person transported to the modern world, eating chocolate for the first time. The little chocolate kisses, off-brand, were grainy with sugar. I couldn't stop myself from sighing.

"You like that?" Isaac said.

At the gas station, a woman stood up and took from the back-seat of her car a baby. I noticed the folds of skin at the back of its neck, its antigravity hair, how bendy it was in her arms, its joints not fully formed. A loitering man threw cubes of ice onto the concrete, and they skittered and clacked and came to a stop right by the woman's red shoes. Was he waiting for Bay, like I had?

"Oh, Beryl, what did you do?" Isaac said, and wiped my coal-black tears with his thumb. He said I smelled like burning oil. That was the burned-up flesh, heavy, filthy, unwashable.

Isaac chucked the star-print chocolate bag out of the window. I whipped my head around to watch it flutter in the flow of cars. With the Ash Family, a broken jar had meant punishment and shame. A broken jar had been devastation. Out here the stakes were too low.

The wind vortex in the Taurus flopped Isaac's hair in all directions. White flowers sprouted on the highway banks but in a second we had passed them. One hawk for every half mile of piney highway. Shadows whispered through the car.

There were far too many things to pay attention to.

Isaac turned on the radio. He put an elbow out the window. He whistled to himself. The radio cut in and out, but Isaac didn't seem to notice. Gray static, then a banjo and a harmony so tight it was syrupy, nothing like Sacred Harp—"*In the pines, in the pines, where the sun never shines, I would shiver the whole night through.*"

I thought about what Isaac didn't know. He didn't know to plant beans in the brassica beds or to breathe gently on the coal to ignite it. He didn't know how a cow looked for green shoots under the snow in January.

I thought about what Isaac knew. He knew how to budget, how to plan trips he wanted to take, how to purchase things he liked. He knew how to live by himself. He knew who he was in the great big world. And he knew about my mother. She had not evaporated into a shower of coins or coal ash. She was waiting for me, at the kitchen table, or sitting on the windowsill beside her solar doll, waving for me as long as the sun shone. I would try to ask for forgiveness as soon as I could find the words.

The roads tumbled by. The trees, the rising and dipping power lines. The flashing angles of a tobacco field, the quick alignments. The ticking power lines, the swarms of birds. I could see every claw and eye, every blade of grass, the fibers on the blades that sucked up the water, and the water itself, flowing smoothly toward the heavens. The sun kept climbing and climbing till the shadows were at their minimum. The earth reeled backward, the road flung up behind our tires like a strip of silk. The trees mumbled. The light buzzed like a hornet.

Who am I? I asked the landscape. Who am I? Who am I, alone now with all these memories? I still don't know, which is as Dice intended. He didn't believe in the "I," anyway.

ACKNOWLEDGMENTS

Thanks to my teachers at the Brooklyn College MFA program— Josh Henkin, Dinaw Mengestu, and Ben Lerner; and at Harvard—Amy Hempel and Bret Johnston for the life-altering gifts of their instruction and support.

Thanks to PJ Mark, for his guidance, knowledge, and generative conversation, and to Emily Graff, for her profoundly attentive edits and for immersing herself in the farm with me. I'm grateful also to Marya Spence and Ian Bonaparte at Janklow & Nesbit, and, at Simon & Schuster, Jessica Chin and Aja Pollock, for their exacting copyedit, Carly Loman and Kimberly Glyder for their beautiful designs, and Samantha O'Hara, Elizabeth Breeden, and Marysue Rucci.

Thank you to Eve Gleichman, the best person to call when you're halfway through a scene and don't know what's happening in it. Thank you to the first reader of the first draft, Julian Gewirtz, to Anastasia Bessias for photos in Durham, and to Lucy O'Leary for introducing me to Sacred Harp and so much else. Thank you to Jay for thoughts on activism and utopia and to Michael Stynes for the mania.

Thanks to all shape note singers in New York and beyond, and to my family, Dan, Nancy, Katie, Trevor, and Charlie.

ABOUT THE AUTHOR

MOLLY DEKTAR is from North Carolina and lives in Brooklyn. A graduate of Harvard College, she attended Brooklyn College for her MFA. *The Ash Family* is her first novel.